Maisey Yates is a *New York Times* bestselling author of over one hundred romance novels. Whether she's writing stories about strong, hard-working cowboys, dissolute princes or multigenerational families, she loves getting lost in fictional worlds. An avid knitter, with a dangerous yarn addiction and an aversion to housework, Maisey lives with her husband and three kids in rural Oregon. Check out her website: maiseyyates.com.

USA TODAY bestselling, RITA®-nominated, and critically acclaimed author **Caitlin Crews** has written more than 100 books and counting. She has a Master's and a PhD in English Literature, thinks everyone should read more category romance, and is always available to discuss her beloved alpha heroes. Just ask. She lives in the Pacific Northwest with her comic book artist husband, she is always planning her next trip, and she will never, ever, read all the books in her 'to-be-read' pile. Thank goodness.

THE SECRET THAT SHOCKED CINDERELLA

MAISEY YATES

WILLED TO WED HIM

CAITLIN CREWS

MILLS & BOON

First published in Great Britain 2022
by Mills & Boon, an imprint of HarperCollins*Publishers* Ltd,
1 London Bridge Street, London, SE1 9GF

www.harpercollins.co.uk

HarperCollins*Publishers*
1st Floor, Watermarque Building,
Ringsend Road, Dublin 4, Ireland

The Secret That Shocked Cinderella © 2022 Maisey Yates

Willed to Wed Him © 2022 Caitlin Crews

ISBN: 978-0-263-30093-2

08/22

MIX
Paper from
responsible sources
FSC™ C007454

This book is produced from independently certified FSC™ paper
to ensure responsible forest management.
For more information visit www.harpercollins.co.uk/green.

Printed and Bound in Spain using 100% Renewable Electricity
at CPI Black Print, Barcelona

THE SECRET
THAT SHOCKED
CINDERELLA

MAISEY YATES

MILLS & BOON

To the Happiest Place on Earth, which inspired this one
while I was on a much-needed family vacation
and contributes to my motto: never grow up.

CHAPTER ONE

RIOT PHILLIPS HAD finally done something spontaneous. And it was turning out very, very badly.

Her name, a gift from her hedonistic mother, had never been representative of who she was. She'd been meek and mild all her life. Cleaning up her mother's messes as best she could, and taking all the money in her savings account for a once in a lifetime trip to Cambodia was not in her wheelhouse, at all.

But her roommate Jaia was one of those people you couldn't deny. Infectious and fun and the kind of woman who effortlessly pulled off a nose ring and got new tattoos of a Tuesday, just because. And when Jaia had said she had some old friends from high school headed to Angkor Wat to explore the ruins and go on a spiritual quest, Riot had been caught up in the moment.

She'd looked at her passport, something she had just in case but had never used. She'd looked at her suitcase—also never used. And she'd decided to just say yes.

And everything had been fine. Until they'd hooked up with Jaia's friends. Lilith and Marcianne took everything Jaia was and amplified it. Everything was more reckless, less organized, and significantly drunker and Riot had been on edge for two days. The hostels they'd been staying in might as well have been a street corner—one was a tree house and when their next door neighbors had gotten amorous the whole thing had... swayed.

Worse, Riot hadn't immediately known why.

And it was drunken Lilith who had howled over Riot not immediately guessing that the motion was caused by thrusting.

But the days spent exploring the different towns they'd been in had been incredible, and when Riot couldn't handle the girls, she was happy to go off on her own.

Then they'd gotten to Siem Reap, the town nearest the ruins, last night to find the hostel full, and Marcianne had talked a man at a local bar into offering them his front room, where Riot had spent the whole night petrified.

Then they'd gone to the ruins and Riot had forgotten everything. All the drama, all the chaos. Because it was so beautiful, so serene and somehow every fantasy she'd ever had about...what might be out there. Bigger and bolder and *more* than her small town in Georgia.

It was a ruin, but the rocks had contained more life, more spirit than anything she'd ever encountered and when she breathed, she felt like she was truly breathing for the first time.

And then it had started to rain.

Not just rain...pour down buckets.

The air was thick and steamy, her dress sodden within seconds, she held the hem up, even though it was really too late to keep herself dry—but she was going to try and make a run for it.

And soon she realized…

She had been left.

The tuk-tuk they'd hired was gone, along with Lilith, Jaia and Marcianne.

She ran out of the temple she'd been in, down the front steps, the stone structure looming behind her, no longer peaceful but ominous. The rain seemed to have cleared out everyone and she was…alone.

Well, this felt like a metaphor for about a thousand painful moments in her childhood.

She took out her cell phone and she tried to call Jaia. It went straight to voice mail. Again and again, while she stood there with rain pouring over her skin.

Then she ducked back into the temple, took shelter in the rock there and walked down a long corridor that was partially open to the elements.

She wasn't cold. But she was utterly saturated. She bowed her head low, water rolling forward down her nose. She touched the stone walls, slick now, and wondered if it was really all that different or special being abandoned in Cambodia versus the abandonment she experienced back home.

Sure. You don't know how to help yourself here. That's what's different.

This was what she got for spontaneity. She should have known it wasn't for her. Not ever.

And then she looked up and everything in her froze.

She wasn't alone.

There was a man standing there. Sheets of rain fell between them, keeping her from seeing him clearly, but she could have sworn he was in a white dress shirt and a dark suit, like he was prepared for a meeting.

In temple ruins. In the rain.

He was tall. At least, he felt tall from where she stood.

It was impossible to say from this distance.

He had his hands in his pockets—a confident stance, rather than a casual one, and she wasn't sure why she knew that, only that she did.

She should run.

She was a woman alone, in the rain, whose dress had become near pornographic with the way it stuck to her in this rain. And he was…a man. A Strange Man. Well, not inherently strange, but a stranger.

She didn't run.

She had nowhere to run to.

So, she simply stood.

And then, he was the one who moved.

Graceful and silent, like a tiger stalking its prey.

As he moved closer, his features came into view. His hair was black, his skin golden brown. His face was sculpted with razor sharp cheekbones, a blade straight nose and a mouth that seemed dangerous.

His eyes were dark and mesmerizing, like the rest of him.

Yet again, she thought she ought to run. But didn't.

She'd also been right about him being tall.

Which set off a further alarm bell. If she was right

about him being tall, she was probably right about him being a predator.

But she still didn't run.

You can't outrun a tiger...

That was not a helpful thought.

She didn't know what to do. If she should speak, or if she should run. She froze instead. And the tiger began to advance.

"Are you lost?" he asked.

His voice was like the sound a tiger made. All low, and felt in the deepest parts of you. She didn't know whether she wanted to cower in fear or...draw closer to him.

"I'm not lost," she said, her voice absorbed by the moss, plants and soft ground, the damp brick. She sounded small.

"Are you in trouble?"

"My friends left me."

Oh, good. Tell the strange man you're all alone.

"I already know there is no one else here."

"And why are you here?" she asked, feeling bold in the moment. But only in the moment, because as soon as it passed she asked herself why on earth she was engaging the tiger man in speech.

"I went for a walk," he said. "I live nearby."

"Just...in a suit? Were you at a funeral?" She'd meant it to sound caustic and it had come out more a question.

His head tipped up, as did the corner of his mouth. "Yes."

"Oh. I'm sorry."

He shrugged one broad shoulder and took another

step towards her. She'd been hoping that if he did draw closer she would see that she'd exaggerated his size, his masculine energy, his handsomeness.

But no.

He burned brighter, the closer he got.

"Sorry helps nothing," he said.

"It's not about helping. It's just about letting someone know they aren't alone."

But they both were.

Together.

The rain continued to pour and her dress was completely stuck to her body. She became very aware of both her choice to not wear a bra, and the effect the cold was probably having on her body.

As if her thoughts had cued him, he looked her over. The perusal was slow and somehow made her feel... heated.

There was something about him. She felt like she knew him, while at the same time he felt utterly unknown. It was a strange push and pull. Safety mixed with danger in a way she couldn't define.

Not real danger. She felt safer with this man than she'd ever felt before.

The danger was in her.

As if he had awakened something in her she hadn't known was there.

"Well, then since we are not alone, tell me. What sort of friends go off, and leave one of their own stranded in a monsoon?"

She had nothing else to do other than talk to him. He was her only way back to civilization.

Her phone didn't have data, so she couldn't look any-thing up. She didn't have a backup plan that wasn't…her flaky friends, which she supposed made her an idiot. So why not?

"I don't actually think they're my friends," she said.

And realized that was true the minute she said the words.

"That seems apparent to me."

"Well, Jaia was my roommate. Is my roommate? Back at home. The other two are her friends, and as soon as we got with them…"

"Old friends taking precedence over new. I see."

"I guess so. I mean, I hadn't really realized how much Jaia was…well she's a flake. This whole trip has been deeply disorganized, and once it started raining they left. Or they met men and they left. Or something. With them, who can say?"

"But no one made sure you were all right?"

"More fool me, I was actually seeing to what we'd discussed doing. I was…" It sounded silly now.

"Yes?"

"I saw this as an opportunity to have a spiritual time." It sounded so dumb and immature, it made her feel exposed, especially next to this man who had an air of worldly sophistication about him. She just sounded like what she was. A silly girl. But she wanted him to understand her, as foolish as that seemed. "By myself. I've… My life has been one long series of struggles and I've finally reached a place where I wasn't so… Where it wasn't so hard. I had some money saved up and I thought I'd come here and experience something new. I thought I'd come and feed my soul for a while because I've always been so focused on survival that part of me has been denied."

"I was here for the same reason," he said, looking up, the rain rolling down his face.

He looked back at her, and she was sure he could see straight through her.

"Oh."

It didn't feel silly, then. It felt like, at least she'd been right about one thing.

"I'm Riot," she said. "Riot Phillips."

He smiled then, in earnest. And it did not make him less intimidating. "Krav."

He did not offer a last name.

Krav.

"You live around here?" she asked.

"I live in many places. Wherever it suits me in the moment. I keep a residence here, and that is where I'm currently staying."

He didn't seem like a bohemian wanderer in the way that Jaia did. But then, he'd been at a funeral, so perhaps that was why.

Maybe the suit was the piece of him that was wrong.

And as she looked at him she thought, yes. The suit was wrong. He was not a man who belonged in a suit. He was a man who belonged here. In the ruins. In the jungle. In the rain.

It was funerals that were wrong.

"Are you…were you here for the funeral?"

"Yes. Though I came a few weeks ago when it was clear my mother would not last much longer."

Her stomach twisted.

"Your mother. Oh, I'm so sorry."

She didn't have the kind of relationship with her mother that brought out any warm feelings in her, but she knew, oh, she knew well, that most people loved their mothers very dearly. And in fairness, she loved hers. It was part of why it was so difficult.

If she felt nothing, then it would all be easier. But she did.

"It is life." He looked desolate when he said it, even though his voice didn't change. "A part of it. And never do I feel more aware of that and connected to it than when I am here, so it felt just the right place for a walk."

He was still a tiger.

But she did not think he'd eat her.

In spite of herself, she shivered. It wasn't particularly cold, but the fabric of her dress was truly stuck to her now. And it was beginning to seep down into her bones.

"Come with me," he said. "You're soaked clean through. My home is just a short walk away."

"Your…home is a short walk away?"

"Yes," he said. "Through the trees."

"The trees but…"

"Follow me."

She did, because there was nothing else to do. And because she felt if she didn't…the very thought of not going with him filled her with a sense of sadness. Darkness. And when they came to the end of the ruin, he went on. Deep into the jungle.

The darkness of the foliage swallowed them whole.

"I don't think there's…"

And then she looked up. There was a glow in the trees, and her jaw dropped.

It was a house. Up in the trees. Not at all like the hostel they'd stayed in last week, but something other-worldly. The roots of the trees grew down over the top of a stone shrine, the banyan tree seeming to hold it like a mother would cradle a child, and it was the trees above the shrine that held the house as well, large pillars extending down to the ground, adding support. A staircase began at the shrine and wound tightly around the tree, carrying them up into the canopy, and into the house.

There was an expansive deck around the whole outside of the house, and he led the way to a door that seemed to open by magic. It was ornately carved, as was the rest of the home, and when they were inside, she was stunned by the care given to each exquisite detail. The carvings inside mirrored much of the temple art, and there were grand tapestries hanging on the walls. The living area was plush, with cushions spread all over. There was a small kitchen area off to the side.

"One moment," he said.

He disappeared into another room and returned a moment later with a silk robe on a hanger. "You should get into something that hasn't been rained on, and I can dry your dress."

"Oh, I…"

Her heart thundered wildly and she couldn't quite say why.

"You may change in there." He gestured off to the left, and she found her feet doing his bidding, even while her mind continued to question both him and herself.

She should ask him to call her a car.

She should ask if he could take her back to…to where? They didn't have a hostel booked. But she could find a hostel on her own. With just a little help. She was going to have to accept that she couldn't count on Jaia and company anyway.

And she would.

After her dress was dry. Because she really was uncomfortable.

When she walked into the room he'd sent her to, it took her a moment to gather her wits because she felt transported. Unlike the front of the tree house, the bathroom was modern, and much more lavishly appointed than she could have imagined a tree house might accommodate.

Who was this man?

She undressed slowly, shivering as she peeled the thin fabric of her dress away from her skin and let it pool at her feet. She realized she was standing naked in a strange man's tree house bathroom and she laughed. She couldn't help herself.

This wasn't the adventure she had imagined going on, but it was an adventure. And maybe that was good enough.

Well, it was happening no matter what, so she supposed what she felt about it was irrelevant.

The robe was luxuriously beautiful. All jade and gold silk with cranes winging their way across the decadent landscape. She had never given much thought to her looks. Being beautiful didn't help her survive and at worst, it attracted the kind of attention from men she just didn't want. But right now, in this strange place in the middle of the jungle, she felt beautiful.

And maybe that should concern her. Because she was alone with a man she didn't know. But she wasn't afraid.

He was still a tiger. It was only she didn't fear what he might do.

She exited the bathroom slowly, holding the edges of the robe needlessly together at her bust line.

And he was there, wearing silk pants in blue, his bare chest on display. She was momentarily stunned by the sight of him. Lean, hard cut muscle exposed and gleaming in the light. Every ridge, every dip, was cut hard and well defined.

And there he was, lounging on the cushions, a pot of tea and two cups in front of him. As if he weren't lethal.

As if he weren't the most beautiful thing she had ever seen.

Krav, he said his name was Krav. His accent wasn't Cambodian, but something else. She'd never heard the name before. But then, few people had heard hers. She could see the legacy of this beautiful country in some of the angles of his face. He seemed like a man who might fit anywhere and nowhere all at once. Like he could find a way to be a part of any culture. But at the same time…he would always be separate.

He was too singular to blend.

"Come," he said. "Have a warm drink."

Outside she could still hear the rain pounding down, hard and insistent.

"All right."

She crossed to where he sat and lowered herself down onto the pillows across from him.

"So you came here for a spiritual quest? Did you imagine it might earn you clout on the internet to take selfies at a sacred ruin?"

She shook her head. "No. I'm not on the internet. Not like that. I've never traveled before and it seemed like an amazing opportunity."

She was about to say something caustic about how it had turned out. But the truth was…it was turning out well. This moment was one she would never forget. As she sat there with this man's eyes trained on her, giving her closer attention than she could remember ever having before, she felt…like this was the adventure she'd come for, without realizing it.

Krav was the adventure.

He poured her a cup of tea and handed it to her. His fingertips brushed against hers.

She suddenly felt warm and didn't think it was to do with the tea.

"You are a strange little thing," he said, just as she raised the cup to her lips.

"Am I?" She asked, lowering the cup quickly. "I thought I was simply unremarkable."

"How can a woman called Riot ever think of herself as unremarkable?"

Maybe it was the man, maybe it was the moment. But she wanted to tell him. Everything.

"The name only adds to it. People expect someone

wild and I'm not that at all. My mother was the child. There wasn't room for two of us."

"I see."

"The name is hers. Not mine. It's about her."

"You could change it," he said.

"Yes. Though there is something…defiant maybe, about keeping it. And continuing to be me."

The corner of his mouth turned upward. "Ah, yes. Now that I am familiar with."

She sipped her tea, and it was the waves of understanding that seemed to grow between them that surprised her most of all. She shouldn't have anything in common with him. But she felt like he might understand her better than any other person she'd ever met.

The hours went by quickly. They didn't talk about deep things. And yet the things they did speak of— favorite foods from their childhood, the seasons they liked best, all uncovered pieces of who they were. And it felt deep. It felt real.

And when he leaned across the space between them and kissed her, it wasn't like kissing a stranger. Because he wasn't a stranger. She knew him better than she'd ever known another person.

Krav who lived in the trees.

Krav whose mother was gone.

Krav, who kissed like a dream but was real. So very real. Warm and far too sharp and hard to bear. He burned bright, and so did she. Like the tiger had taken her for his own, not to eat, but to claim.

She'd never been kissed before. It came back to the fact that she had never trusted men and never wanted to.

Her mother had made a mess of her life over men and Riot had wanted…independence. Freedom. But she'd never felt half so free as she did right now, kissing this stranger in the trees.

His movements were expert, his hand on her cheek warm, his thumb sliding over her cheekbone and creating a hot sensation that started there but rioted through her. Down to her chest, down between her thighs. Until she burned, all of her.

"Krav," she whispered.

His dark eyes burned into hers and she trembled. And she understood now why people made crazy decisions in the name of desire. Why Jaia was always tragic about some man or another. Because this moment, where she'd met a stranger in the rain and gone back to his house, seemed perfectly reasonable and somehow in the back of her mind she knew that it shouldn't.

But it didn't just seem reasonable, it seemed necessary. To part her lips for him and allow greater access. To let him slide his tongue against hers and taste her like she was an indulgent dessert.

She felt like an indulgent dessert. Or maybe a whole riot, contained in a girl who had never felt anything like that at all.

He tugged the shoulder of her robe down and the slick fabric fell away, revealing her shoulder and then, her breast. She might have gasped in shock if it didn't seem natural. If it didn't seem like exactly what was supposed to happen next.

Her nipple beaded tight and his eyes sparked with interest. And she felt…

She had never wanted a man's attention before, not particularly. And so being the unexpected focus of his was something she could scarcely comprehend, much less anticipate.

And it was everything. He was everything.

This was the moment.

That certainty whispered inside of her. A core truth of everything she was.

This was why she had come.

Maybe it was why she had been born.

To feel beautiful under the hands of this man. To feel the exquisite pleasure that came from his hot lips trailing over her neck, down to her shoulder, her breast. The way the tip of his tongue traced the edge of her tightened nipple, before sucking it deep into his mouth.

Her head fell back and she moaned with pleasure. She hadn't really understood pleasure until now. Arousal, sure. But this was different. He was in control. He was the one giving it. Determining the pace and pressure. Where he touched less, where he tasted. How deep. How glorious.

This was her giving the power over to him, and somehow feeling all the more powerful in return.

Riot wrapped her arms around his neck and kissed his cheek. He pulled his head back and looked at her, intensity shining in his gaze. And then he kissed her mouth again. Hard, intense. And she fell back into the cushions, guided by his strong arms, making her feel weightless. Like she was floating.

His kiss was devouring and she had to laugh because perhaps he was going to eat her after all…

And that slightly amusing thought turned molten when he began to kiss a trail down her body, separating the sides of the robe as he went until he was between her thighs, his hungry gaze trained on the most intimate part of her. And then he put his mouth there.

She arched against him, a scream rising in her throat. This was beyond her fantasies. This was beyond anything. The tiger had indeed come to devour her. And she had been right not to run away.

His tongue and fingers created magic in her. Left her breathless. Left her writhing beneath him and begging. He turned her inside out. Made her question things she had never questioned before, all over the stroke of his tongue against her sensitized flesh.

He moved his large hands beneath her rear and held her up, a pagan offering for his consumption. And yet the pleasure was all hers.

The climax overtook her like a wave, and when it shattered her she was left spent and breathless, trying to cling to something, anything that would keep her grounded to the earth.

Krav was all there was.

Then he was above her, his dark eyes intense and she realized he was naked now, his beautiful body on display in the dim light of the room, the dips and hollows of muscle and glistening golden skin sending her to a place past thought.

But she didn't get a chance to look at him for as long as she wanted before he was over her, settling between her thighs. And then he thrust into her and caught her gasp of pain on his lips. It was a shock.

But he didn't seem to notice, and it didn't take long for the feeling of impossible fullness to begin to recede, giving way to the same pleasure she'd found beneath his mouth but…different.

They were connected. And hadn't she felt like she knew him better than she had ever known anyone only moments before?

That had been nothing compared to this.

They were like one. And the beauty of it, the immense physicality of it, made her want to cry. And she couldn't imagine this thing being traded cheaply around clubs and after dinner dates, she simply couldn't. Because that wasn't what this was. It wasn't cheap or easy or tawdry. Not to her. And it never could be.

It was beautiful, magic. Meant to be.

And in her whole life she had never felt meant to be. She felt like a mistake, and always had. At every moment, at every turn. Like an unwanted tagalong to someone else's experiences. But not this. He needed her for this.

He needed her now.

And as he began to tremble right along with her, as his desire began to match with hers in a desperate race to the finish, she knew then she had never felt so whole. So complete.

Like she belonged.

In the world.

In the moment.

And then her pleasure became a living thing, taking flight inside of her and sending her to the stars before bringing her back down to earth, a sanctuary of glitter and his strong arms holding her steady and keeping her from shattering completely.

She clung to him, and his own movements became fractured, uneven, and when he found his release, it sent her to heights her own had not.

In that moment, he needed her.

He needed her.

And she had never felt so alive. So herself.

He needed her so many times that night she lost track. There on the cushions in the living room, and then in his room, with a large canopied bed.

And she would never again misunderstand what that motion next door might be. Though she would say now, it was weak in comparison to what she'd experienced.

Krav was a dream. A fantasy.

One she didn't want to wake up from.

But when morning came, he was there, looking at her like she was a revelation. And so she stayed. And stayed.

The days and nights melted together, and she began to think that this might be everything.

By the time she was able to get a hold of Jaia, she told her that she wouldn't be finishing the trip with her.

Because she had met a man.

And it was so satisfying to be the one to have found someone. To be the one having a wild, delicious affair.

To be the one falling in love.

Krav was beautiful. Her Tiger. This man who had taken everything she thought she knew about herself and upended it. They stayed in the tree house for a while. But then after that, he took her to a brilliant hotel in Siem Reap, and they got reservations at the most coveted table in the entire country, where she was served gourmet delicacies that thrilled and delighted her.

"We should go to Europe," he said.

She had left her waitressing job before the trip, it was always easy enough to get hired for another job like that, at least it had been for her.

There was the apartment, but that was taken care of until she and Jaia were meant to come back from Cambodia.

There was no reason to not pack up and go with him. Anywhere. Everywhere.

"I feel like there's so much about you I don't know," she said. "And I have told you everything about my life."

"Surely not everything," he said, grinning as he held a bite of chocolate cake up as a temptation across the table. "I am absolutely certain there is more that I don't know."

"There is certainly no more to be seen."

She was shameless with him. And she had never imagined that she could be shameless. But he lit her on fire, from the inside out. Turned her into a stranger, and she wanted to stay this stranger.

This woman who was wild and sensual, who had no boundaries in bed with this glorious, gorgeous man who ignited need within her with a simple look across the room.

But she knew that she was living in a fantasy. Around the edges of this, that reality hovered.

He had to have a job. He had to have a real life. And she was beginning to sense that it wasn't here.

But he was not forthcoming with information about himself at all.

"I do have work," he said after they'd spent a week in that glorious hotel. "But I tend to do it while you sleep. And yes, soon… Soon I will need to get back to life. But for now…"

"But what is that life?"

"It is none of your concern."

And that should've been the first indicator to her that it was not for him what it was to her.

But as one week turned to another, and another, from England to France to Switzerland, she forgot to be cautious. She forgot about Jaia. She forgot about her apartment.

About the life she'd walked out of like it was nothing.

She was in love. Quite simply for the first time in her life, she was desperately in love.

One day he looked at her across the bed they shared.

"We should go to Italy for a while."

It occurred to her then, he was Italian. And while she realized that he must be Cambodian in part, and he spoke Khmer with ease, the accent of his English had been different than the ones she'd heard in Siem Reap.

He was Italian.

They went and stayed at an estate on the Amalfi Coast, and it was the most blindingly beautiful place she had ever seen.

And every day, she fell more desperately in love with him.

But it wasn't until she missed her period that she began to be concerned.

Because she wouldn't be unhappy if she was pregnant with his baby. But she was afraid… She was very afraid that he would be.

He was wonderful to her. Always. Even though he worked more now that they were in Europe, it was always gourmet meals and sex all night with Krav.

He was insatiable. Completely and utterly and she loved it.

But she was no closer to knowing him than she had been before, no matter how much she liked to tell herself otherwise. No matter how much she liked to tell herself that she must know him because she knew every inch of his body. Because she knew how to bring him to pleasure. How to make him lose control. Yet no matter how much she tried to tell herself all of that, she didn't think he was going to receive news about a baby easily.

It was that darkness she sensed beneath it all. That predator.

There came a point when she couldn't ignore the missed period any longer, so while Krav was working she went into the village and procured herself a pregnancy test from a drugstore. She went into the bathroom and took the test. And when it came back positive, she began to cry.

She was happy. She was. But she had a terrible feeling that it wouldn't be easy.

She dressed herself up as perfectly as she could. He had provided her with the most beautiful clothes. And she had his chef prepare a dinner that she knew was his favorite.

It was such a funny thing, that she felt she could ask the chef to prepare something specific. She wouldn't have done that even a week and a half ago, but she was beginning to become so settled into the life that they'd made. Is it a life if you still know nothing about him?

She just had to hope that tonight he revealed that he had the same attachment to her that she did to him.

There was a storm starting to rage, and she thought it was ominous. Though it must be either a good omen or a very bad one. Good possibly because this was how they had met. Bad because... Well, typically, a storm didn't signal anything good.

But the table was set beautifully, his favorite pasta dish prepared to perfection.

And she had tried to make herself as beautiful as possible. As if there was a threshold that might make this all okay.

When he walked in, for a moment he looked so dark it stole her breath away. But then he looked at her and smiled.

"Dinner and you. What have I done to deserve this?"

"I just wanted to have a special evening."

"Then a special evening we shall have."

Outside, it was pouring rain now.

They sat down to dinner, and she waited, with all of her nervous energy, trying to force herself to eat so that he wouldn't think something was wrong.

"I have something to tell you," she said.

He looked up at her over the table, and she knew. Before she even spoke, she knew.

That he'd always had the power to devour her if he wanted.

To destroy her.

And that he would.

"I'm pregnant."

His fury was immediate. Like a lit match. And when he moved, he was that Tiger. Instantaneous. Powerful. He was across and standing in front of her in no time at all.

"You're what?"

"I'm pregnant."

"No. That cannot be."

"It's true. You didn't use a condom the first night we were together. How can you say that isn't true? I think there've been many times since then when you haven't."

And the girl she had been back when they had first met would've been embarrassed to talk about this, but not the woman she had become. "How can you look at me and say that there isn't a way?"

"Because it isn't acceptable. I do not want a child."

"Well, I am having one. So now it is simply a question of…"

"No. I want nothing to do with it."

"You can't mean that."

"I do. You don't know anything about me, and that is by design. I will never, never have a child."

And before she could think about what she was doing, she stood and pushed away from the table.

"Riot…"

"Don't talk to me," she said. "Don't touch me. How dare you. *How dare you.*"

"For all I know you're pregnant with someone else's bastard and you're trying to fob it off as mine."

"How dare you," she whispered.

And then she turned and ran out of the room. Ran out of the house. The rain was pounding, but she ran anyway. But she slipped and fell onto the cobbled stones. And felt a violent cramp in her stomach.

She stood up, a sob on her lips. And she felt warmth on her legs.

"Riot," he shouted.

"Go away," she said, tears pouring down her face. "I'm losing it anyway. Everything is lost."

He picked her up and carried her inside. He put her in the shower, then wrapped her in a towel and tucked her into bed.

He left her there.

The next morning he was gone.

But a car arrived for her.

Ready to whisk her into the heart of the village.

And he wasn't there to say goodbye to her. He was gone, her bright burning tiger.

This was over.

When she arrived at the hotel—one of his—there were instructions waiting. She could stay there as long as she wished, and then after the concierge would arrange for her to go anywhere she wanted.

She thought of her tiny apartment back in Georgia.

She had shared it with Jaia but she'd abandoned it—and her—for this life in Europe, like it wouldn't have an end. But it had.

She had no job to go back to.

But now she could go anywhere. Do anything. And Krav had given her the key to that, even as he'd crushed something in her she thought she'd never get back. It felt like a metaphor and one she was going to seize.

She had the ticket. She just needed to be brave enough to take the first step.

She'd been lost in a fairy tale for a moment, lost in pleasure. It was over now, but there was something beyond that.

But if she'd learned one thing in life it was that she couldn't waste her time, her energy or her emotions on other people. He didn't want to be in her life.

Better than that, he'd given her the path to a new one.

This was the journey she'd been brought here to go on. She just hadn't known it.

And so she went to England, because she'd always wanted to go. She'd started in London and ended up going north, to a small village where she worked in a café and got to know everyone.

She went to a doctor, where she found out she hadn't miscarried after all.

She'd bent at the waist, sitting on the medical table and wept. Joy. Sorrow. All cascading through her like endless rain.

How was it possible?

A baby. The baby wasn't gone. Krav was gone. The life she'd thought they would have, that was gone.

Because the man she'd thought he was…he didn't exist.

But this child did.

Her child.

Hers.

Not Krav's.

Just hers.

The doctor held her hand while she cried, and then he gave her a bunch of pamphlets explaining her every option. She took them all, because it seemed responsible. But she didn't need to look at options.

She was keeping the baby.

And she wasn't even afraid. She'd found a life, a community. The older woman she rented a room from had been sweet and nonjudgmental, happy for her in a way Riot knew her mother certainly wouldn't have been.

It would be okay. Everything would be okay. She'd do just fine here in this little village that had adopted her as their American mascot. They liked her accent and they liked her. And this was all part of the new adventure she was on. One that was certainly happier and more filled with hope than anything before it had been.

Everything was perfect—except sometimes she thought of Krav and the heat between them.

And how he'd broken her heart in ways she didn't think she'd ever recover from.

She'd trusted him. In a way she'd never trusted another person. Enough to be naked with him. Enough to feel safe. She'd finally believed…

She'd finally believed love was possible. That for her, it was possible.

The realization that it wasn't had nearly destroyed her. But now she had a new reason to put herself back together. And so she did.

Everything was perfect—except one morning she went to pick up fresh baked scones from a bakery down the street to bring to the café and she was hit head-on by a reckless driver.

Everything was perfect—until she lost consciousness and a swirling darkness claimed her as its own.

CHAPTER TWO

"MR. VALENTI, IT'S about the girl."

Kravann Valenti looked across his desk at the man standing there. And then looked behind him, at the expansive view of Rome in all its bustling glory. He was tired of Rome.

He was tired of everything.

He had been tired of everything until he'd met Riot Phillips.

She had been standing in the ruins like fate that night, and he had been the fool who'd decided to grab hold of her.

Unexpected. And he had been in a low place in his life, and he was utterly furious he had allowed anyone into that moment.

He had no one to blame but himself.

Perhaps his father had been right after all. Perhaps there was weakness in him after all. A weakness that had needed to be beaten out of him.

It didn't work, did it?

She had wrecked his life.

She had been all he'd wanted, all he'd craved. He'd

never been like that, not with anything. Control mattered above all else, and he had none with her.

He'd never kept a woman beyond a weekend, and Riot had been with him a month. One month of sex. He hadn't been able to get enough of her.

Then she had told him she was pregnant.

If there was one thing he had always known it was that he would never have children. And suddenly she didn't seem like simple fate. She seemed like a twist of it. The enemy of everything he'd built. Of all that he'd sworn to be or not to be.

He was not a man who did regret. And yet regret had been his very breath since that night. She had run from him, like he was a monster. And then she had fallen.

Everything is lost.

He'd known then he had to let her go. Because he had never thought he was his father, and that moment had brought him closer than he'd thought possible.

The darkness in him…it had won out.

The image of her there, bleeding, weeping…

It woke him at night.

Shook him awake with its insistence. Evidence of his demons. Demons he would never escape no matter how much he wished he might.

He had not personally looked into what Riot was doing since she had gone. But he had asked that his people keep watch on her.

The Valenti Company was the only reason his father had ever had anything to do with him. A man at his wit's end after his oldest and only legitimate son had died, he'd gone to Cambodia and stolen his bastard from the arms of Krav's mother, making him the heir to the family fortune.

It was not because Sergio Valenti had any soft feelings for a son. It was because he believed in carrying on the family business, and believed it had to be done by Valenti blood.

And he had been the only other direct line to his father remaining.

It had given him much.

Money, education, power.

But it had taken a vast amount from him as well.

His mother had loved him.

But she had been powerless to stand against the powerful Valenti Company when it came to defending her rights to her child.

Krav himself had been five.

He could scarcely remember anything before coming to Italy.

Just vague pictures of a room with bright pink walls and a soft voice speaking to him in his native language.

Then he'd been thrust into a world with unfamiliar nannies, words he didn't understand and a distant, tyrannical father.

He'd survived it. And he'd thought he'd survived it well.

His mother remained his one weakness. He ached for her, all of his life. Like there was a hole in his chest where his heart had once been. It caused him pain, always. His father had been quick to point out that pain like that was nothing more than human frailty, and Valenti men could not surrender to such things.

He had only done so with her.

Her death had…

It had rocked him in a way he had not imagined anything could. And then Riot had been there.

Riot. A ridiculous name for a girl with blond hair and an accent thick and sweet like honey. She had looked like a forest nymph with her hair all curled from the rain and her brightly colored dress plastered to her body by the rain, her cheeks pink from the sun, her nose scattered with freckles.

And her touch had been a revelation.

He had felt more in those moments with her than he could recall feeling in the whole of his life.

He gritted his teeth and kept his focus determinedly on the scene below. "What about her?"

"She has been injured."

"What?" he turned sharply, and for the first time really looked at the man delivering the message.

But it was not his face he saw.

It was Riot.

Her face full of joy and wonder as she'd looked at the tree house. At him. At everything.

And then devastated that night…that last night.

Injured.

He thought of her lying on the ground, broken. Then he thought of that night he'd broken her. That night all his poison had spilled out and destroyed the world they'd lived in.

Dio, what had he been thinking?

Those months with her. All sun and sex and brightness and he'd been pretending. It had only been a matter of time before the darkness leaked out of him, and it had.

From the first time he'd seen her to the last, she'd gone from pure joy to pure anguish. And it was him. All him.

She was hurt now, though.

And all he could think of was going to her.

"When?" he asked.

"This morning. She was in an accident. She has been living in a village in the north of England."

He asked the question he feared the answer to most. "Is she going to live?"

"It is not certain." He felt that like a blow. "She's unconscious."

He was moving already. "Get the helicopter ready. We are going to England." He had to see her. He had to go to her.

He would not touch her, not again.

But he had to go to her.

"Yes, *signore*. But…there is one more thing."

"What?"

"She's pregnant."

The words rang in his ears like a gong. "Pregnant?"

"Yes."

She hadn't lost the baby.

It had been eight months since he'd seen her. She could have met any number of men in the time since then. Gotten pregnant in the time since she had lost the child she had carried with him.

But he could not ignore the feeling that raced through his veins when he heard the word. Something primal.

Something like the beat of a drum that surpassed thought and reached down to the very heart of him.

To a place that defied reason and logic.

His.

That child was his.

All was not lost.

He had not broken this.

And this was his second chance. One he did not deserve, and perhaps…

Perhaps one he should not claim.

He had been more monster than man that night.

But she was unconscious in a hospital, and she was carrying his child.

And monster or man, it mattered not.

She was his.

The man spoke in hushed, apologetic tones. "They do not know if the child will live, either."

If he hadn't sent her away she would not be hurt.

If he hadn't sent her away, the child would be alive.

They had to live.

Both of them.

He would fix this. He was not simply a man, monster he might be. But he was a Valenti. And a Valenti did what must be done.

He would move heaven and earth.

He would take the pen straight from the hand of God and he would damn well write a new ending.

"We are going to England now."

When Riot woke up, she wasn't in her bed.

That was her first thought as she groggily opened

her eyes and tried to find a comfortable position. She couldn't. Her arm wasn't mobile and there was a strange beeping sound. And she…ached.

Her eyes fluttered open and she realized she was in what might have been a hospital suite. Except it was… fancy. But there was no denying there was medical equipment everywhere.

She tried to remember how she'd gotten there, but she couldn't. She tried to remember…

She had to call Jaia.

Her roommate would come and get her. Heaven knew she couldn't rely on her mother.

She and Jaia were supposed to go to Cambodia in a couple of weeks. Jaia had decided to go and meet some of her friends on a whim and she'd invited Riot to come along and Riot had thought…why not.

She felt a stab of disappointment. Depending on how badly hurt she was she might not be able to go on the trip.

Maybe it hadn't been such a great idea anyway. After all, it would have cost her so much of her savings.

But then…

She had never really done anything adventurous before. Her life was just…

She had tried so hard not to be her mother. Not to be a riot, really. And somewhere in there she'd become a gray, pale nothing.

One that was in a hospital bed, though.

She looked around, trying to see if she could find a button to push to call a nurse or…someone. As she did she took in more details of the room.

It looked like a bedroom. Though, not an ordinary one. It was luxurious. With deep red wallpaper textured like velvet and gold edging on all the doorposts.

If she weren't in a hospital bed, if there weren't beeping machines and IVs and all of the other medical accoutrements, she wouldn't have ever thought she was in a hospital.

Where was she?

For a moment she knew a zip of fear because this wasn't…normal. And no matter how hard she tried she couldn't remember how she'd gotten here. She couldn't remember the last thing she'd done.

Well, she had a most recent memory. She was in her apartment eating cereal for dinner and listening to Jaia talk about how staying in hostels was fine and she'd done it all through Europe and they'd be perfectly safe.

But that didn't connect to this moment.

It didn't explain how she'd gotten here.

She finally found the call button, or what she thought might be one, and pressed it. Repeatedly. Desperately.

The door opened and in swept a woman, not in a hospital uniform, but in a…pinafore that reminded her of something she'd seen in period pieces, down to the starched white apron.

"Ms. Phillips, you're awake!"

"Yes," she said, feeling groggy and confused. "I… you know my name?"

That wasn't actually weird, of course she did. It was probably on all her patient information. She'd surely had her ID with her at the time of whatever accident she was in. But she didn't seem…injured. She was sore, but she wasn't bandaged or anything.

She touched her face just to be sure.

Not a bandage on there, and no blood or anything on the extremities she could see.

"Of course." She raced over and began to look at the machine, and as she did she took her phone out of her pocket—a piece of tech that seemed incongruous with her old-fashioned outfit—and dialed a number quickly. "Yes, Doctor, she's awake. Please come as quickly as you can."

A hard knot of fear began to grow at the center of her chest.

"Is my being awake…a bad thing?" she asked.

"Not at all." The nurse—Riot now assumed she was a nurse—looked down at her. "But it is a bit of a surprise."

"Why?" Fear was now a desperate, living creature clawing at her chest. "Why is it a surprise?"

"Ms. Phillips… I should wait until the doctor gets here to speak more of it."

The door opened again and Riot thought it must be the doctor.

But it wasn't.

It was a man. Tall and broad, dressed in a black suit. His hair was jet black as a raven's wing, his eyes nearly as dark. His skin bronzed, his cheekbones razor sharp, his nose a finely honed blade. He was striking in a way that stole her breath.

He was utterly singular and unique and yet…

And yet something echoed in her soul. A recognition.

But she had no idea who this man was. None at all.

She'd never seen him before in her life.

But when he stepped into the room she felt it. Like a seismic wave moving through her body. He brought with him a new pull to the earth, a shift in the stars.

He was power.

She knew it, intuitively. She didn't have to know who he was to know that.

He was more than a man. He was…

A tiger.

That thought came from nowhere and whispered in her mind, in her soul. Goose bumps spread over her arms and she rubbed at them.

"Mr. Valenti, I don't think—"

But one look from him and the nurse's words fell into silence.

Then he looked back at her and if she hadn't already been stuck in bed, his stare would have pinned her there.

"You are awake," he said, his voice deep, with a beautiful accent that begged the listener to draw closer to him.

Even as everything in her screamed danger.

"Y-yes," she said. "I am awake. As this woman here has observed. And called for help. But I'm not sure why it's significant? Or why…or what happened. Or… or anything."

One of his dark brows winged upward. "You don't know what happened?"

"I don't. And I have no idea why I'm here or who you are."

He seemed to not know what to say to that and she

knew—somehow, like she knew anything about him—that he was not a man accustomed to not knowing.

"Riot," he said, her name rough on his lips, sending a shattering sensation through her.

He knew her name, her first name, and why that seemed to make such a difference, she had no idea.

"Riot," he repeated. "You've been unconscious for a month."

"A…a month? That's impossible. I was planning to go on vacation with my roommate and then I woke up here."

"You've already been on vacation with your roommate," he said.

She frowned. "No…no I haven't. I've never been outside the country before."

"And which country do you think you're in now?" he asked.

"I'm in America," she said. "Georgia, I would assume. Where I've lived all my life."

"No, Riot. You're in Rome. In my estate. And you are to be my wife."

CHAPTER THREE

SHE WAS AWAKE, and she did not know him.

The fact was, Krav now had the perfect opportunity to send her away. She didn't remember him. She didn't remember Soriya.

But he had told her she was to marry him anyway.

Kravann Valenti did not second-guess himself. He had not been raised that way. At least not in the second part of his life. His father had been a mean, dictatorial bastard. To make him strong, he'd said.

To make him worthy of the name Valenti.

And Krav had never once acted with the intent to honor his father. It was simply he could never allow his father to be right.

He could not allow his father's fears of Krav's weakness to have any bearing on reality. The only time he had ever shown softness was in the hours following his mother's funeral. When he'd found this creature who lay before him now.

There was a reason he'd sent her off, and quickly.

But now she was here.

And he had just told her she was staying.

But it was no matter.

He had done well enough with the child so far. He had nannies… But why continue on having nannies when the child could have her mother. He had been incensed when he had found the adoption brochure in her things. She had been going to give his child up, without ever giving him a chance to be a father. Not that he knew anything about being a father, but it was the principle of the thing. A child should have their parents. And one of those parents should not be a maniacal sociopath hell-bent on nothing more than the upkeep of his name.

One thing he knew for certain, he wanted Soriya to have her mother. He needed Riot to protect Soriya from his darkness. To act as a buffer.

And she didn't remember anything…

And what of when she does?

It wouldn't matter. By the time she did remember— if she ever did, things would be different.

He was rewriting the story.

After all, she did not have his full name. So it was likely she had only been considering giving the child up for adoption because of financial reasons. As his wife, she would have everything she could have ever wanted and then some.

"I'm… I'm to be your wife?"

"Yes," he said. "You do not remember me, *cara mia*?"

She shook her head, and he was astonished to see her eyes filled with tears.

"What is it?"

"I can't believe I don't remember falling in love. I cannot believe that I don't remember that somebody in this world loves me."

And if he were another man, he supposed he might feel guilt in this moment. Because there was no love between them. Certainly, passion had flared that night in the tree house. There was no denying that.

But love?

Krav did not even know what that was.

He felt a fierce protectiveness for Soriya that he had never felt for any other creature on this earth. A kind of protectiveness that transcended his own sense of self-preservation. It was like having a part of him walking out in the world. He would not characterize that as love. For it was not pleasant.

It made him even more feral, if such a thing were possible.

And when it came to keeping his child's mother here… Well, he would do anything to accomplish that. No guilt involved at all.

"Please," the nurse said. "Mr. Valenti, with all due respect, we must have a doctor here to examine her. She needs an MRI. We need to ensure that she is not placed under any distress."

"This is not a soap opera," he said. "I can hardly see what knowing a little bit about her life is going to do as far as damage goes."

This nurse… She knew nothing about their circumstances. Everybody working in the house at the moment was under the strictest confidence. He could not have the broader world knowing about Soriya, not yet. She was a month old now and had never been taken away from the estate grounds.

And, in spite of the fact that he himself understood few emotional connections, he had made sure that she had been brought into Riot's room every single day by one of the nannies. If there was one thing he knew... It was that a child needed his mother.

He had done. Badly.

And so he had made sure that Soriya had known her mama. And that she had understood she was merely sleeping. Taking a very long nap.

And now she was awake.

"Valenti..." She closed her eyes, and she looked dizzy.

"Do not tax yourself," he said.

On one score he did agree with the nurse, he could not immediately tell her about the baby. She did not remember anything after her trip to Cambodia, then he imagined the child would be quite the shock.

The DNA test had already confirmed that the child was his, so there was no question as to the fact that she had conceived her during that night.

And as she had no memory of that night...

It would be likely she would find the whole thing impossible.

If she found it distressing that she had missed falling in love... If only she knew. That there was no love between them, only a broken, dark passion that had exploded that night. And had undone everything he had ever believed about himself.

He was a man of great control, but never once had he thought of using protection with her.

He had her over and over again that first night, and he had not thought of it.

The doctor arrived shortly after, and examined her. "In theory," he said, "she is in good health."

He was speaking Italian, and Krav had the realization that Riot wouldn't be able to understand. But that would give him the chance to explain after, and be yet further in control of the narrative, and that suited him just fine.

"So there is no reason to withhold information from her?"

"No," the doctor said slowly. "At least, not in my opinion."

"Good."

"I want to check in with her from time to time, and you must keep me apprised as to her memory."

"Yes," Krav said, waving a hand. "But now I feel that we should be left."

"I assume you do have things that must be handled between the two of you."

"Yes. A great many things."

During the visit with the doctor, Riot had gotten out of bed. They had exercised her while she was in a coma, which had ensured that her muscles were not entirely atrophied. And while she had been unsteady on her feet, and required the use of a walker, it had not taken long for her to begin to move around on her own. "I remember how to walk," she had said. "I remember everything except… I guess I don't remember the last…"

"Ten months at least," he said. "Your trip to Cambodia happened that long ago. And you've been in a coma for a month."

"We met there?" She asked, perched up in bed, only the two of them in the room.

And he was surprised then, how much he still wanted her.

He had managed to shut down the ache while she was unconscious. And while he still felt… Something, every time he was near her, he had managed to transfer those feelings to his desire for Soriya to know her mother.

Now he was there, he could not deny that his desire for her was as it had always been. Purely, deeply sexual.

And now was not the time to ponder it.

"I went to Cambodia," she said, softly, not looking at him.

"Yes, you did."

"I can't believe I had a whole adventure and I don't even remember it."

"Well, *cara*, you are still on an adventure."

Her head whipped around and her eyes widened. "That's right. I'm in Rome, aren't I? And I assume you don't mean Rome, Georgia."

"I do not," he said, looking at her.

He had grown accustomed to her face, but sleeping. She had looked peaceful these months, lying in bed as if she were under an enchantment. The doctors had held little hope of her waking, but he had been unwilling to give up on her.

Soriya needed her mother.

And what do you need?

Need.

It burst through him like a bomb.

His need for her.

She was here. Speaking to him. Not just asleep. He felt like part of himself had woken up too.

She wasn't looking at him like he had just broken her whole world.

She was looking at him like she had that first day.

That was what he had, here and now. A second chance at a first day with her.

"I'm actually in Italy. With a man and I'm…engaged." She looked at him as if she was trying to place him. "How did we meet?"

"We met at the temple ruins," he said, deciding to keep the conversation as honest as possible.

But it was clear Riot wanted love. He didn't have the ability to give it to her. But it cost him nothing to weave a new story for them. And why not?

She hadn't been planning on keeping the baby, but she would settle into their life here.

She would be happy. And as for the truth…once she was convinced of the rightness of all of this the truth wouldn't matter.

"And you swept me off my feet?" she asked.

"Something like that."

"No really," she said. "Tell me."

She was looking at him all open and sweet and he remembered her being much more guarded when they'd first met. She trusted him now. She wasn't looking at him like he was a predator set on devouring her.

He idly wondered if this was a moment another man might feel something like guilt.

"Your...friends ended up leaving early. It was raining. We were the only two people left at the ruins, and you came back home with me." It was impossible to keep his voice from growing huskier. Impossible to hide the rising desire inside of him because thinking of that night made him think of how it had been.

If he pushed through the memories of grief, if he ignored why he'd been there in the first place, he could remember the way her skin had felt beneath his hands. The way she'd looked up at him in wonder as she'd found her release...

"I did?"

"Yes."

"Then what?"

She looked so guileless, and if he didn't know for a fact she'd just woken up after being in a coma for a month he would have thought it was an act. Not that it couldn't be an act but he doubted she'd be that quick to slip into one.

No, whatever Riot was...he'd never thought her an actress.

A sorceress, perhaps, for no other woman had ever managed to get under his skin in quite so accomplished a fashion.

"Our connection was immediate," he said. "And physical."

She blinked. "No. Now I know you're lying. Sorry, there is no way I went back to your place and…no."

"No way?"

"None," she said, shaking her head.

"I hate to disappoint you, but you did. You had known me all of one hour when you took your clothes off for me."

She laughed at him. Sleeping Beauty had the audacity to laugh at him. "It didn't happen that way. I'm a virgin."

Then she seemed to remember herself, putting her hand over her mouth, color suffusing her cheeks. "I don't know why I said that. I don't know why I'm talking to you like this except you say I know you, and now you're telling me I slept with you moments after meeting you and I'm sorry I just…can't make that make sense. Not when I know what I know about the rest of my life."

"But you don't know anything about the days leading up to your trip. Or what happened on it," he pointed out.

A virgin?

Was it possible?

She wasn't one now, that was for certain. But it had never once occurred to him that the sensual woman he'd taken into his arms that night had never been with another man.

"I guess I had a whole personality transplant. Believe me, I'm not adventurous. I…"

Something else changed in her face just then and it galled him that even now he couldn't read this woman. Even now she was a mystery to him.

Women were not mysteries in his world. They filled a very specific purpose, fed a specific appetite and then he didn't think of them again.

It was how people were in his world.

They outlived their usefulness, and then they were gone from it.

Now he had a baby, and practically speaking, babies served no use at all. But he would have her, forever.

And now there was Riot, and he was going to have her forever too.

And she mystified him.

"I must be adventurous," she whispered. "I must be. Because I went to Cambodia and I met you and we…we did, didn't we?" She seemed hypnotized then and his heart did something it had never done before.

He had no words for it.

An ache, a squeeze and a thunder all at once, as she leaned forward with a questioning look on her face. And she placed her hand on his chest. Over that muscle that was reacting to her even now.

Her eyes met his and the wonder he saw there mirrored what he'd seen when he'd entered her body that night they'd been together.

He curled his fingers around her wrist and felt everything begin to burn.

And then an ear-shattering wail split the silence.

Riot went still. "What is that?"

CHAPTER FOUR

HER MIND WAS REELING. It had been blank when she'd woken up but now it was…it was overly full. With this place, with this man.

Engaged? It seemed impossible.

She couldn't remember anything, and she really had no idea how she had gone on her trip, a woman who had never been kissed, and ten months later found herself engaged to the most beautiful man she'd ever seen in her life.

Who was also obviously wealthy?

None of it made sense.

But she could feel something between them. Something like she'd never experienced before and she'd felt compelled to draw near to it.

But the crying baby had stopped everything.

"Where is the baby?" she asked, her heart thundering in desperation.

"It is not time to have that discussion."

Panic. Desperation. Terror.

"Why not?" she asked.

"Because it is not."

But she didn't listen. On her unsteady legs she got out of the bed and ran. She stumbled forward, her knee coming down hard on the carpet, which bit into her skin and she cursed the ridiculous nightgown she was still wearing.

The baby.

There was a baby.

She'd been asleep for a whole month.

She opened the door just as he reached for her, pulling her back against his hard body as it opened to reveal a woman standing there, holding a tiny little bundle, cradled to her chest.

The baby had dark hair, her skin golden. None of Riot was visible at all. She looked for her own features, desperately and didn't see any.

She saw *him*.

But there was nothing that decisively stated that she was there as well.

But she felt it. *She felt it,* and she couldn't say what it was.

She knew so little right now. She knew nothing about how she had gotten to this place in her life. And she didn't look at her fiancé and know anything.

But looking at this child, she knew.

"What's her name," she whispered, his hands still holding her in an iron grip.

"Soriya," he said.

It was a beautiful name and she wanted to ask what it meant, but that desire was overshadowed by her need to hold the baby. She was fussing and hiccupping and the woman holding her might as well have been invisible because she didn't matter to Riot at all.

All she could see was Soriya.

"Give her to me," she demanded.

"There is explaining…"

"There is no explaining," she said, pulling out of his hold with Herculean effort. "The child is mine, I know she is."

"We do not wish to upset you," he said, his voice firm.

"Do not treat me like a child. This is my baby. Give her to me," she demanded in a voice she didn't entirely recognize. But the woman holding the baby—a nanny she assumed—immediately did as Riot said.

And then she placed the soft, warm bundle into her arms and the whole world seemed to change. Again.

She'd woken up in a life she didn't know. And this should be yet more confusion. But it wasn't.

It was all suddenly clear. Because while she didn't remember him. And she couldn't understand how she'd come to be engaged to him, and she really couldn't believe she'd chucked twenty-two years of virginity out the window in an afternoon, she could believe this.

This child.

She knew her, down in her bones, maybe because her body had knit her together. She knew her.

And the grief that overwhelmed her for a moment took her breath away.

She didn't remember falling in love.

She didn't remember the touch of his hands on her body.

She didn't remember carrying this baby, or telling

him about the pregnancy. Was he happy? Had they been filled with joy? Did they have to move the wedding date up or…they must have decided to wait until after she was born.

And the birth…

She had missed all of it.

Had forgotten her stomach growing rounder by the week. Had slept through the labor pains. How could she have delivered while asleep?

It was too much to take in. She'd slept with this man. Had a relationship with him. Had his baby. All of it was gone.

Except…

It wasn't all gone.

This baby was hers, and whether it made sense that she knew it or not, she did.

She hadn't held her baby. The baby was a month old and she'd never held her.

Suddenly her chest felt like it was caving in on itself. It was all too overwhelming. She'd been awake for hours after the baby had been separated from her for so long and no one had brought her to Riot.

"Why didn't you bring her to me immediately?" she asked, angry that there had been hours where she could have been holding her child and hadn't been.

"Concern," he said, his voice hard. "It is difficult enough for you to believe all that passed between us. To lose this from your memory…"

"She is mine," she said.

"Yes."

"I know," she whispered. She did. She knew it with her whole heart. Her whole soul.

Suddenly everything felt terrifying and precarious. He knew so much more about her than she did, and the only good thing was that he must love her. No one else in her life ever had. But if he loved her, and he had taken care of her so it seemed that he must, he wouldn't do her any harm.

He wouldn't take Soriya from her.

And she suddenly felt desperately, horribly afraid. Not of this unprecedented situation that she found herself in, but that she might actually be asleep now. That this was a dream.

Because how had the girl that she had been when last she remembered, woken up to be engaged. Woken up to be the mother of this perfect, beautiful child. It didn't make any sense. She had never been lovely or compelling or desired.

Her own mother hadn't wanted anything to do with her at all, much less her father.

And somehow, she had managed to get herself into the situation where… Where she was different. Where everything was different. It was like waking up in an entirely new life.

It wasn't like that, it *was* that. And she couldn't… She would never be able to…

And she realized she didn't even know his name.

"I'm sorry, we have not been properly introduced."

He looked at her, as if she had said something extremely surprising. And she supposed that she had. But she didn't know what was surprising right now. She felt at sea, and utterly ignorant of everything. And he knew everything. He knew about the baby. Everything about her. Riot didn't. She hadn't even known she was pregnant.

"Kravann," he said. "Valenti. If I had friends, they would call me Krav."

"Oh."

"Yes. It means nothing to you, I take it?"

"No. It just doesn't… None of this… I don't remember anything. I don't remember any of this. I don't remember you. But then… I'm not entirely certain that I remember myself. Because I just… I am not interesting enough to have met you and gone back to your place and…" She realized that she was still speaking in front of the nanny.

And then he gestured to the woman. "Leave us."

Riot took the baby in her arms, holding her close. She was so warm and weighty. She wanted to cling to her forever. She had never felt anything like this, the strange sense of peace that stole over her even in the midst of all this turmoil. And if there was one thing she knew right now it was that this child was hers. Regardless of whether or not she remembered it. This child was hers.

"We will find our way," he said.

And she wondered if he had been worried about her. If he had been keeping a bedside vigil. It was difficult to imagine this man worried. He was… She had never known a man like him, that was certain. Her experience with men was limited, it was true. But even so, she felt that he was the sort of man that wasn't common in the least.

He had an air of authority about him that was entirely different from any other person she'd known.

And all of this…

"I just have so many questions," she said. "I feel like I need to… Piece together the whole last ten months immediately."

"You do not have to," he said. "We have the rest of our lives, Riot. The rest of our lives to determine who we are. You do not need to put yourself back together in five minutes. Head injuries are complex, so I have been told many times over the last month."

"Can you start with telling me what… What happened to me?"

"No. I think we should start with getting you moved to a better room. I think we should start with you getting cleaned up, and then having dinner."

She was in a nightgown, and she couldn't deny that there was likely some validity to what he was saying, but that would require that she separate from Soriya.

She held the baby closer.

"She has been with me this last month. She will be fine with me for a few moments more."

He took out his phone, and opened something, pushing a button inside of the app. And moments later, two members of staff she had not yet seen appeared.

"Yes, Mr. Valenti?"

"Please take my fiancée to her room. She will be in different quarters now. Help her select an outfit for dinner. Show her to the bathroom and draw her a bath."

"Yes sir."

And with that, Riot found herself being ushered away

from Soriya, and from Krav, and she felt like the world had been upended yet again.

They were her anchors, she realized, even though she couldn't remember either of them.

Because this whole world was foreign, but if it was Krav's world, then she could at least work out why she was in it.

It didn't take any imagination at all to see why she would've been tempted to go with him.

"Is he… He always like this?" she asked.

"Always like what, miss?" one of the women asked her.

"He's quite… Autocratic."

"I found him to be quite soft in that moment," the other woman said. "Typically he is…"

"He growls like a tiger," the other finished.

And they smiled at each other. A burning sensation of jealousy sparked in Riot's stomach. And she knew that was silly. How could she be jealous over a man she didn't even know? Anyway, they were engaged. In theory.

The entire house was grand, and she had barely had a chance to take it in, but when she was ushered into the room that was to be hers, the breath was stolen entirely out of her lungs.

It was…

It was so different than the rather intense, Gothic appearance of the rest of the manor.

It was light. White with soft pink accents everywhere. The bed was like a cloud. All white and cotton fluffy pink with gold for the poster frame and gauzy netting wrapped around it.

It was so open and airy, so different from the room she had just come from. So different from... From anything she had ever seen before, and yet somehow it was perfectly what she would've chosen for herself.

Was it strange, though, that there was this room here prepared for her and they didn't share it?

She wondered if that was just how rich people did things. She knew that royalty often had separate bedrooms. Maybe it was... Maybe it was something the wealthy tended to do. She wouldn't know.

She hadn't known any wealthy people, not in her whole life. And he was clearly...

She tried so hard to remember. She tried so hard to cast her mind back.

Really, it was no mystery how he could've gotten her to let her guard down. He was the most beautiful man she had ever seen. And she might've thought that she wouldn't have very many chances like that in her life. To sleep with a man who was quite that beautiful.

How horribly inconvenient that she was no longer a virgin and she couldn't even remember having sex.

Of all the things to be upset about, that was perhaps a very silly one, but she did feel upset about it in the moment.

"What would you like to wear?"

One woman went over to a vast, ornate wardrobe and threw the doors open. And inside was the most delicious array of clothing Riot had ever seen.

Organized by the colors of the rainbow, deep jewel

tones and pops of bright color dazzled her. It was like a dream. She didn't like to admit it, but the fact of the matter was she was a magpie. She loved beautiful things. It was only that she had been able to own very few of them.

Her home back in Georgia was a small collection of curated things that she had saved up for, that she loved.

Because when she could buy something nice, she savored it. And now there was this entire room full of delicious things. All gifts, and there was something that made her feel breathless in that.

But then, for him, these gifts must come so easy. For her, everything beautiful had always represented hours of work. It had to have great value to her, because if it didn't, why would she put in so much work in order to have it. Money that went out had been painstakingly saved.

And she couldn't decide if it meant more or less that it had come from him.

Maybe it doesn't matter. Maybe you're just trying to attach meaning to things because you can't find an anchor.

Now that could be very well true.

She needed to get back to him. She needed to get back to Soriya.

"Mr. Valenti will want you ready in the next hour. That is when he eats dinner."

"He eats dinner at the same time every night?"

One of the women nodded. "Yes. He does. He is a man of exacting schedule."

That didn't surprise her. He seemed... Exacting. And

she was hungry for details about him. Because he was apparently a singular man in her life. A sea change in a suit. And she knew nothing about him.

There were things about him she could not quite… *grasp*. Her mind was desperately trying to fill in all of these blanks, but if she did not know that he was her fiancé she would've said that he… He did not seem like a man with a great well of emotion inside of him. There was something hard and dark about him. Something that felt quite dangerous. But that wasn't the kind of person that she was drawn to. It never had been.

She had never quite understood the appeal of the bad boy. In theory, she had decided that she liked nice men.

Of course, she had never got around to dating one. Because any man who proclaimed to be nice never was. And as far as nice men went… That was all she had ever found.

And for some reason, she chose a dress that was the color of a peacock, all shimmery and rich, and then allowed herself to be led to the bathroom where she found a deep tub that they filled with warm, scented water. Flowers were scattered over the surface, and a silk robe left out for her. And then she was left to her own devices.

She sank slowly into the water, and sighed. One thing she did know was that it had been a very long time since she'd taken a bath.

She couldn't believe that she was missing all of this time in her memory. It didn't seem possible. That so much of life had just…evaporated. The part that she had forgotten, and the part that she had been asleep through.

Asleep.

No. She hadn't been asleep. Obviously, she had been in an accident. But she didn't even know the details about that.

She tried to push it to the back of her mind, slowly beginning to wash herself. But her mind went back to Krav.

And as she moved her fingertips over her own skin, it was far too easy to imagine that the hands were his.

An electric shock went through her body.

How could she be thinking about… That? How could that be the leading thing that she… Well, if what he'd said was true about their meeting, that had been their first connection. And while she couldn't quite imagine it, maybe that was… Maybe that was the key.

She had met him, and apparently, she had been over-come by the chemistry between them. She could feel it even now.

Even with all of this… Even with so many bigger, grander things at stake… She was thinking about things that had never concerned her prior to meeting him.

She got out of the bath, swathing herself in the silk robe, and looking in the mirror. Her eyes were bright, her skin pink. She looked a bit sallow, beneath the color that had been brought on by the bath, and she let the robe fall away, examining her body in the mirror. She looked at her stomach, and tears filled her eyes. Stretch marks. A bit of extra skin.

A scar where the child had been delivered…

So that was how she'd had the baby when she'd been asleep.

Tears filled her eyes.

She had carried a baby. A *child*. And she couldn't remember...

There was a firm knock on the door. "Miss?"

And after that, there was no time to be standing there feeling sorry for herself in front of a mirror. She was hurriedly dressed and her hair brushed. Makeup applied to her face, and when she looked back in the mirror, she was yet again staring at a stranger, but not for the same reasons.

She made her way from the room, led by her entourage to the dining room.

And there he was, standing at the head of the table, wearing a dark suit. The room was vast, ornate, and heavy like the other room she had been in was. Not like that stunning bright bedroom of hers.

There was something old money about this. Something dark.

"There you are," he said.

But there was a weight beneath the words that set off a fire in her stomach.

"Yes. Is Soriya here..."

"She is down for her nap. She often takes a small nap just at this time then wakes again for a snack before going down for the night."

She couldn't deny she was disappointed by that. But suddenly she was ravenous. And her hunger overtook everything else.

Dinner was beautiful. And for a moment, she forgot about all the things she had forgotten. For a moment, she allowed herself to believe that her last memory was yesterday, and today she was standing in this beautiful, palatial home with the most glorious spread of food in front of her that she had ever seen.

For a moment, she allowed herself to believe that her life had simply transformed in an instant.

And she felt like…not like a sad, confused girl, but for the first time like perhaps she was a secret princess.

The idea made her eyes sting.

She had seen a movie when she was a teenager all about that. About a girl whose long absent father was secretly a king.

And she, secretly a princess. And sometimes, Riot had wished that was her life. That she was royalty. And someday somebody would come and take her away from her mother and give her a completely different life.

Instead, she carved out a life for herself, once she had accepted that fairy tales weren't real.

But now she felt like she was in one, and just for a moment, she wanted to embrace it. Wanted to feel it.

"Have a seat," he said.

She did as she was told, taking a seat in the chair across from him.

Being this close to him… He was even more beautiful than she had realized.

"You are…remarkable," he said. "I should imagine that most people who have gone through the ordeal you have do not come out of it looking half so well."

"I bet there aren't very many people who have gone through what I have," she said. "This seems more like a soap opera than real life."

"I told myself that quite a few times while you lay there. It was… A low point."

"For you?"

"I'm the kind of man who believes that he could fix anything. But I could not fix you. I brought in the best medical help that I could. But I was told that nothing but time would wake you. If you woke at all."

She hadn't considered that. That she might never have woken. She would never have known about Soriya. Would never have remembered Krav.

What if she had woken but years later? Missing so much time…

It made her chest burn.

"But I did wake up," she said fiercely.

"Yes," he said. "You did."

"I don't know where to begin."

"We will be married as soon as possible," he said.

But something in her jumped in fear. "I don't even remember you."

"It does not matter. We are a family. And we have waited all this time to be so. You shall be my bride."

"A bride who doesn't know her husband?"

He looked at her, his dark eyes serious, compelling. "I seduced you once. I have no problem doing it again."

And she shivered. Because the very idea of a man like him turning his focus to…seducing her… It made her…

Well, her body sang with the possibilities.

"I want to know about you," she said. "I don't remember anything. I'm sure we already did all the boring getting to know you sort of things, but…"

"My father was very wealthy. As was his father. As was his. I think you understand where this is going. The Valentis are very old Italian family."

"Right."

"The empire has expanded. We own a great many hotels. There is also a manufacturing arm. Property development. There is very little that we do not have our hands in. I am as financially secure as a person can be."

"I don't... I don't even understand that. I've never been financially secure a day in my life."

"You are now," he said. "You have nothing to worry about. All of your needs will be met with me. All of Soriya's needs will be met."

That rubbed against something wounded in her soul.

Her mother had resented her so much, and a huge part of that had been because of the financial instability they found themselves in. At least, that was what Riot told herself. The alternative was that she just wasn't lovable. That no matter what, her mother wouldn't have cared. So, she liked to excuse her on the basis of stress and fear. Because it made things easier.

Why couldn't she have forgotten that, but remembered him? This man who was beautiful and offering to take care of her.

Why was so much of him a blank space?

"How did we fall in love?"

He leaned back in his chair, his elbow resting on the arm of it, his dark eyes fathomless. Compelling.

"I told you how we met. It was undeniable. This thing between us."

"It must've been. Otherwise, I never would have...

I was raised my whole life to be very cautious about strangers. And particularly strange men. I built up a pretty healthy immunity to them. So, I can't imagine that encountering you alone in a ruin would've made me feel altogether very confident."

"You were not," he said. "You were skittish at first. But you needed a ride. I brought you back. You didn't leave."

"And then what happened?"

She was looking up at him with expectation. Her breath coming in short, sharp bursts, her eyes wide. She was greatly anticipating the story he was about to tell, and up until this moment, everything he'd said had been true.

Krav had never considered himself a liar. But he had never worried over much about it either. If a lie would do better than the truth, there was no harm in it as far as he was concerned. And he had decided before she had come out to dinner that he had one goal. To make her his bride. To make this thing between them last.

He could not be the sole parent in Soriya's life. It would be a mistake. Beyond a mistake. He had vague memories of the way his mother had held him. Of the way she had taken care of him. But vague memories were all he had.

The things that he remembered with sharp clarity were the harsh beatings that his father had doled out. The cruelty. The way that he had belittled him. And he would never…

He would never do that to Soriya. He was not afraid of being his father.

But there was a gray space that he feared almost more.

He was a man who prided himself on being an expert in all things. But he was not an expert on how to care for a child. How to give them what they needed.

And he feared his negligence would cause irreparable damage.

He was a cold bastard.

And that was why lying now seemed easy.

There was no reason not to.

She wanted a love story.

He thought of their days together. The nights. If he had been another man, that would have been a romance. But of course, he had shattered the illusion in the end.

He could see that she needed a love story. So why not give it to her? Why not give her the love story that she needed to be happy?

Maybe somewhere in there he would find that space again.

Where she had looked at him with joy and he had felt...

The days had stretched on there, like endless summer days he'd heard about but never had. The Valenti heir could never be still. Could never take a break. Could never rest.

With her, sometimes it had felt like rest.

He had tricked her into seeing a man, and not the monster he knew he was.

He wanted that again.

She needs it, that's what matters.

"It was like you had always been there," he said.

"I cooked for you. We stayed at the tree house for a while after. Then we moved on to my hotel in the city. From there we went back to Europe. We took a tour."

"I must've gotten pregnant very quickly," she said.

"Yes," he said. "Though, we…were often overcome with passion."

Her cheeks went scarlet, and he wanted to touch her. "What happened? When I found out?"

"You were scared," he said. Because she must've been. Then again, he felt that it was best if there was a ring of truth to all of this.

He saw that moment again in his mind.

I'm pregnant.

She had been happy.

He had taken that happiness and crushed it in his fist.

He had thought…

But what if it had gone differently?

He took his mind back there, to that moment.

For one moment, it was like he was there, at that dinner. Looking at her in that stunning dress as she said those words to him again.

I'm pregnant.

And this time, he made a new choice. The Krav in his vision changed.

He made a new story.

"But I told you… I told you not to worry. I told you that we would be in this together." And he could see it, in his mind. It was the strangest thing. He could imagine holding her against him, taking hold of her chin and tilting her face upward. Kissing away her tears. In this story, he was a man he had never been. One who knew how to be tender if it was required.

"Have you been married before?"

"No," he said.

"But you were ready to marry me?"

"Yes," he said. "I was… I don't have any other children, either. I did not plan on becoming a father. But once I found out… There was never any question of what I would do."

And that again was true.

"Oh." And she began to cry.

"Why are you crying?"

"Because… You say that as if…as if fathers just take care of their children. As if a man would obviously take care of the woman whose baby she's having. But…that has not been my life. My father wanted nothing to do with me, my own mother didn't care for me. And that I remember. But I can't remember you… I can't remember us. And it breaks my heart. Because I wish so much I could remember that moment. I bet it was the best moment of my life."

And he hardened his heart, into stone. Into obsidian, because he could not afford to be moved by this.

Hell, he had never in his life had to try to not be moved by anything. Except for her beauty. Her beauty was…

It had been the thing that had gotten in and undermined his control in the beginning. And it hadn't changed much now.

"We will put it back together. That I promise you.

And then… You will know that you should be my bride. My wife."

"Thank you," she said.

"Knowing that we are in love. Knowing that you love me… It's the greatest gift I could've ever asked for."

And he knew that meant he must show her the truth of it as best he could.

He must weave together a story that was so compelling she could never find the lie. She would never want to. If she knew the man he was, she would not feel this way.

If she knew his flaws. His darkness.

She would run away again, as she had that night.

He would have to hope that she did not remember the truth.

CHAPTER FIVE

RIOT HAD BEEN afraid to go to sleep that night. She had been asked to be taken to Soriya's room, and there she had stayed. She had held her baby, gazing down at her and trying to understand how her life had taken such a strange new shape so quickly.

And then she had simply rocked her, held her. She had very little memory of going to bed. But when she woke up that morning, cocooned in impossible softness, she was nearly afraid to open her eyes. If she did, would she be gone? Would her baby be gone?

Would she wake up and find that she was actually just still Riot, sad and alone in Georgia having had no adventures, and no life-changing loves?

But she opened her eyes and saw that pink canopy cloud, and she breathed a sigh of relief.

She would take not remembering if she was able to wake up here. She would take it every day if she had to.

Krav was nowhere to be found that morning, so she went and got Soriya out of bed, and played with her. She was so…she was so happy with how easily her daughter took to her.

She found herself weeping often throughout the day, and she wondered if there was a time when she wouldn't feel overwhelmed by emotion over the situation. But she didn't mind. Not now.

"He brought her to see you every day."

She was getting assistance from the nanny still, it was helpful, and she didn't want to take a steady caregiver away from Soriya while she was still getting used to Riot.

It hurt. It hurt to realize that this other woman had spent more time with her baby than she had.

But she was a soft, grandmotherly figure, and as long as Riot thought of her that way, it settled all right.

Particularly since her own mother would never make a good grandmother to Soriya.

She wondered about Krav's mother. Wondered if she was still alive. If Soriya would have any grandparents…

"He did?"

"Yes. It was very important to him that she knew you."

She was touched by that.

Later, they went outside and she laid out a blanket for Soriya, and the nanny left the two of them alone to simply enjoy their time together.

She smiled as she watched her little girl crawl around, from the blanket to the grass.

And she looked up at the blue sky and wondered how she had gotten quite so lucky.

It was still like a dream, but over the next few days she woke up every morning and it seemed to remain.

She made going and lying on the lawn with Soriya

a routine. And it was wonderful. If there was anything that settled uneasily in her it was her relationship with Krav. She couldn't quite… She couldn't quite square up the way that she felt around him with the fact that they were supposed to be in love. There was attention there. Something that she couldn't quite readily define. He was so kind. And incredibly patient.

But her afternoons were happiest when it was just her and Soriya. Because at least there everything seemed simple.

She stared up at the sky, her beautiful child next to her, and for the first time, things in her life felt…

Perfect.

Krav watched her from his position on the balcony. He pressed his hands firmly into the marble as he gazed down at her below.

The sight of her with the child made him feel an intense sense of possessiveness.

That he had nearly lost them both seemed unconscionable now.

But they were here. They were here and they were his. And it was time. She had been awake for a week, and he had kept a respectable distance. Trying to gauge exactly what was happening with her memory.

It seemed to him—Doctor though he was not—that there was no point waiting around to see if it might return. She was happy. He would do his best to make her his.

And once those things were accomplished, there

would be no question about her remaining with him. With Soriya.

It was what she wanted, after all. Or had been. He was not a man given to self reflection, but he knew that he had reacted…badly. He was not a man given to regret either, but it had been a constant gnawing regret ever since.

But now she was back. And it was his chance to rewrite what had occurred before.

He would not question the gift.

For months he had lived in a darkness he couldn't get through.

That he had taken this beautiful creature and shattered her.

That he had caused the loss of her child.

Their child.

It hit him now, harder than ever, for that child was Soriya, not merely a possibility but a human being, so small and helpless and dependent.

This new story…

Riot was here, Soriya was here.

He didn't have to go back to that moment.

He walked down the curved staircase onto the grass below, and went to stand before Riot, whose blond hair was spread out all around her like a halo. She sat up, her cheeks turning pink, and he felt an answering desire echo in his stomach. No matter how many times he had had her, he had never been able to satiate the need that he felt for her.

She was too beautiful. Too perfect.

And the way that she fit in his arms, the magic that

they created between their bodies, it was more than simple sex, and always had been.

He had been on the verge of sending her away before she had found out she was pregnant.

Because the heat between them wasn't dying down, it only seemed to be growing more intense, and he did not have a place for that in his life.

He was not a man who did permanent. Or even close.

And now here he was, bound and determined to make this forever.

But if there was one thing he would not do, it was repeat the sins of his father.

He very nearly had. Perhaps not in the sense that he had done the exact things his father had done to his mother, but in the sense that he had failed. Failed his child. Failed the woman who was bearing that child.

He would not fail them again.

"I rarely see you during the day," she said, sitting up and pushing her hair off her forehead.

She was such a lovely, delicate thing.

She scooped Soriya up from the blanket and held her close to her breast.

"I was looking for you."

"We come out here every day," Riot said, smiling. "She loves to be outside."

"Good. She has not been away from the estate yet. That is what I wish to speak to you about. We have not…that is…our relationship was private. As was your pregnancy. And given the circumstances surrounding Soriya's birth…nobody knows that she was born. And no one knows that you are part of my life."

"And it will matter," she said softly. "Because you are part of such an old family."

That wasn't even the half of it. He was one of the richest men in the world. And the media hounded him like they would a movie star.

Perhaps even more so, because he was so private. So, he was a point of interest. Somewhat unknowable.

"There will be interest in the fact that I'm getting married. There will be interest in the fact that I've had a child. I could send an announcement out to the media, but I do wonder if it would perhaps be best if we were just…seen together."

"What was it like before?"

He hesitated. "We… We kept a low profile. After you and I were together in Cambodia. We traveled, a bit. But we stayed away from Rome and other major cities. We went to the Amalfi Coast." He watched her face. Watched to see if that jogged any sort of memory. He hoped it did not.

"I see."

"It is fairly easy to keep away from prying eyes in those places. And I have many residences."

"Was I your dirty secret?"

She had been. But not because of the things they did together. Because of the things that she made him feel. He thought nothing of trotting out mistresses to the public. But he had felt protective of her from the beginning. And the thing between them had not felt common or indeed like anything he felt like sharing with the public.

He had not felt like sharing her.

He had shown her something in him he had hidden

all his life, that night after his mother's funeral. He had let her see him.

He had raised his barriers again after that, but he had...

He had felt the need to hide her, to hide them, to draw a curtain around them and keep that weakness she'd brought out in him a secret.

"So what exactly are you proposing?"

"That we go out. As a family."

The smile that lit up her face felt like a stick of dynamite going off in his chest. "Yes, please. I would like that."

"You're feeling up to it?"

"I feel fine. Other than the fact that I cannot remember what has to have been the most significant year of my life, I feel wonderful. I've never been so happy."

Krav brooded on that as they got ready to go into the city. She was still living in his house, but they were not sharing space. It was entirely different from when they had been in the midst of their affair.

She had often spent whole days naked in his villas. He would dismiss the staff for the week so that she could lounge by the pool and do nothing and he could come home from work to ravish her.

She had been all he wanted.

And he had certainly not thought of living with her when sex was not the primary objective.

How things had changed.

Though his desire for her had not. When she came down the stairs wearing a white dress that skimmed over her curves in an easy manner, and fell to her knees, his breath took a leave of absence.

And then there was the way she cradled the child…

"Would you like to hold her?"

"No," he said.

Her smile faltered. "I don't mind."

"You missed the first month of her life. Hold her."

"Okay," she returned, keeping the child cradled to her breast.

He extended his arm, and the two of them walked out the front door, to the limousine that was waiting for them.

"This seems… I can't even believe this," she said.

She fussed around buckling Soriya in her car seat, and then looked at him, as if seeking reassurance.

"All looks well," he said.

Typically, the nannies did this. He did not…hold her. She was tiny and frail and he…

He broke things that were fragile.

"Good," she said.

She slid into the limo, and looked around, her eyes wide.

"We will be going to one of my favorite restaurants."

"Did we do this a lot?"

"Sometimes. I often like to keep you at home to myself."

The innocence in her expression nearly undid him.

It reminded him of when they had first met. By the end of everything, she had learned what he liked.

She had become accomplished at pleasing him, and

any embarrassment she seemed to have about things of a sexual nature had vanished.

It was fascinating to see a return to who she had been before.

"Why?"

He chuckled. He did not know if this was the time to bring up the physical connection between the two of them.

What he wanted was to build the scaffolding for something that would be strong.

He had the chance to change the truth. And why wouldn't he?

Why wouldn't he?

"I like to have you to myself," he said. "Then when my desire for you overtook everything else... There were no barriers."

It had been a calculated risk, but it had been the right one. Because whatever she remembered or didn't, this remained between them. This fire, this heat. It was why they were in the situation in the first place. The unrelenting chemistry between the two of them transcended everything that Krav had ever known.

He was a man who had known many women.

He was expert in pleasing them and walking away having felt nothing but release.

What had burned between them had always been something undeniable, something else entirely. And he had told himself for a long time it was because of when they met. Because he had been diminished since his mother's death.

But now it felt like perhaps that was far too simple a truth.

Now it felt like perhaps there was more. Like there had to be.

She seemed pleased by that.

"I just wish that I could remember..."

"Perhaps it is not a matter of remembering. Only discovering."

He remembered. He remembered everything perfectly. Up until the bitter end when it had all exploded.

When you destroyed it.

It had been necessary, or rather it had felt so at the time.

But now...

Now here she was again. All of them together.

"Maybe," she said. "I've been trying to wrap my head around the fact that I'm a mother. It's difficult for me to see where you fit in."

"Let me show you."

And he had never wanted to be gentle with someone in all of his life, but he wanted to be gentle with her. Right now, he wanted to learn to do things and be things that he had never once desired to be.

Right now, he wanted to be the man that he had needed to be when she had told him she was having a child. The man he had been unable to be. He had months to sit with that. To sit with the loss of the pregnancy. And then the miracle of finding out she hadn't lost the child after all. Then the uncertainty of her own health.

And then she had woken up remembering nothing. It gave him a chance to change it all.

The restaurant was open-air, right out on the street where they could easily be seen. And it was his favorite. Not because of that, but because of how amazing the food was.

Whenever they had shared a meal together, she had always enjoyed it. But he had spent that time willing her to finish, so that they could get down to what he truly wanted. Which was always stripping her out of whatever she was wearing and being inside of her again.

It wasn't that he didn't want it now. But there was something about the moment that he didn't mind lingering in. Something about the moment itself that seemed like enough.

And it allowed him to truly watch her as she ate her food. As she delighted in it.

"I have never had anything so amazing."

She had always enjoyed the food when he had taken her out, and it hadn't occurred to him that she didn't remember any of those meals.

"You have," he said. "You just don't recall. I fed you well during our time together."

She laughed. "Well, there is something to be said for getting to discover this all over again. If I can have some humor about it."

Their eyes caught and held, and desire arced between them. There was no denying it.

"Maybe there will be something to be said for discovering other things for the first time all over again."

"Though, by your very admission, your first time with me was your… Your first time."

"I didn't tell you?" she asked.

"No. You didn't. We never spoke of the past. Past lovers, I mean. You told me only small details about your life."

"Well, the story of my past life is only sad."

"I do not think you are sad."

A small smile curved her lips. "That is something."

"I'm glad you think so."

"And what about you? Did we talk about… Your past?"

"I'm much more interested in my potential future. With you."

She let out a satisfied sigh, and then a chocolate cake was put in front of her and she grinned brightly.

"I'm sorry that we didn't attract any media attention," she said.

"What are you talking about?" he said. "We've been having our picture taken this entire time."

Her eyes widened. "We have? How did I not realize?"

"You aren't used to it. But I am. The thing about the paparazzi now is that the ability to take photos is on your phone. They're able to be much more subtle when the mood strikes. Oftentimes they still like a telephoto lens and gross invasions of privacy, or sticking a camera in your face. Though, they do not enjoy doing that with me so much."

"Why?"

He smiled. "They're afraid of me."

She shivered, her shoulders twitching back and forth.

"What?" he asked.

"Sometimes I sense that about you."

"What?"

"That you are to be feared. That you are... A predator." She laughed. "I don't know why I think that. I realized as soon as I said it how silly it sounded. Because you've been nothing but wonderful this entire time. It's just that..."

A disquiet grip took hold of him. She could see it. The darkness in him. And he had let it out, the full weight of it when she had told him about her pregnancy, and she didn't even remember that, and still she knew.

But he would not unleash it on her again.

He had broken her, and he had nearly ruined all of this. More months, he'd been sure he had. He had kept watch on her through his people and yet never allowed himself to look in on her, not even once.

Had never allowed himself to directly ask about her.

Because he had not deserved to see her.

Not after the way he'd sinned against her.

But now...now things were different. He was making it so.

There would be a way to do this. She would be his wife. They would share a bed.

She would believe that he was in love with her. And that would be enough.

She would care for the child...

All would be well.

"Well, I'm glad that you realize I'm not one."

"Of course not," she said. "You're just a very handsome man."

It was such a sweet, but new sort of complement that it caught him off guard. Touched him in places he did not expect.

"Handsome?"

"Well, it's nicer than dangerous, isn't it?"

"Indeed," he said.

"Come," he said when they finished. "Let us walk."

They had an expensive pram for Soriya, and Riot pushed it, marveling at the city around them. She had never seen Rome before. At least, he assumed so given everything he knew about her.

And they had never come here together.

"This really is your first time here," he said.

A wave of relief seemed to move through her body. "That is actually good to know. It is unsettling. Not knowing what I don't remember, and what I actually haven't done."

"Yes. I can see that."

"I'm happy to be here with you. Really doing this for the first time."

And even while she was pushing the pram, she let go of the handle, and wrapped her fingers around his. They had never held hands.

Not even when they were at the peak of this thing between them.

Holding hands was…domestic. They had never been domestic.

But here they were, with a child, strolling down the street like they might've been…normal. And it would make for exactly the sort of picture he had been trying to have taken, but for some reason he could not bear it.

Slowly, he withdrew his hand from hers, and he could feel a slight withdrawal coming from within her, but she said nothing.

"I have made an appointment for us," he said.

"An appointment?"

And then he ushered her into the shop that was open only for them.

Her eyes widened when she looked around and saw all of the dresses hanging on the racks. Dresses that would fit her. He knew well how to shop for Riot's body already, and he had taken that knowledge and sent it ahead to the designer.

"Since we are to be married. I thought it would be a good idea for you to begin the selection process for your gown. You can have semicustom of course, but all of these are available, and can be altered in any way."

"I've never... I've never seen anything like this. And there's no way... You can't..."

"I'm a billionaire. I can do whatever I want. We could buy a plane and fly to space today if you wish. But I had thought we might start small. And with something that we actually need."

"A wedding gown. I..."

And then she started to do something truly distressing. She began to cry.

And he didn't know what to do. He simply stood there, frozen. And he was not a man who did loose ends. He wasn't a man who did uncertainty. How did this woman continually put him in a position where he had no idea how he was supposed to react?

He had said nothing hurtful.

And she was weeping. Like a child.

"I'm sorry," she said. "It's only that... No one has ever done so many nice things for me. And I am so heartbroken that I don't remember meeting you. I think you changed everything. You did. I woke up from a coma and now I feel like I'm in a dream. You have given me…" And then she launched herself into his arms, her face pressed against his chest, and he could feel the moisture from her tears seeping through his shirt.

And he felt… He was on fire. He had not held her softness in his arms like this for nearly a year. This woman… This woman who had come into his life and upended everything… He had to watch her lie in that bed motionless for a month. He had her out of his life for eight months. It had been…torture. All of it, but this was no better. This was…

This was like nothing he had ever experienced before, and what he truly wanted to do was crush his mouth to hers and show her how things really were between them.

The intensity and the need. And do something to rid himself of the yawning ache at the center of his chest.

But he could only hold her.

"I'm sorry," she said, wiping at the tears on her face.

"It was just so unexpected. You know my mother always treated me like an imposition." She looked down at the pram. "I will never do that to her."

Conviction took hold of him. And while he didn't share anything about his father, his life, he wanted to share now.

And why not? In this new moment, when he was not the same man who she had run from that rainy night. But when he was the man who had heard of her pregnancy and reacted with joy. The man who had taken her into his arms and kissed her, who had proposed.

The man of the lie. Not the man he was in truth.

"My father treated me like his thing. I was nothing more than the heir to his fortune. He did not love me. He loved nothing but himself. And that would've been fine if he had the decency to have someone in my life who did love me." And he ignored the parallels between himself and his father right then. Ignored the reality of his relationship—or lack thereof—with his daughter.

He did not hold her. He had not. But he was doing the right thing. His father had wrenched him from the arms of someone who had loved him and brought him to a place where he had felt like nothing more than an obligation.

He would not do the same.

Her face was close to his, and it would be the easiest thing to grip her chin and hold her steady while he tasted her.

But if he kissed her once, he would not stop there.

He did not understand how to do a slow seduction. Not with her.

It was the softening that seemed to be required, that was what was so difficult. He wanted to drag her into the sitting room and have her. Show her why they had made this child. Why she was here. Why he could not forget her.

But she had forgotten him.

It struck him then, the hilarity of it.

For he had forgotten any number of women to pass

through his bed, and they were always trying to win him back.

But this one. The biggest regret of his life. The one who had taken everything and turned it on its head, she had gone and forgotten him.

He supposed it was poetic justice in a way.

He would laugh, if it did not make his insides feel like they had been lit on fire.

She separated herself from him when the designer walked into the room. And she wiped the tears from her cheeks, and he wished that he would've done that instead.

It was a strange desire. One he barely recognized.

Soriya slept while Riot tried on different gowns, her beautiful figure swathed in silks and satins. And he simply sat and watched, the fire that had been banked for weeks now beginning to flare bright inside of him.

"I thought it was bad luck for the groom to see the bride before the wedding," she said.

"I think we had our share of bad luck already, don't you?"

She smiled. And then disappeared into the changing room again.

The problem with every dress that she tried on was that all he wanted to do was take them off of her. He had never imagined having a wife. And now… He was being bombarded with imagery that made it extremely clear that he was going to have a wife.

He already had a child.

He clenched his teeth together, tight.

"We will take three," he said. "The first, the fourth, and the last one."

"I don't get to choose?"

"Did you want to?"

"I'm… Somewhat angry that you chose my three favorites."

"Good," he said. "We have proven as compatible as ever. Memories or not."

"Why three?"

"You can choose whatever feels right on the day."

"That seems extreme. Maybe we should have gotten the spaceship."

"Don't be silly. They will be marginally less expensive than a spaceship."

"I guess so."

"Anyway. Billionaires launching themselves into space is so done these days. Three wedding dresses is slightly more avant-garde."

She laughed. And it delighted him. There was no other word for it. He could not think of another thing that had delighted him, not since her. Not since every moment he had spent with her all those months ago.

And he was fascinated, that the man he'd become in this storybook romance he was writing could feel delight. Could laugh. Could make her laugh.

They wrapped the dresses up, and soon they were headed back to the estate. She let her head rest against the seat, her eyes resting on Soriya. "This was the best evening. Thank you. I feel… I'm not even sure I need to remember." She sighed heavily. "Like you said. Maybe it's more a matter of discovery."

And that was when he was determined. Determined to give her something good to discover. A new story.

She had not mentioned a ring, but surely she would notice soon enough that she didn't have one. He would give her what she should have had. When she told him she was pregnant she should have had a proposal. A ring. And he would give her that now.

Give her a romantic escape. Give her a reason to ground herself in this life. To discover that she wanted nothing more than to be with him. Then to be with Soriya.

Because he could remember all too clearly the woman he had devastated. The way that she had tripped and fallen and bled. The way that she had been gone from him, and he had been certain that he had…that he had destroyed her.

He wanted there to be something else in place of that. Even for him.

He would prepare the grandest proposal that there could be. And he would give her everything a woman could ever want.

In that he was determined.

CHAPTER SIX

SHE WAS STILL floating the next day. She felt like a high school girl with a crush. At least, she thought that might be what she felt like. It was still so strange, suspended in this bubble that didn't even feel like reality. Even going out into Rome hadn't made any of this feel more real. There was just something so…strange about it. And she wanted to believe it. She really did. He had bought her those gowns…

You don't have a ring.

She had noticed that. But there were many reasons that she might not have a ring.

She had never asked him about the accident she was in either. Was he in it too? It was weird that she didn't know.

She would talk to him about it. Last night, she had actually spent some time with him, and it had been nice.

She could imagine being his wife. She didn't think she had ever really spent that much time imagining what it would be like to be married. She had just sort of excluded that from her potential future. But she could imagine marrying Krav. If there was such a thing as a perfect man he might well be it.

Soriya was definitely the perfect baby. She had little experience with children, but she was loving all of this.

She was starting to feel a little bit more grounded when Krav walked into the dining room that morning and announced that they would be going to Paris. And that was disconnected from any reality that she had ever known. "Have I been to Paris?" she asked, which she realized was a strange question.

"No," he said.

"Well, I'm glad of that. I would hate for my first time in Paris to be lost in the mists of my mind."

She hated everything that was lost in the mists. She wished that she could remember…

But there was no point being upset about that. Not really.

She was taken care of. He was taking her to Paris, after all.

Her stomach fluttered.

She wondered when the physical part of their relationship would…when it would begin again.

She had spoken to her doctor, and she knew that she was technically still recovering from giving birth.

Or rather, had been until recently. She was no longer bleeding, and she wasn't sore in any way.

She had been told that meant she could return to… regular intercourse.

Something that seemed kind of hilarious to her because she couldn't remember having intercourse of any kind.

It was the private jet that succeeded in stunning her. And she would have thought that Krav didn't have any more surprises in store for her. She understood that he was rich. It was just that she was also beginning to understand that she didn't understand what rich meant. In her tiny town in Georgia, she had associated it with people with large flashy cars, homes that were comically palatial, with all manner of space that sat there unnecessary, simply creating more volume as if it was entirely for the purpose of shouting, *I could stuff all my extra cash in this space if I wanted to.*

That was not rich. Not in the way Krav was.

There was wealth, she was beginning to realize, that was not shouted about on the streets. Rather, it was factual. A part of the way that he moved.

Every nook and cranny of the ornate estate that he lived in spoke of this wealth. The way that he could command the entirety of a boutique, yet did not call attention to himself.

In fact, he seemed the sort of man who would be happy to have no attention on him ever. But his bearing didn't allow it.

Everyone stared at him. Whatever room he was in, whatever street he walked down, she had observed that people couldn't take their eyes off of him.

And neither could she.

The attraction between them…

He had not touched her. He had been solicitous to the point that she wondered if he still felt attraction for her.

But she felt it. Felt that slow burn inside of her, so utterly foreign.

She tried to imagine herself as the kind of sex kitten who would've gone back to his place minutes after meeting him.

It was difficult to do.

Almost impossible.

She had never wanted a man before him.

She did want him though. So that was consistent.

Even amidst all the confusion. All the...everything. She wanted him. She felt a deep curiosity about what it would be like to be touched by him. And an anger at the woman that she had been in that time before her accident, that woman who had kissed him. Touched him.

She was jealous of herself.

That thought made her laugh.

"What?" Krav asked.

"I just...nothing," she said, looking down. "It's silly."

She turned her focus to the beautifully appointed jet.

It had several rooms, and Soriya had been taken back to the nursery by the nannies. She didn't love the involvement of the nannies, but Krav was very concerned about her sleep. Especially given all that her body had been through.

She appreciated it. But that was another thing she was jealous of. The world had had an entire month with Soriya that she hadn't. Krav had had that entire month. She...she had been sleeping. Sleeping through the birth of her child.

"I was actually just thinking that I am a bit jealous of myself," she said.

"In what sense?"

"It's almost like I'm the other woman," she said, feeling he touched her face. "I mean, because I've... I've been with you. But I don't remember. So it feels like... like it was an entirely different person. Not me."

"And you are jealous of yourself?"

His voice was practically a purr. Though, not the purr of a house cat.

"Well, you don't have to look like that."

"Like what?"

"So damned pleased with yourself."

"And how should I feel, knowing that my fiancée wants me?"

"Did you think that I didn't?"

He shifted, and his expression went to something like granite. "Things have changed between us, have they not? I take nothing for granted. As you said, it is... You are not a different woman, but it is as if we are living in a different timeline. Our past is erased. And so we must make what we can of today so that we might find tomorrow together."

"I don't think that will be difficult."

"I'm glad to hear it. Would you like a drink?"

She had not had alcohol since waking up. She was a moderate drinker anyway, but she had been very careful because of her mind and memory. She wasn't breastfeeding Soriya, because being in a coma the first month of a child's life, did make milk production problematic. Another thing that had been taken from her.

But she didn't want to focus on what had been taken from her. She wanted to focus on what she had been given.

This thing that felt like an utter surprise from the

universe, all things considered. But she did feel the need to know what exactly had happened.

"What happened to me?"

"You were in an accident," he said.

"Was I by myself? Or were you in it with me?"

"You were alone. It is a regret of mine. You were driving early in the morning. You were hit head-on by a driver who had been out reveling all night."

"I must have been out very early," she said.

"Yes," he responded. "You were. It was… When I got the news of your accident… I have never felt out of control before, you must understand that. And yet you have challenged me at every turn. Challenged what I know about myself. And about my own power. I would argue that it is good for me, except to have not enjoyed a single moment of it." There was a rawness to his admission that felt unfamiliar. That was ridiculous, since all of this felt familiar.

But this was different. She just knew that it was.

"Then what?"

"You were taken to the hospital. And it was decided that you needed to deliver right away. It was quite precarious, that entire stretch of time. Not knowing if… If you or the baby would live."

"How awful for you," she said. "It would've been awful for me, but thankfully I remember none of it."

"You weren't conscious," he said. "You had a head injury upon impact."

"And so they gave me a C-section," she said.

"Yes. And Soriya was born. They monitored her closely, as she was early, but she was well. Healthy immediately. You… Your body protected her. Almost at the expense of itself. It was truly a miracle."

"Well, at least there was that."

"I brought you back to the estate. I did not wish to leave you to the care of the hospital. I hired my own staff to care for you, twenty-four hours a day. And a month after the accident, you woke up. But you did not remember any of the previous time we spent together."

"You've done so much for me. I'm sorry to have re-paid you by forgetting you."

His gaze took on a distant look. "You're here now. That's what matters. In many ways, our relationship has progressed quite quickly. It is not as if we were a couple for many years."

"It's all very spontaneous, and I have to admit I tend to not be very spontaneous."

"No. Neither do I. And so it is a strange thing, I find. This union."

"You don't have any regrets, do you? Because you could get rid of me. You could've told me anything."

"I brought you here and kept you for a reason."

And she wanted him to say that it was because he loved her. Because she had assumed that he must.

But he had never said the word, she realized then.

But he must. He must. Because everything had moved so quickly.

You did get pregnant…

It made her wonder. If that was the only reason. But then, her mother had gotten pregnant, and it had meant nothing to her father. She didn't even know him. So it wasn't as if pregnancy meant by default that a man would marry you, stick by you, give you twenty-four-hour care in his palatial estate.

No. It didn't mean any of that. And so, she supposed she shouldn't worry so much about what words had been used or not.

And maybe, soon she would have the courage to ask. But until she could say it to him… She supposed she couldn't ask that he say it to her.

Though she was beginning to feel like… It was so strange. She couldn't remember even kissing the man, but she was beginning to feel like this was love.

She knew that she loved Soriya. It was instantaneous. The moment she had seen the child not only had she known that she was hers, she had been infused with an intense conviction that she would protect this child at all costs.

And that she would love her, at the expense of all else.

Because she did love her. With everything.

And so, maybe it wasn't so strange that she felt like she was falling in love with Krav.

Maybe it wasn't so strange at all.

And now he had answered her questions. About how it had happened.

She was glad she couldn't remember the accident, actually. How terrifying it must've been. But it was so hard to imagine what she would've felt in that situation, because she had no access to the girl that she'd been at that point.

So many things had changed in her life in the last ten months, and she couldn't remember any of them.

It was such a strange thing.

The plane touched down in Paris almost too quickly, and she would not have ever said that she would wish for a plane ride to go on longer, but the jet was just so lovely and comfortable, and her glass of champagne had warmed her.

She felt relaxed and…happy. That was the most amazing thing about all of this. She couldn't remember feeling quite so simply happy in all of her life. Maybe she was shallow. Maybe it had to do with all the money. And while she thought it might help, she really thought it was because of the addition of Krav and Soriya to her life.

"Does Jaia wonder where I am?"

"Jaia abandoned you, and I don't think she has worried much about you since," he said as they got into a limousine that was waiting for them at the airport.

"It's really no wonder that I'm so happy to accept my life here with you," she said. "Everyone in my life before was so…"

"Useless," he responded, the word carrying an edge, even as he grinned.

But that grin looked dangerous. And it felt like a knife-edge against her soul.

He knew her. Her flaws, her vulnerabilities. He remembered everything she'd ever told him. And he was…she felt things with a certain level of confidence where he was concerned, but it was nothing she could confirm. Nothing she could put into words.

She didn't *know* things about him. She only felt them. Whereas she was a book he'd read cover to cover and retained every word.

It felt exposing. Unfair.

"Well. Exactly."

"They are not worthy of you. I do not believe she ever inquired about your whereabouts. Though I think you did tell her that you had gone off to be with me. Likely, she's jealous. As I believe her greatest conquest during your trip was to shag a backpacker in a sad hostel."

She couldn't help it. She laughed. "That is so mean. But you know, Jaia probably enjoyed that."

"Indeed."

"I guess I shouldn't feel terribly proud of myself that when I decided to shag someone, he happened to be a billionaire."

He chuckled. "You didn't know," he said. And his eyes went molten. "You didn't know who I was."

"I didn't know you were rich?"

"No. The way that we met, it was not obvious."

"I'm… I like that."

She did. She loved the fact that she had simply met him and it had been right. This thing had bloomed between them.

They were whisked off to a penthouse apartment in the center of the city and what was practically a motorcade of their household help, and all of the baby items that they required.

The penthouse was yet another angle of beauty. Ultramodern, rising high above the classical architecture of Paris.

All glass and crisp clean angles high above lovely stone scrollwork.

It was unbelievable.

And she couldn't help herself, she twirled in the open space of the living area, with the Eiffel Tower behind her, and when she stopped, she was breathless, and he was right there. And she felt… Like it would be the most natural thing in the world to close the distance between them and kiss him.

And she knew she had done it before. Suddenly, she was overcome with the conviction that she had kissed that mouth hundreds of times.

There was heat in her belly that felt familiar, that same sort of certainty that clicked into place when she *knew* something about him that transcended a specific moment or memory.

But there on the heels of that heat was something…dark.

Something that held her back.

Suddenly there was a pain in her chest that felt so real she couldn't breathe past it, and it held her in place.

Kept her from touching her lips to his.

"What is it?"

"Nothing," she said. "I'm just… So excited to be here. With you."

She pushed the pain aside. She pushed the heat aside.

What she had, all she had with any certainty, was this moment.

She would choose to live in that.

They took a walk through the city. With Soriya in her pram, they saw the Eiffel Tower, the Champs-élysées, and they walked along the Seine. She was delighted and overwhelmed in the best way by all of the artists on the street selling their wares, and the bustle of the people around them. It wasn't only that she hadn't been to Paris, it was that she had been to very few major cities in all of her life. She was used to the pace of a small town.

And the speed and intensity of both Rome and Paris were a revelation.

After they were done with their walk, one of his beauty teams appeared, and ushered her into her suite, where she was given a facial, had her hair styled, and was wrapped in a haute couture gown—red and draped over her curves.

She looked in the mirror, and she didn't know herself.

Which should be something she was accustomed to by now, but she just wasn't.

The woman staring back at her was sophisticated. Her makeup expertly done, the bold red lip a choice she never would've made on her own.

But this was the woman that Krav loved. The one that he was going to marry.

Where is your ring...

And her heart fluttered, because she wondered... She wondered if tonight would be the night.

And as she looked in the mirror, she made her decision. Ring or not, tonight she was going to kiss him. Old memories, old feelings...they didn't matter.

She could sit in the unfairness of it all. That he knew more about her. That there were great swaths of their relationship she couldn't remember.

Or she could make new memories.

She wanted that. She wanted to follow that path.

She would start on it with a kiss, and see where it led. Because she was tired of being jealous of herself. Of a version of Riot that she couldn't access.

She had never once lived up to her name. At least... Not

in her memory. So she would make a new one. Tonight. Where she was Riot, and that name meant something.

She was a bit nervous leaving Soriya, but she wanted to spend this time with him.

And she wondered if she would feel this tension no matter the circumstances. When she exited the bedroom, and went back to the living area, he was there.

And he took her breath away.

He was wearing a custom black suit that conformed to his lean muscled body. He looked taller, which she would've said was impossible, as she barely came to the top of his shoulder.

He was stunning. Arresting in all of his glory, but even now as he wore the trappings of civility with such ease, she sensed that wildness beneath. That tiger.

That danger.

And she wondered if she would always feel that as she stood there and looked at him. If she would always sense that underlying darkness.

And if she would ever know why.

If she would ever fully understand. "I hope you like dancing. I already know you like food."

"Yes. You do know me well."

But I don't know you.

That disquiet echoed inside of her, but she did not give voice to it. Because hadn't they spent all this time getting to know one another again? Hadn't he been kind and solicitous?

He had.

It didn't make that feeling go away.

But she ignored it.

She took his hand and let him lead her to the elevator, and then down to the street. There was a car waiting, this time not a limousine. This time a sports car, shiny and red, matching her dress.

They did not have a driver, rather he got behind the wheel, top down, and they drove through Paris as the streetlights began to illuminate. And she was grateful then that she didn't remember her car accident, because this was blissful, and she would hate for any notes of fear to sneak in and steal this from her.

Riding in a beautiful car with the most glorious man she had ever seen beside her.

The restaurant looked like a private residence, and the inside had much the same feel. Intimate and small, with very few tables.

"It is not the sort of place with a menu," he said.

She didn't know what that meant. But she was excited to find out. And find out she did, they were given a selection of the chef's favorites, the freshest foods that had been available today at the market, and turned into culinary masterpieces on the fly.

She felt drunk on food alone by the time they left the restaurant, walked down the street to another nondescript building which turned out to be what amounted to a speakeasy.

And for the first time since she had opened her eyes and seen him, he pulled her into his arms there on the dance floor. And her entire body was suffused with heat.

Held up against his strong body she…yes, she knew why she had gone back with him moments after meeting him. And the only reason they were waiting now was because of her amnesia, she knew that. He was concerned about her. And that was the only reason. Because otherwise they would have… This was undeniable. But suddenly she felt afraid.

She'd had a child since they'd last been together, and she had a scar on her stomach that hadn't been there before.

Maybe she wasn't as beautiful now. Maybe it hadn't been so much about her physical recovery, but about the fact that he didn't want her anymore.

"You're beautiful," he said, as if he could read her thoughts.

"Oh," she whispered.

"More now than ever. Riot, you are the most beautiful woman I've ever seen in my life, and it was true from the moment I saw you there at the ruins. And it is even more true now. All that you have withstood. All that you are. Beauty and strength. You have endured such cruelty from the world. And I will make it my mission to protect you from any more."

From the dance floor he led her up to the rooftop, where he got on one knee and opened up a box with a beautiful diamond ring, as fireworks went off over the city, illuminating the Eiffel Tower. As if he had made this moment just for them. Or perhaps he had. For when a billionaire proposed to you, she imagined there were very few limits on what was possible.

"Yes," she said. "I would marry you tonight."

And without rising from the ground, he grabbed hold of her waist and tugged her down to him, and on a growl, his lips crashed into hers. And she went up in flames.

CHAPTER SEVEN

SHE'D SAID YES. She was his. He would marry her as soon as possible, and she would be his. But first, he would brand her, with all of the passion that he felt in his veins. All of the desire that had been roaring in him like a beast all this time. All these months. Ever since he had first seen her.

It had never stopped. Monster, man, he did not see a difference between the two. And right now, he did not care. She'd said yes, and she would be his wife.

He held her face to his, as he kissed her deeper, his tongue sliding against hers, his need so intense he was not sure he possessed the fortitude to do anything other than strip her dress off now and have her on the rooftop.

He might've paid for a certain measure of privacy, but he felt as if that might be pushing it.

He consumed her, and she whimpered, arching her body against his, and he knew her. That was the unfair advantage, he supposed. He knew exactly what she liked, what she craved. He knew how to make her scream his name, how to make her beg for more. He had done it any number of times.

And yet for her this was the first.

That steadied him. Forced him to pull back, to soften the kiss, to turn it into a question rather than a command. Because for her this was the first time all over again.

He had taken her virginity once, and in many ways now he would do it again.

And what would he change? Now that he knew. Now that he knew he was the only man to ever touch her. Now that he knew he would have her forever.

His.

But had he not known that from the first moment?

The real mistake had been denying what was so apparently true. The real mistake he had made had been in believing Riot would not put him off his course.

Yes, that was the real mistake.

Now, he had corrected course. Now, he had made it so she would be his forever.

And when the years bled into years and they had been together longer than they'd been apart, the real story would be this one.

Not his mistakes.

Not his darkness.

They would both be with him.

She and Soriya, and everything would be as it should.

"Shall we go home?"

"Yes," she whispered. He cursed the fact that he had chosen to drive tonight as they waited for the car to be brought around to the front. He wished they were in a limo, so he could put the partition up and have her in the back seat. At the very least push her skirt up around her hips and bury his face between her thighs as they rode through traffic.

That would at least do something to satiate the desire that was growling inside of him.

Instead, he would have to content himself with knowing he would have her. Finally.

The drive took too long.

By the time they were back in the building, in the elevator, he could not wait a moment longer. When the doors closed, he pulled her into his arms, pushed her against the elevator wall and wrapped his hands around her wrists, forcing them up above her head as he kissed her neck, down to her shoulder, her collarbone.

"Krav!"

"Do you want me?" he asked, looking up at her, the intensity in him burning bright.

"Yes," she sobbed. "Please."

"Do you know what you're begging me for?"

She shook her head. "But I feel it."

"You want me to tell you. Because I know. I know just what you like."

And he did push his hand beneath her skirt, pressing his thumb against that sensitized bundle of nerves at the apex of her thighs and rubbing her slick flesh there. The first time he had touched her in all this time. He circled that sweet spot, and watched as her eyes went glassy. Watched as she began to surrender herself to this need. Her breath became short, choppy. And she began to roll her hips in time with the movement of his hand.

"You like that," he said. "You like it much better when I put my mouth there. When I lick you slowly, and taste every ounce of your desire for me. When I push a finger, and then another inside of you and mimic what we both really want. You like that a lot."

"Krav…"

"I'm not finished. You like me to do that until you're screaming. To eat you as if I am starving. And I am. With you I always am. You like to be teased." He took her hand, and guided it down to the front of his pants, moved her fingertips over his cloth covered erection. "You like for me to disrobe, and tease you with this. To toy with entering your body, but not quite. To deny you what you really want. Which is to be filled. You love that. You like to beg for it. And I like to make you beg."

Her eyes fluttered closed. "Look at me," he commanded, and she obeyed. "You're about to beg me now, aren't you?"

"I need… I need…"

"I know exactly what you want. And once we get inside the penthouse, I'm going to give you everything that I promised you here. And more. But you will beg for it."

"Yes," she said. Too soon, the elevator reached the penthouse. He had wanted to be in her instantaneously, but also wished to draw out this torture. She wasn't the only one who liked to be mad for it.

It was what they both liked. To push themselves. To make themselves wait for that moment of bliss. Sometimes they managed a mere thirty seconds. There had been a time in Cambodia when they had gone to dinner, and had made it into the entrance of the apartment, they had barely closed the door before he was inside of her. But they'd also had whole nights of teasing, teasting, denying themselves that ultimate release for as long as possible.

With her, it was always an adventure.

Tonight, though, he did not have the fortitude for games. Not long ones. Soriya was safely in bed, the entire place clear of visible staff, just as he had asked.

And he led her from the living room straight into his room.

"I want to see you," he said.

Her shoulders contracted in on themselves, and she suddenly looked shy.

"What?"

"I look different."

"You look beautiful."

And he took her in his arms and kissed her again, lowering the zipper on that dress as he did. Then he stepped back, and his desire became a living thing that he could no longer control.

Her curves were more generous than when they had first met. And she had a scar, where their daughter had been brought into the world. All to him evidence of strength, of that time she could not remember.

Of that time that was lost to her, but buried in his memory forever.

That time they had been apart.

The time he had been sure he had broken her, but there she stood before him, not broken at all. In no way diminished, not even by him. And it was miraculous.

He unhooked the strapless, lace bra she had on and revealed her beautiful breasts to himself. Finally. His.

Her body was familiar, but this was like discovering her again.

"I know where I want you."

He took her hand and led her to the edge of the bed, then pulled her panties down as he sat her right on the edge of the mattress, spreading her thighs for him. He dropped to his knees. "I told you exactly what would happen," he said, looking up at her and reading her nerves accurately.

"Yes," she said.

"Will you beg for it?"

Her knees began to close. "I don't remember…"

"But I do. Trust me when I tell you, I have tasted you many times, and I am starving for you. I've been deprived of you for far too long."

Longer than she knew.

Ten months without this body. Ten months without sex at all, though he realized even if he'd had a hundred women since Riot had left his bed it wouldn't matter.

There had been none, but even if there had been, he would want her just as badly. Because sex on its own would never satisfy. Not again.

It had to be her. Only her.

"Please," she whispered.

And he took that plea.

He pressed his mouth against those slick folds, tasting that sweet nectar at the apex of her thighs. He sucked her, lost himself in her. In the sounds of pleasure that she made, in the way that she grabbed hold of his head and held herself against him.

She wanted him. She wanted this.

And he wanted nothing more than to drown in her.

He pushed his fingers inside of her, thrusting as he ate her, as her pleasure overtook them both.

"Please," she begged. "Please." He sucked hard, and he felt her explode, her orgasm almost everything he needed.

Almost.

"You," she said. And she began to work the buttons on his shirt, and he helped her, stripping himself naked, gratified by the rush of breath she let out.

"You're so beautiful," she said. "Oh… Krav."

And she leaned in, and kissed his chest, his abs, and he knew what she intended, but not tonight. He did not have the fortitude to withstand it. So instead, he lowered her down to the bed and pushed the head of his arousal through her folds, rolling his hips back and forth until she was sobbing. *"Please."*

"Please what?"

"In me," she said. "I need you inside me."

He grabbed hold of her hips and lifted them up off of the mattress, and he thrust home. Her cry of pleasure echoed in the room, and he began to move, losing himself in the rhythm of them.

The rhythm that only they had ever found together.

And he forgot. He forgot the game. He forgot what he was trying to do for her, because he could only feel. He could only feel this need. This desire. This everything. It overtook him, consumed him.

It was no longer about her first time.

It felt like his.

He thrust into her, grinding against her pleasure center, and she cried out, her orgasm rippling through her, and setting off his own. He growled, losing his control, thrusting into her one last time and spilling himself into her.

"Riot," he whispered.

And she held his head to her chest, stroking him as if he were a beast in need of taming.

But perhaps he was.

Perhaps he was.

"I love you," she whispered. "Krav, I love you."

He had done it. He had restored the things that had been lost between them. And she would be his.

His mouth curved into a grin as he pulled her into his arms and she rested her head on his chest.

He had won the war.

The war against himself, and all the darkness in his soul.

Riot was his. And there was no question about that.

CHAPTER EIGHT

WHEN SHE WOKE up it was raining.

Krav was still holding her in his arms, and she could hear his heart beating steadily against her ear. She could also hear the rain falling on the roof. Splattering against the windows.

It created the strangest echo inside of her.

For some reason, she felt compelled by it. There was a balcony off of the master bedroom, and she slipped out from the warmth of the covers, the warmth of his hold, and stood there for a moment. Looking at him.

None of his intensity eased in sleep. It was all still there. Except it seemed… Unvarnished.

There was nothing to soften it while he dreamed. His strength, the inherent danger of the man radiated off of him and sent a chill down her spine. And why should it?

He had been nothing but a romantic lover to her. Nothing but a man of extreme solicitousness. There was no reason to feel this chill.

She loved him.

She could see so clearly now how she had fallen for him.

The things that he had done to her body were magic. And no wonder she had given herself to him with such ease.

But it was more than that. He had given her the world. Quite literally. And for a girl from small-town Georgia, it was everything. It was like nothing she had ever even known to dream of. Private jets and Paris. Proposals beneath fireworks in the shadow of the Eiffel Tower.

How could she not love him?

She walked across the bedroom and stood in front of the glass door that led out to the balcony. She watched the rainfall, splattering against the surface. And then she opened the door.

She was naked, but for some reason she didn't feel self-conscious. She stepped out into that rain, and the drops began to roll over her skin. And there was a flash in her mind. Standing there at the root with him across the space from her.

Everything had changed in that moment. She knew it. She felt it. And most importantly, she saw it. Not because he had told her, but because she remembered. The rain. She had been soaked through to the bone, abandoned. Afraid. And he had been there. And she had wondered if she was walking to her doom or to her salvation, and she had chosen to walk toward him anyway. She always chose to walk toward him.

She hadn't known, even then. If he was a man or a monster.

Heated images flashed into her mind. That night in the tree house. It had been a tree house. She had given herself to him without thought. Because there had been no room for thought. His hands on her body. His mouth on her throat. Would he use his teeth to destroy her or give her pleasure? He had given her pleasure.

And she knew now why it had all seemed so strange. Because she had unlearned so much about life that night. And built something new. New affirmations inside of herself that changed the very foundation of who she was.

It amazed her, that realization that so much of the changes had taken place over the course of a single night. But they had. Utterly. Absolutely.

And the rain continued to pour down her skin, and as the drops washed away the fog in her mind, she could see further and further into time.

They had not separated after that night. Not ever. She had been in his bed every night after that. She felt like she was running through an open field, racing toward something in the distance.

Sun and truth, even as she stood still in that cleansing rain.

Rain.

Rain again. She was running through the rain. On the streets, cobbled and uneven. And she fell. But what happened before? What had happened before that moment? She could remember holding her stomach. Low. Blood.

And as clearly as if she was experiencing it now, she remembered looking up, raindrops hitting her face. Melding with the tears on her cheeks.

I'm losing it anyway. Everything is lost.

And it was his face she saw. But there was none of the

gentle lover there. It was the Tiger. Only and ever. Dark and fearful in his symmetry. And there was no terror over whether he would devour her, for he already had.

In that moment, everything had been gone. Everything she had believed about herself, all of the new truths that he had built that first night, decimated. The future. Everything she had hoped for. Everything she had believed in him. But most of all, he was gone. The man that she had grown to love was gone, all of his artifice ripped away, revealing the truth of him. That deep, horrific darkness that she had sensed was beneath the surface all that time.

But she couldn't connect the whole memory. Only that picture. Only that face.

And the blood.

She stumbled back inside, soaking wet and shivering, and Krav sat up in bed, threw the covers to the side, revealing his glorious, sculpted body.

But she felt nothing more than wild, insensible terror. "What did you do?"

"Riot…"

"No. I need to know. I remembered the rain. I remember the rain and the day that we met. I remembered why I went back with you. I remembered… You changed me. You made me feel like I was beautiful. But then it rained again, and you made me feel like I was nothing. You destroyed me. You destroyed us, didn't you?"

"Riot…"

"No," she said, moving away from him. "You never loved me. You don't love me." He had never said it. He had never said it, but she had believed that he did because he had to. Because how could they be here building this beautiful life together with their beautiful child if he didn't love her?

"You never loved me. And you… You sent me away. You did."

She couldn't remember, but she could feel it now. She could feel the utter brokenness in her soul. As if her heart had been severed from her. That was that moment. He had done worse to her than anyone else in her life ever had. Because he had made her believe that there could be more. He had made her believe that he cared. And she had been a fool. She had ignored all of the things that her spirit had known. Had sensed. She had chosen to see only his beauty, and to ignore his darkness. She had chosen to believe that just because he could make her feel good didn't mean he would eventually destroy her with that danger.

She had mistaken the fact that a predator could be beautiful for a promise that he would be *good*.

But he was still a predator. And he would destroy that which stood in his way. Krav was a man who consumed beautiful things, sated himself on them until they no longer served him.

She knew it. In that moment she knew it.

He was not a beautiful man with the touch of predator. He was the Tiger.

All the way through.

Anything else was simply a facade. A gleam of gold and stripes to distract, of burning eyes, dancing fire that hypnotized and left his prey stunned, immobilized, willingly standing there waiting for the strike. And strike he had.

She had wanted so badly to remember… She had wanted so badly to remember.

The falling in love. But it didn't exist. Oh, she had fallen in love with him. And he had slaked his lust with her.

He had *used* her.

Nothing more. She had told him everything about herself, and she couldn't remember him because he had told her nothing. Nothing. The only truths she had ever learned about him were during that first night. That first night when he had told her about his mother. But it had been nothing more than basic facts. Nothing more than the barest hint of information. There had been no real emotion behind it. She had put it all there.

Because she had wanted to see it.

She had created a beautiful life for herself, and he had been there, the scaffolding for it.

But this…

He had lied to her. He knew that she didn't remember, and he had lied.

"Tell me," she said, her throat tightening. "Tell me the truth."

"We should be together," he said, his voice scraped raw.

"Why? Why should we be together?"

"For Soriya," he said. "She needs you."

"I can take care of her fine on my own."

And that statement jogged more of her memory. It was the after. She had left. She had left him after that night in the rain, after the bleeding and the pain.

And suddenly, grief spread out through her chest like a poison.

She had lost him. And for a while she believed she had lost her pregnancy. But she had gone to the doctor when her period didn't resume a few weeks later, and they had confirmed the viability of her pregnancy. The bleeding didn't mean she had miscarried.

But she had spent the pregnancy alone. And Krav hadn't known.

"What happened to me?" she asked, her heart pounding so hard it made her dizzy. She was sick with it, with this.

Staring down the man who had become the ultimate villain in her life. And she'd fallen in love with him a second time. It made her wish for that blankness again. It made her wish she knew nothing, because knowing this truth about him, about herself, was too much to bear.

She'd fallen for this man a second time. Even though somewhere inside herself she had to have known what he was.

"I told you the truth," he said. "You were in an accident. It was how I discovered you were still pregnant."

"Oh. Because you thought that I had lost the baby. And you... You sent me away anyway."

His expression hardened. "You left."

But she could see herself, curled up in a massive bed in his empty house. Then could see the staff carefully taking her to the car...

So gentle, all that betrayal. Wrapped in soft sheets and sent away in a limousine.

But it was rejection, a mortal wounding all the same.

"Because you wanted me to. You might not have thrown me out into the street, but you made it clear you wanted me gone, and if I hadn't left you probably would never have returned to the villa. Don't rewrite it even now that I remember. But you're right. Then I wanted to. I never wanted to see you again. Ever. You destroyed me. You took my dreams after you gave them to me, and there is nothing crueler than that, Krav. And you knew that if I remembered… You know if I remembered I would never want to see you again."

If only she could remember what had led up to that moment outside. If only she could remember. But it was like her brain had the door firmly shut on it. Like it didn't want to know.

"I made a new life for myself. Away from you. Away from your rejection. Why did you get to hold her first?" The question came deep from her soul. "Why? Why should you have memories of her birth when I don't? You didn't want her."

And that statement threw the door open on all the memories. "I told you I loved you," she said. "I wanted to make a life with you. I believed that we could."

The devastation was raw and real. That dinner. The way that she had hoped and believed. That he had loved her the way that she loved him. And this was just the same. He had lulled her right back into that fantasy. And this time… Oh, this time it had been even more cruel. Because he had made her believe… He had made her believe. Again. What a fool she was. And he was happy to make her one.

He moved toward her, and she jerked back. "Don't touch me. How dare you. You made love to me with me thinking you… With me thinking I loved you. When we both know I don't. Not anymore. Not ever. I want to go. I'm leaving. I'm taking Soriya back to England."

"I'm afraid that is not possible," he said, his face shadowed in darkness. "You are to stay with me."

"I don't want to."

"And how do you think that will go for you, Riot? I am one of the richest men in the world. You have just sustained a head injury. I have been caring for Soriya all this time... And I cared for you."

"You rejected her."

"You ran away and nearly caused yourself to miscarry. I did not chase you out into that storm."

His words were hard and harsh, and she knew they were a lie. She knew he didn't even believe this version, and yet she could see him trying to hold it up over himself as a shield now.

This was the Krav she'd forgotten.

The man who used his cruelty to guard any tender places in himself. To push anyone who got too close far, far away.

"Is that what you tell yourself? Your cruelty wasn't the beast that ran me right out of your villa? I did not miscarry. I went on to make a life, I got a job, I had a home..."

"You have a home with me. You will still be my wife."

"This changes everything."

"It changes *nothing*."

His words landed, a cruel blade at the center of her chest. "It changes nothing to you if I go from loving you to despising you? It changes nothing if you go from having a wife who stays with you willingly to one who is a prisoner?"

And again, she saw the truth of him. He lifted a shoulder and shrugged. Worse, he stood there naked, as if it bothered him not at all, while she felt increasingly vulnerable, soft and exposed.

How could you go up against a man such as him?

A man who felt nothing.

"I want to leave," she said.

He took a step toward her, his eyes all black fire. "I don't care."

"You would keep her from me?"

"Yes. Because in the end, you won't go. Not if I keep her. And so, I will have what I want."

"Why did you do this? Why do you care? You've never..." And it was like a light had been shone into all the dark places in this glorious life, this glorious home. No more illusion left at all. "I've never even seen you hold her."

He had made sure she was cared for, but he never touched their daughter.

He never showed love.

And her mind, her heart, her soul, had been so desperate to fashion him into what she'd wanted him to be that she hadn't seen it, not really.

The blind spots hadn't come solely from her lack of memory.

She wanted love so very badly.

His love.

She'd wanted his lie to be true, so she'd ignored anything that had shown it for what it was.

"She is a Valenti," he said. "She will have my name,

my protection, and all of my power behind her. And she will have her mother. You had literature on adoption in your car…"

"I was given pamphlets by a doctor, and didn't clean out my purse. You don't know anything about me, Krav, you don't want to. You listen to my story, and yet you heard nothing. You don't know who I am. You don't care to know."

"What matters is that you are her mother. She needs her mother."

The words were rough and wild. How could he seem to feel nothing and everything all at once? She couldn't understand this man, and she'd believed once that she did.

Because she could turn him on? Because they'd shared sex and passion?

It was such an innocent thing to believe.

She'd had all his intensity focused on her in the bedroom and she'd believed it had given her the key to knowing him.

But it was a darkness that ran deep, and she couldn't see the bottom of it. A terrifying void that drove him, that haunted him.

He seemed cold and unfeeling, and yet it was more. He burned.

But the flames were black.

"And the jailer?" she asked. "Standing in place of a father?"

"It isn't like that."

"Isn't it?"

"I will protect her. I will protect you." The promise

was guttural, honest. Of all the things he'd said, she knew this was honest.

But he was missing the truth of it.

He had the power to hurt them both. More than any other person on earth.

"From everything but yourself?"

"I did not ask for this."

"Oh, you didn't ask to be a father? You just had sex with me without a condom."

He growled. "I did not ask for this thing between us."

This thing.

This passion.

It tortured him, she could see it. He didn't lie. And it hurt her. To know that the most beautiful thing she'd ever felt had been anathema to him all this time.

"What a victim desiring me has made you," she spat. "I cannot imagine how difficult it is." He took another step toward her, and her traitorous body responded. To the beautifully sculpted lines of his nude form. Everything in her wanted to launch herself at him. Scratch his face, and then kiss him. Hurt him, and then make love to him.

She shuddered. In repulsion. But not at him, at herself. At what he had made her. For he had changed her, at her very core. Her very foundation, and she had believed it had been for the best, but it had not been.

He had turned her into his creature, and she hated that girl.

At least the woman she had been, scarred though she was by her mother, without friendships, or attachments, had been independent. What was she now? "I hate you," she said. "As much as I ever thought I loved you. You have killed us. It will never be the same again."

"It was never love for me."

He burned in this flame, but it didn't consume him. And it threatened to make her ash. It was too hot for her. Too devastating.

"I won't marry you," she whispered.

"I believe you will."

The threat in those words did not escape her. He would take Soriya from her if he had to.

"I want my own room."

"By all means," he said, his voice hard. "Keep this one."

He did not bother to dress, he simply strode from the room, closing the door tightly behind him, and leaving her. She collapsed to the ground, and there was nothing. Nothing but the sound of the rain and her own piteous weeping.

Riot Phillips had thought for a moment that she was loved.

And what a cruel trick it had been.

She had all her memories now, she had the truth.

And she wished desperately that she could go back to living a lie.

Because it had been such a beautiful lie.

You can't live a lie.

You can't.

So this was the truth. All sharp and jagged edges. But what did it gain her?

There was no dignity to be had here. No respect.

She was utterly reduced.

You will remake yourself. You have every time.

And this time you have Soriya.

And that right there was the bright, burning conviction she needed.

A fire that would burn hotter than that demonic flame in Krav.

She was a mother. And she could remember now. That pregnancy. And how it had gotten her through the heartbreak of losing Krav.

It had sustained her. Soriya had sustained her.

She put on a robe, and walked out of the room, moving slowly to evaluate whether or not Krav was still in the main part of the penthouse.

She crept into Soriya's room. She looked down at her tiny, sleeping daughter. "I will not be my mother. And whatever happened to your father... I will do better. I will not allow you to become twisted and bitter. Or sad and lonely. You will be better for having me. I will not be weak. And I will not lose you. I will do whatever it takes to protect you. I promise." And she realized then it was Soriya who was protecting Riot. For she was giving her purpose. She was giving her strength now. Something bigger than simply her own heartbreak.

Because she was broken. She could be as angry as possible, holding that up as a shield to herself but as much as she despised him now, she had loved him.

And that was terribly painful.

But she was resolved.

She would do whatever she needed to do to be with Soriya. It was her hill. She would die on it.

And given that she was living with a tiger, that was very, very likely.

CHAPTER NINE

HE HAD BEEN caught in his own trap. He had spun a web so very deceptive, that even he had begun to believe it. Had begun to erase the truth of what had happened between them the night she had told him of her pregnancy.

Had begun to believe in the connection that they had created.

But it was a lie. A very clever one, but a lie nonetheless.

And now... Now she hated him.

She had not lied. She had spoken with the full force of truth.

I love you.

I hate you.

He had heard both things from her last night, and both had been true.

But it did not change his resolve.

He knew what he had to do.

But...

She would never let him touch her again.

There was a strange echo in his soul that reminded him of when his mother had died.

It felt like grief. He always felt as if he was standing

some distance away from his emotions. Examining them from afar, looking at them with some dispassionate distance.

And so, this was not a crippling feeling, rather it was simply there.

She was right. He had never held Soriya.

Because he had that distance. And it was a valuable thing. It served him well.

It mattered.

He had been torn from his mother's arms when he was five years old. He had not seen her again until he was an adult, who could make his own decisions and do what he wished with his time.

He had found her. The reunion had not been what he had hoped.

She had been so broken, bent by all the years of sorrow and poverty. Of a hard world and emotional devastation.

She hadn't liked to look at him. In his suits. She hadn't liked to hear him speak.

Still, she had mattered to him.

But it had been too late for him.

When he had been ripped away from her, it was as if he had been torn from his own heart.

The intensity of it had been too much for his small body to bear, and he was convinced it had damaged his ability to connect after. That and the general cruelty of his father. It had provided him with protection, and he did not regret it. But she made him wish…

She made him wish things could be different. That he could be different.

He'd had moments of it. When he'd been trying to

change this story for the both of them. He'd had moments where he'd found gentleness in himself he hadn't known was there.

But that wasn't real. It had been an act.

It had to have been.

Nothing good in him could survive, or thrive or last.

The next morning, she was adamant that they leave. She was like ice as she looked at him.

"I just want to go back to the villa. Where there is… *space*."

Unspoken he thought that was also…where he had not touched her.

"You're through with Paris?"

"I have a feeling I will be through with Paris for the rest of my life. I don't know that I should ever like to return here."

"That is a shame. Paris has quite a lot to recommend it."

"Paris can go to hell."

He had never seen her bitter.

After their… Their breakup, he supposed, all those months ago, he had not seen her again. She had been sad then, but he had not been on the receiving end of her anger.

But now he was. And it was quite stunning in its force.

"We will marry next week," he said.

"How nice for us," she said.

Their plane ride back to Italy was astonishingly different than the ride over. She did not look around the plane and delight. She did not flirt with him.

She sat, ashen, and she held Soriya the entire time. Like a tiny shield.

And he had not realized… He had not realized all the warmth that she injected into his life. Until she had taken it from him.

She had only been awake for a couple of weeks, but even while she had been in a coma, he had been able to imagine what they might build.

You bought into your own lies. More fool you.

It didn't matter. He was accomplishing his end. She wouldn't leave now. Wouldn't leave Soriya. She would marry him.

And someday… If there was one thing he knew it was that the desire between them would overcome this anger.

She would not withhold her body from him forever.

That made him feel better.

He knew that she wouldn't, because it was inevitable. Because they were inevitable.

Whatever she might think.

"Why are you like this?" she asked, with only twenty minutes before they began their descent.

"Why am I like what?"

"I have racked my brain, Krav. And one thing I do know. You never shared yourself with me. The night of your mother's funeral is the closest that I got to knowing anything about you. But I don't even know… I don't know your story. Your parents. How did they meet? I don't know who raised you I don't know…"

"I didn't know my mother," he said, deciding now to simply tell it. It did not have to touch him to explain the truth of it all. "Not really. My father was on vacation in

Cambodia, he had an affair. With a beautiful woman who worked at a bar he went to. He was much older than she. He had no children. And he needed them. Some years later, he discovered that she had given birth. To a boy. He wanted me. Not because he cared about anyone or anything but himself. He took me from her, and left in my place a sum of money. But she had no choice. She had no choice. I was taken away from everything I had ever known. My home. My language. My mother. Taken to Italy and raised by a man who inflicted nothing but pain upon me. You're right, I have not held Soriya. I'd rather never touch her than do to her what my father did to me. I can protect her without… Without being him."

"What makes you think you would be like him?"

"It is a chance I would rather not take. When you spent your life raised by a monster, it is bound to seep into your blood."

"Krav… He took you from your mother?"

"Yes. I had spare little time with her before her death."

"But you kept a home in Cambodia…"

"Yes, my father always had a hotel there, it was why he was there in the first place all those years ago. I went to visit my mother as soon as I became an adult and began to form an uneasy… I don't know. We would see one another sometimes. Eventually I decided to have a personal residence there to…to reconnect. With the food, the language. My people. I was raised Italian. That will always be the biggest part of me, and there is no going back and rewriting that. It was the place I spent most of my life. But Cambodia was my foundation. And… I felt an impulse to try and go back to that."

"It's as much a part of you as Italy."

"I suppose. Though, not in practice."

And now he had told her. Dispassionately, the truth of things.

And she seemed… She seemed as if she didn't know how to react.

"You never told me any of this."

"I don't speak of it."

"You nearly did. That first night we met."

"I was not myself. I was not here."

And obviously he did not mean on the plane. He meant in his father's world. In his father's world, there were rules. And they had to be followed. Otherwise, there were grave consequences.

And yes, it had been different. In his homeland, the land of his mother, grieving her loss.

"What did your father do to you?" She asked. The pressure in the cabin began to change. "We have begun our descent," he said. "There is no time to get into what my father did to me. But suffice it to say, whatever monster you think I am, you're not wrong. I was made to be this way. I was made to be able to run the Valenti empire with no weaknesses standing in my way. No attachments. He succeeded in making me into his…his creation. Perfectly cold and capable of doing whatever needed to be done. I'm sorry that you were brought into this."

It was the truth. The most honest thing he'd ever said. It felt…freeing to admit it.

"Are you?"

"Yes," he said.

"Then you can't be entirely without feeling."

"My feelings are ghosts. I might know they're there, but I can't grab hold of them. And the minute I try… they vanish."

The plane landed then, and they got in a car that carried them back to the estate.

"We will live separate lives," she said, when they got back to the estate. As they stood in the vast entryway. And suddenly, he remembered standing there as a boy. And how large and imposing everything had been. How large and imposing his father had been.

"As long as that life is contained here."

"Why do you feel the need to control it if you don't care?"

"It is…it's the only thing I know."

And he didn't know what that meant. Only that it was true. And it echoed inside of him long after the words were spoken.

But as time marched on, as their wedding drew nearer, that persistent feeling of grief wouldn't go away.

And he remembered…

He remembered when she had not. When she had believed he loved her.

It had been easy in its own way. All he had to do was take her to nice places, speak to her with kindness. All that he had to do was pretend the past didn't exist.

It had felt…

It had been a strange sort of freedom. The first time he'd felt detached from what his father had made him.

He didn't see why they couldn't do it now. He didn't see why.

And what he wanted was to find his way back to that, he realized.

It stunned him. The realization that he wanted something. The realization that he missed…her. Of course, when she had gone the first time he had missed the sex. That had been what he told himself. But they'd only been together once. In all this time, only once.

And it was not simply that he missed.

He missed her, and he missed the child being around. She was around less when Riot wasn't there. Of course. It made sense.

He had been filled with certainty. That nothing mattered but the wedding. Joining her to him. But he was beginning to realize it wasn't enough.

To live in this space. Of darkness. Of utter coldness between them.

No.

And on the eve of the wedding, he made a decision. He was going to win her back. With her full memory, he would win her back.

He could not fix what was broken in himself. But she felt like the key to something.

When she'd loved him, he'd been in control of his darkness in a more profound way than ever. He wanted that back.

He would make it so.

She would love him again.

Of that he was certain.

CHAPTER TEN

SHE WAS DOING her best to be as happy as possible. But she had lost that feeling of being the luckiest girl in the world. It had been there for a while. And it had been so intoxicating. The feeling of having it all.

She had Soriya. She lived in a beautiful place.

She might be desperately lonely, but that was not really any different from the life she had before she had known Krav.

And at least she had a child.

That was an unexpected gift, and something she hadn't thought she wanted.

To be a mother.

But there was healing taking place inside of her soul as she mothered her child.

As she was able to find space to heal over the ways her mother had not been there for her.

She was able to consciously consider how to be there for her own daughter.

She was able to put that intention into words and plant them deep inside of her own heart as she held her, saying to her as they lay out on the grass in the estate.

And sometimes she would look up and see Krav, gazing down from the balcony over them.

And she did her best not to look back.

Did her best not to think about him at all.

But it was hard.

She had said that she hated him as much as she had ever loved him, and that was true. It was just that… Sometimes she felt like the hatred existed right alongside the love.

Especially after what he had told her about his past. About his father. His mother.

He had said it with such detachment. It was difficult to understand exactly what he felt about it.

But she had been turning it over inside of herself. Deciding what she felt about it.

And it was an incredibly difficult thing to parse.

So mostly, she chose not to.

But she was marrying him. She was marrying him. That was… Such a strange thing.

She had also been grappling with all of her memories. That was the problem. She had gotten that broken, bad memory back. The truth of what happened when she found out she was pregnant. And she felt utterly silly for having romanticized it now. But she had also gotten back the time they'd had together. And there had been joy in it. And she had seen a lightness in him, and she didn't think it was a lie.

It was only that… Finding out he was going to be a father had terrified him. She could see that now. That of course he would react to fear with anger. And she could understand that there was fear because of his own past. His own childhood. It made her soften. Which irritated her.

But there was so much more to him than he thought. Than was easy to see.

He'd said he was cold. That his feelings were ghosts, but she'd seen how untrue that was.

His rage was not a ghost. It was a whole dragon.

And if he felt that with such intensity, he must be able to feel everything else.

It was all buried, twisted and mangled beneath the rubble left behind by his childhood. And that made her feel…

She didn't want to find any sympathy for him. Not any softness. That way lay a certain measure of madness. Because she just wasn't…immune to him. As much as she wanted to be. And the man was forcing her into marriage…

You could leave. You could fight him.

She pushed that thought away. She wasn't particularly interested in thinking about the ways in which she was responsible for the situation she found herself in.

It was easy to think only of the way that he had stormed into her life. Easy to think of herself as a lamb being led to slaughter.

She thought of that even as she was wrapped in her white wedding gown the day of the ceremony. Yes, a sacrificial lamb. That's what she was.

Spotless on the altar before him.

So much drama.

But Riot embraced the drama, as the bouquet of red roses was handed to her.

And she wondered who this farce of a wedding was for. If the doors would swing open and the church would be full of people who were strangers to her.

But the Cathedral was empty. Empty of everyone except for him. The nannies that held Soriya acting as witnesses.

He was alone. And that stood out as stark as the fact that she was too.

And right then, as she walked down the aisle toward him, with no one forcing her or marching her in that direction, she suddenly saw all of those missing memories again. But she saw them differently.

She had walked toward him in the ruin. She had gone with him back to the tree house. When he had pounced, when he had kissed her, she had returned it. With just as much force and greed as he displayed.

And that made everything feel different.

Did a lamb return volley when the Tiger pounced?

No. And she knew it.

Only a tigress did that.

Only a tigress would ever stand against something quite so fearsome.

And she saw in that moment every responsibility that belonged to her.

She had wanted him, and she had had him. She hadn't asked him to use protection. She hadn't cared.

She had wanted him, and so she had taken him. She had wanted to leave her life behind, and she had allowed him to do that, she had allowed him to not share with her because she hadn't wanted her fantasy disrupted.

And when he had sent her away, she'd been heartbroken, because she had allowed herself to see him with rose-colored glasses, and she had done it not out of innocence, and not out of a misunderstanding over the way that the world worked, but rather because she knew quite a bit too much about how people were. The abandonment of her own mother, of her father. She hadn't wanted to lose him, and she hadn't wanted to know that he might not be as wonderful as she had first thought him to be. No, she hadn't thought him wonderful at first, she'd thought him dangerous.

She had just wanted him to be the fantasy, so she had willfully set out to make him into one, and she had broken her own heart. He had never made her a promise. Not ever.

She had hoped, because she was still optimistic despite whatever life had thrown at her. And she wondered if...

She wondered if what she had really wanted all this time was to have adventures but to be able to blame other people when they went wrong.

She might've been bitter at Jaia for the lack of planning on the trip, but she hadn't contributed any planning to it. She had paid her own money and gone sailing off after her friend. Knowing that she was flaky.

And then she had gone off with Krav, with no more planning about where she would end up.

And so, every pitfall was someone else's fault, wasn't it?

But no. They were her choices. It was her heartbreak. She had chosen it.

Just as now she was choosing to walk down the aisle

toward him while she told herself she hated him. And yes, he had put her in a difficult situation. He had put her in one with options she didn't like.

But that was not the same as being forced. Even now, she was walking down the aisle toward him because part of her hoped.

Because whatever she said, whatever she told herself, she had not lost hope. Not entirely.

About what they can have. About who he could be. But she had to stop being passive. She had to stop fantasizing. And she had to be honest. She could not see herself merely as a victim. She had to see herself as an active participant in all of this.

And if she wanted more from him she had to demand it.

No. She had never done that. Instead, she had fallen desperately in love with him, with a facade, because she had allowed herself to fashion him into the image of something that she wanted him to be.

So maybe she needed to set about learning more about him. And see if she could fall in love with that man. The one that she had professed to hate.

He had hurt her. And yes, when she had woken up, she hadn't remembered that he had done that. So what she had learned from that experience was that she would fall for him again every single time. Because there was something in him that was undeniably for her, no matter what. She could call it chemistry or sexual desire, and surely there was an element of that involved. But it also couldn't be quite that simple. It couldn't be quite that limited.

She thought of all that and realized her own power as she was walking down the aisle toward him.

It stunned her.

And as she stood before him, as he took her hand and brought her to that place in front of the priest, she was faced with the enormity of what she was doing.

She was making vows to him. Becoming his wife. And that was not a temporary state. If she was going to stand there and promise him forever, then perhaps she needed to be prepared to fight for it.

At least give it a try.

A real try, an honest try.

Grappling with the man that he was, and not simply the one she wanted him to be.

Maybe he could change.

Maybe for Soriya it was worth the endeavor.

And maybe for you?

She had not touched him since that night, and now they held hands and faced each other.

"Do you promise to love, honor and obey one another, as long as you both shall live?"

"I will," he said.

And then the question was posed to her. What did that mean? Had he even paused to consider it? Or was it merely part of his plan to keep her with him? She looked into his dark eyes, and she wished that she could fully understand what it was that he wanted from this. He wanted Soriya to have a mother, but was that all?

What she was realizing about herself, just now, was that there were issues handed to her in childhood that she was aware of, but that did not mean she fully understood the ways that they impacted her life.

And she could see some of them as she looked back on her interactions with Krav.

It was just not as simple as she would like it to be.

And so when she said, "I will," she did so knowing that she didn't truly understand what she was saying. Or what it would mean for them. What it would look like. She did so knowing that they had a long road ahead of them, and that she could not let him have the final say in this marriage.

On what it would be.

And when it was time for them to kiss, she made a decision. To go into that kiss. To go into him.

Their mouths met, and her heart nearly burst through her chest. This thing between them had always been so glorious, so wonderful. This was the easy part. This desire. Except it cut her now. Made her feel a deep sense of desire, loss and pain. And of hope. And it was the hope that hurt her most of all. That thing with wings, but she worried that if she flew too high, that in the end, it might abandon her. That it might be part of her destruction.

They were pronounced, man and wife, and they joined hands and walked down the aisle, to their audience of two, and when they had exited the sanctuary, she looked at him.

"Have no fear," he said. "I have no designs on claiming a wedding night. You are free to spend the rest of the day as you wish. You are my wife, you can go spend my money abroad if you wish."

"I think I would like to go home. And take care of our daughter."

"Then you are free to do that if you wish as well."

"Does cruelty make you feel better?"

He paused. "Are you attempting to score points?"

"No," she said. "I am simply asking you a question. Does cruelty make you feel better in this instance? Does it make things seem clear to you? Because I understand that we do things in an attempt to make them seem simple. I personally liked to rewrite what I wanted into fate and fairy tales. Because it meant I didn't have to be responsible for the decisions. So does being cruel absolving you from needing to be better?"

"You think I'm being cruel, but I am just being that which I was made."

He believed that. She could see it. But she felt in that moment that she knew differently. That she could see the way that he was working to simplify all of this for himself. To justify.

And she didn't know why he needed it. She just recognized the same thing that she witnessed in her own self. And he left her there, but there was another car to take her back to the estate. They did not go together. He did not seem concerned in the least about appearances of any kind.

Their relationship had already been in the media, and they'd made no announcements about their wedding, so they had drawn no attention for the event.

She wondered if it would've been different, had she not remembered.

You know it would've been. You would've worn that dress in front of a sanctuary full of people.

Yes. She would have. He would've given her the wedding of her dreams. He would have been the solicitous groom. And he would've taken her to a beautiful hotel, where he would've laid her down on silken sheets after and given her a glorious wedding night.

And she wished, in that moment that she could have the fantasy back.

It would've been so much easier.

It was this damn reality. That was what made things so difficult. And she wasn't angry at herself for seeking the mists of fantasy. She knew why she did it. It was just she couldn't do it. Not now. Not with everything she knew. Not with everything she was. Everything she had become.

She ate dinner alone.

She spent the evening holding Soriya, rocking her. Reminding herself that this was why she was doing what she was doing.

No. Because at some point you need to be doing something for yourself.

That realization cracked her open.

She saw her mother as selfish, so she had determined that she would simply become the best mother to Soriya that she could possibly be.

She had thought that her own desire shouldn't come into it. That it couldn't come into it. And she realized with absolute clarity that was just as potentially damaging as being a selfish mother.

She had to know who she was. She had to be able to show her daughter what life could be.

She couldn't see herself as a lamb. Because she wasn't one. She was a tigress. Wasn't she? She was too. She had survived everything that she had been raised with. She had done it well. It wasn't that she didn't have issues. But she was acknowledging them. She had survived. She would give Soriya better. And she would make sure that she knew from the beginning that she was a daughter of a tigress, and that she would be no less. That she was brilliant and wonderful, and that she deserved the whole world.

But she would have to demand things for herself. Otherwise…

Those lessons would be empty. If she saw Riot meekly accepting this sham of a marriage, a life without love, if she saw her wandering around like she was a woman in chains, then how would a message of empowerment mean anything?

And anyway, it was just more hiding. To go from a fantasy straight to martyrdom. To decide that she hated him when nothing inside of her was anything near that clear or simple when it came to her feelings for Krav.

No. It was more. It was everything, just as he was.

Everything ugly and complex, but the good things remained.

And that was when she made her decision.

She kissed Soriya on the forehead and laid her down in her crib, and then she went down the hall. She was dressed in nothing remarkable. It was not a wedding night ensemble.

They made love in Paris, but she hadn't remembered the truth of them. She did now. She remembered the way that he had hurt her. But she also remembered the foundation of their connection. The heat between them, so undeniable. The way that she had always craved more, even if they had just finished making love. The way he had transformed her, from someone who was afraid of this sort of desire, to a woman who had embraced it.

The memories were complicated. And so were they.

And so was she.

In her sweats.

Without knocking, she opened the door to Krav's bedroom.

He was standing in front of his nightstand, shirtless, wearing the dark pants that he had worn in the wedding, and nothing more. His feet were bare, and just as it had seemed that first night they were together, there was something so intimate about that.

She wished that they could go back there. To Cambodia. She remembered vividly seeing him in the clothing native to his country—the silk sarong in a rich blue, flowing over him like water, rather than the rigid, fitted suits he wore away from there—and how…right it looked. How fitting.

This life was one that had been forced upon him. In the same way he was trying to force it onto her. But perhaps he knew no other way. And perhaps he didn't think anyone would choose this life, this life with him, if there wasn't force involved. What else had he been shown?

He had shared with her, and she had tried her best not to feel sympathy.

He had not shared it seeking sympathy. He had not shared it with emotion, but that didn't mean it wasn't there.

It didn't mean it wasn't there.

"What is it you want?" He asked, straightening, setting his watch down on the nightstand.

She looked at his chest, broad and covered in dark hair. She was hungry for him.

Emotional turmoil aside.

But she wasn't here simply because of the hunger. Simply because she was driven by desire for him.

No. She was here to try and make a new map of them. To draw them back to each other, so that they might be able to meet somewhere.

She did not wish to live in this house with them living different lives. Moving on different paths. She wanted to find a way to join him.

She was hurt. She was still terribly hurt by him. And this wasn't going to make it go away. Not entirely. This wasn't even really forgiveness. It was just reclaiming. And she needed that. She needed it desperately.

"I want my wedding night."

She stripped her sweatshirt up over her head, and she had nothing underneath it.

And in spite of the fact that nothing she was wearing was particularly sexy, she could see him respond.

The fire in his eyes was instant. Burning bright.

"Why?"

"I don't know," she said. "But it's my choice." She pushed her pants down her hips, and took her underwear along with them. She had been naked in front of Krav any number of times. Countless times, and she had all of the memories now. She had been shameless with him. And she would be shameless now.

"But you didn't force me into this marriage, I chose it. I'm choosing to be here now. Because what I want matters. I don't want a cold marriage. I don't want to simply be married to you and wander the corridors pale and listless, behaving as if I am one of your victims. I'm not a victim. Anymore than you have victimized me. I made choices that brought me here. I made a choice to be here now."

"But, do you want me?"

"Yes. You know that I do. That has never stopped."

"But, you do hate me," he said, his eyes lit with black flame.

"Yes," she said. "Part of me does. Part of me will never understand why you treated me so cruelly. I loved you so much, Krav. And you destroyed that. You looked at me as if I was nothing. As if you hated me."

"I never hated you," he said. "Only myself."

The words hit her like a blow. He said them as if they were a simple statement of fact. Something that cost him nothing. And yet…she felt it. Deep and echoing in her soul.

"And what do you feel for me?"

"I don't know," he said. "Because I lost the ability to truly feel my emotions the day I was taken away from my mother. And I'm not saying that to garner sympathy. You have asked an honest question, and you stood there and gave me honesty, so I'm trying to do the same. It doesn't cost me anything to admit it. I'm broken."

"Why? Because he said you were?"

"No. Because he was. And he raised me to be. And it doesn't matter if I know, maybe in ways that he never knew such a thing about himself, the fact remains the same. I have learned to stand back and look at my feelings, but I have not learned to actually experience them."

"I don't believe that. I believe that there's more."

"Don't. Don't go down that road with me. I don't actually want to hurt you."

"You're willing to. Emotionally."

He nodded slowly. "Yes. I am."

"Perhaps I'm willing to hurt us both. I told myself when I met you that you were a predator. And I felt nervous. As if I were prey. But I never behaved like prey, did I? And I won't behave like it now."

"Riot," he said, his voice rough. "I want to possess you. And that is the truth of it. I have from the moment I saw you."

"I want to possess you," she said. "You were the most beautiful man I had ever seen."

"But you can't."

"Can't I?"

She moved toward him, and pressed her body against him, and she could feel the evidence of his desire for her pushing against the front of his slacks. "You want me, and you cannot help yourself. Was there another woman? In all the time I was away from you?"

She would accept the answer, whatever it was, but the idea of him touching another woman made her see red.

"No," he said. "I have not been with another woman since the first time I laid eyes on you."

"So I have you already, don't I? You came for me.

Even though you said you didn't want a child. You came for me. What made you change your mind?"

"I didn't want her," he said, his voice jagged. "I simply knew… I thought that you didn't want her."

It angered her to hear him say that. She knew it was…she knew where it came from. That it triggered deep pain from his childhood. But it still wounded her. "You know now that I do, and you still married me. You still want to keep us. You want to keep us together, you just want to keep us at arm's length…"

"It isn't that I want to, it's simply that it's how it is. It's how I feel."

"You lie. But not most especially to me. Most especially to yourself. You lie to us both."

"Are you here to screw me, or are you here to talk?"

"We can do that if you'd like," she said. "That's what we did. A lot of it. Though…sometimes I was making love."

"I never was. I never am."

He was pushing her away. She could see that. He never knew what he wanted, and she could see that too. He wanted her close and the minute it was too much, he broke.

She didn't want to allow it, not now.

"And that's why you care so much for my pleasure."

"Why don't you stop talking," he said. "And see to mine."

A surge of power filled her, and she recognized her choice in this. That she wanted to do this. That she wanted to use his desire for her against him.

Her feelings were not simple. Because her anger at him was still there.

It was just there was more than that. And for all that he said he couldn't feel his emotions, she felt them all.

She was overwhelmed by them. Rage, desire, need, and love. Still love.

She hadn't ever wanted this. Something so messy. She had her fill of difficult people. And yet somehow this was different. Because he wasn't detached from her.

Her mother would go in and out of her life on a whim. Her friends had done the same. But he couldn't. He'd married her. Whatever he said, he had married her. He had taken steps to keep her with him forever, and that was different. He was different. And so... She was willing to take this on.

She wanted to.

She sank to her knees in front of him, working the belt on his pants, opening them, revealing that glorious, hard length of him.

She had always thought him beautiful.

She loved his naked body.

She had always liked the look of men, but she had never been tempted enough by them to do anything.

He was a constant temptation.

She leaned in, sliding her tongue over his length, the way that he had taught her to pleasure him.

She took him deep into her mouth, sucked him until he was groaning with desire. Until she had the power. All of it. And she knew it well.

Until she couldn't wait any longer. Until she needed him between her thighs, not just her lips.

She stood then, pressing against the center of his chest, and he sat on the edge of the bed. She straddled his lap, bringing herself down onto his hardened length and impaling herself on the evidence of his desire.

She let her head fall back as greed overtook them both. He gripped her hips, and brought her down hard onto him every time she moved, increasing the intensity even while she set the pace.

And they didn't kiss. It was more primal than that. And there was too much… It was still too much anger.

But he was hers. And he was in her. And she needed him. Needed this, in ways that she couldn't articulate.

"Krav," she said, rolling her hips forward.

"Riot."

And he came inside of her on a roar, and she followed him over the edge, need pulsing through her, memories.

She made love to him knowing that they had met in a rainstorm. Knowing that they carried on a torrid, physical only affair that spanned continents. Knowing that he had rejected her. That he had sent her away thinking she had lost the baby. Knowing that he had lied to her. That he had manipulated her.

And wanting him anyway. Having him anyway.

And when it was done, their foreheads pressed together, their breathing jagged.

"I don't know what our marriage will be," she said. "But it will not be in name only."

"Be careful," he said, tracing a line down her throat with the tip of his tongue before kissing her. "You may not be happy that you've opened up this possibility."

"Whatever we are, how can we find out if we build fences around each other?"

"I live my whole life with the wall between myself

and the world, Riot, and marriage will not change that. Sex will not change it."

"Maybe it isn't for you. Maybe it's because it's changing me."

"As long as I get to have you. Doesn't matter."

She wished that it did. She wanted to tell him that it should. But instead, she simply slid away from him and collected her clothes. "I assume you won't stop me from keeping my own room?"

"Is it what you want?"

She wanted to protect herself, and she understood that was the urge driving her now. But for now, she was going to give in to it.

"Yes."

"All right."

He was still naked, still breathing hard. And yet speaking with such cool dispassionate emotion that it would be easy to believe he hadn't been affected. If she hadn't just had him inside of her. If she didn't know better.

And when she went back to her room, she gave in to her own complicated feelings, and started to weep.

Because she might've resolved to take action, and to be strong, but that didn't mean it was pain free.

No, this thing was difficult. This thing was a fight.

But at least now she had admitted that.

She was his wife, but not by command, by choice.

And that meant the marriage would be something of her choosing.

CHAPTER ELEVEN

SHE HAD NOT come to his bed again since the wedding night. It had been three days, and it was all he had thought about.

She had been a revelation, had Riot.

He had been restrained, allowing her a measure of control when what he wanted was to pull her to him and keep her with him all night.

But there was something reckless in her emotion, as if he could see her balancing on a knife's edge, willing to risk anything, and… He was not a man who admitted to fear, but he was a man who knew better than to push a woman when it was ill advised.

As if you have ever been in a similar situation with another woman.

No. Never. But then there was no woman other than Riot.

He was left unsettled by the entire experience, and he would like to say he was not a man who did unsettled, anymore than he was one who did uncertainty or fear, but he felt as if he had done a host of things he didn't normally do since Riot had come into his life.

And it was difficult, because he didn't do entanglements, and yet just like they had done at that simpler time, they shared meals together at night. And it was unavoidable that they talk.

And she knew things about him, about his past and the way that it made him feel, and now, about the things he did every day.

Because she had begun to ask. And he did not deny her answers to the questions.

About his life. His mother. His business.

She was different than she had been before.

He had not been forthcoming with information about his life, and she hadn't pressed. But she pressed now.

And he could feel her winding herself more tightly into the fabric of who he was.

And she would do all this while holding the baby.

He felt protective over the child, but…

He had still not held her.

And soon enough, she would be bigger. And you did not hold larger children anyway.

He could not remember being held.

And one night, he was walking down the halls, and he heard plaintive wailing. Usually, Riot wasn't far behind when the baby was upset, or the nannies. But nobody came.

He pushed open the door, and walked into the room, it was shrouded in darkness, and so was the tiny bundle.

He stood there. And watched her cry. He stood there and watched her cry because…

He had convinced himself that somehow his touch would be more damaging than his distance.

The child was crying, and he was doing nothing.

He had been this lonely child. Denied a hug, and comfort, and the arms of a parent. And here he was, doing the same.

He was a coward.

He would've said that he was not a coward, he would've said that he wasn't afraid, but he was a man steeped in fear, and he could recognize that then. He was not disconnected from it. It took him over. It made him feel choked with it. Not with the fear, but with disgust for himself.

He took a step closer to the crib, and closer still.

Then he reached down, and touched that tiny, flailing hand. And she stopped. And curled her fingers around his.

This tiny girl holding on to him with everything she had. And he remembered. Clinging to his mother. And he had convinced himself because of that memory that a child needed a mother. Because he had been devastated by the loss of his own, brought to a world where he had a father, but that father had meant nothing, that father might as well not have been there.

But he had needed both. And he hadn't had them. Not really. The tragedy was not that he had been taken from his mother and raised by a father, but that no one had raised him as a parent truly should.

And that was the crime. And here he was, perpetuating pain of a different kind. Passing it on to this child who was innocent, who didn't deserve this.

Who needed him to find it in himself to be more. To be better.

It was because of Riot that he was standing here even now.

Because of who she was. Because of her bravery. Because of the way she had treated him these past days, even when he didn't deserve it. Because of the connections she was trying to build.

His chest felt heavy with it. With the realization of it all.

And in that moment, he realized that no matter his intent, he was going to keep that cycle spinning. Unless he did something. Unless he changed.

He leaned down and, using the same technique he had seen the nannies and Riot use, supporting her head, he lifted her out of the crib and cradled her to his chest.

And the strangest sensation overtook him, and it wasn't simply possessiveness. It wasn't simply a desire to protect. It was that, but it was more. The absolute conviction that he would not just die for this child, but he would live for her as well.

That he would do everything he could to ensure that she didn't experience the pain that he had in his life. But she wouldn't experience the pain Riot had either.

And this was why, he knew. This was why he had never held her before. It was because he had known that if he did this, he would have to change.

And he had decided who he was a long time ago. It was protection. To throw up all the walls that he could as quickly as possible around himself and ensure that nothing and no one could reach him.

He had cemented himself in his earliest days, a defense against his father. Not allowing him to decide who Krav was going to be. Not allowing himself to be movable.

He had done it to consolidate the core of who his mother had made him. To save a piece of himself from that assimilation. To keep his heritage. To keep his happiest days.

And so, change had been his enemy.

But he had to do it now. And it wasn't about force.

No. His father had used an iron fist to try and effect an evolution in Krav.

Instead, it was the delicate, tiny fist of his daughter, wrapped around his finger that had changed him.

It had been the kiss of a woman at the ruin. That had begun this journey. This moment. This change.

It was like a blow to him. He could barely breathe past it.

He stood, and cradled her, swaying back and forth as he did so. And then he looked up, and he saw Riot. Standing there in the doorway. With tears on her cheeks.

"She's asleep now," he murmured, laying her back down in the crib.

"I didn't know she was crying," Riot said.

"It's all right." His chest felt tight, and he didn't want to speak of the things he had just recognized. He didn't know why. He didn't know why it was so difficult. To stand in front of her with all of this rolling through him and try to make sense of it. Try to find words for it.

Instead, he moved away from the crib and walked toward her.

Put his hand on her face, and leaned in to kiss her.

They hadn't touched since their wedding night, when their coming together had been intense and wild.

But when he kissed her this time, it was softer.

He broke away from her, pain lancing his chest, and he turned and walked away, out onto the expansive balcony that ran from the nursery along the side of the estate. It overlooked that place where she usually lay out with Soriya. Where he usually stood over them and watched, but didn't partake, because he held himself back.

And it was raining.

He looked back at her, and she stepped out onto the terrace with him.

"Why is it always raining?" he asked.

When he met her.

When she left him.

When she'd remembered.

"Maybe it's trying to tell us something," she said.

And she walked toward him, the sky truly broken open now, beginning to go from light to downpour.

But she didn't flinch.

Instead, she put her hand on his face. "Maybe it's trying to grow something new. That's what rain does. It creates new life."

He swept her up into his arms, lifting her up off of the balcony, and kissed her.

Kissed her without end, as the water washed them both clean. He carried her down those stairs of the balcony, to the place that he had watched her, but not joined her before. The place that he had held himself back from.

So much holding himself back.

She stripped his clothes from him, he from her.

And they were naked, down on the blanket that she kept there, raindrops sliding down their skin, as his hands skimmed over her body.

She was beautiful and wild, delicate and strong all at once.

She was everything in a way no one else ever had been.

And she had been from the beginning.

Krav was a person who had spent his life in isolation.

He had held onto a dream about where he was from. About his mother. But they were disconnected. He had visited her often, but they had never felt like mother and son. And in the end she was so ill he wasn't even certain she knew it was him who was there.

And he had attended that funeral in that same isolation. Sitting in the front with everyone around him giving him a wide berth, because even if they were family in a distant sense, they didn't know him.

He had been robbed of that. Not just his mother, but a community.

He had been brought to Italy where he hadn't been given one. And yes, he had wild success.

Money. People flocked around him because of that. Because he had power.

Women wanted him because they thought he was handsome, but most of all because they thought he could give them something.

There were a great many men who didn't look like him, who had any number of feminine acolytes because they could write a check and make the world's problems seem that much smaller.

None of what he had, none of what he'd built had anything to do with him.

But Riot had been there. She had been with him. She had seen him.

And they had made something together that night. Just as they were making something now.

It was more than desire. Connection.

Tiny, tenuous golden threads, woven around them and through them.

Shoring up the broken places inside of them. Knitting them back together. Leaving veins of gold dust where before there had been darkness.

Emptiness.

Nothing.

And when he sank into her beautiful body, he was electrified. Lit up from the inside out.

But that light shone on the darkest of things, and they didn't scurry away. They were there. Staring back at him. There was nowhere to hide.

And it made him want to retreat.

But he couldn't. Because she was all around him. Soft and smelling like sunshine and rain. Like revelations.

His release was something more than pleasure. It emptied him out. And what remained…

What remained…

He rolled over onto his back, the rain cascading down his chest as he lay there, eyes open in the torrential storm.

And she covered him. Put her body over his and curled up against him, her hand over his chest. They were together. And he remembered, when she had been on the ground before him with all that rain.

He remembered, the way that he had treated her. Even while his heart raged against him. Those feelings...

Those feelings he tried so hard not to connect with.

Is it just the way it is, or is it something you've made?

He sat up. "We should go inside," he said. "You will be cold."

"Will I be?"

"I'm afraid you will be, yes."

"I'm never cold when I'm with you."

But there was something in her eyes that made him think she was lying.

"I don't think you mean that," he said.

"I would like to mean it," she said. "From now on. I would like to mean it."

He knew that she had felt cold with him. Because he had turned her away. And in turn, he had turned away from her.

But no, he wanted... He wanted her love. He wanted her love.

And he recognized that he was going to have to... be different. Do different things. But surely there was a way to keep what needed to be kept secure, kept secure. Surely there was a way...

"Ask for whatever you want," he said. "And I will give it to you. Even if it's half of my wealth."

"I don't want your wealth," she said. "I mean, I'm quite happy to live in it. But I just want us."

He picked her up again, naked this time, and took her into the house wet. He brought her into the shower, and let it warm them both.

Then he carried her to bed.

And he made love to her again in the softness of the sheets. And he thought… This was more than he had ever sought to build for himself.

He had been given back a piece of something.

He may never have a whole heart.

But perhaps she could be that heart.

When he did things that pleased her, then he would know. He would know that it was right. That he was right.

He would know.

And he slept with that knowledge, with that comfort.

He might be broken beyond repair. But there were places she had put him back together, and where he could not be… She could be his compass.

He held her. All night long.

And for the first time in memory, he dreamed of the future.

And he did not despise what he saw.

CHAPTER TWELVE

THAT NIGHT WITH Krav had been transformative. Whatever had happened between them… Whatever had happened in him. He had held her.

And he had kept on doing it in the days since.

They had begun to share a bed every night.

But it was different than the time they had spent together on the Amalfi Coast. Different than that reckless, sexual affair.

Not that what was between them wasn't deeply sexual, it was.

But there was something else to it. He truly let her
make love to him.

But he…

He was still holding himself back. Of that she was
certain. He was still… Fighting something. Fighting
the two of them.

It was a subtle thing, but she felt it. That there was
a resistance inside of him that didn't want to crumble.
And yet… He had softened.

It wasn't that she didn't still look at him and see a
predator. She did. Because he was. Every bit as dan-

gerous as he had always been. But something in him had changed.

Still, she didn't quite… She didn't quite know where they were at.

And she didn't quite know how to approach him. He had hurt her. Many times. And if there was anything she had learned in life it was how to protect herself. She had been foolish with him on multiple occasions. Had held her beating heart out to him only to have him reject it. Or worse, crush it beneath his boot heel.

She didn't want to do that again. For obvious reasons.

A fool's errand, as it was.

And then he suggested they go to the Amalfi Coast.

And she had no idea if she was ready to visit the site of her previous degradation. But she agreed. Because… She felt compelled to follow this path they were on.

She felt like there might be answers there.

It was a joy to watch him take part in packing Soriya up for the trip. Watching him participate in fatherhood, rather than simply presiding over it as a man who was being forced to bear witness to it.

He was the one who packed her diaper bag. And bundled her up, ready for the trip. And on the plane, he was the one who held her.

"I've never held a baby before her," he said when they were comfortably in the sky.

"Never?"

"No. I was… I was very isolated in my life."

"Can you tell me more about your childhood?"

"Will you be charging hourly for the session?"

"No. But I just… I want to know. One of the things

that I promised myself was that I would be a good mother to her. No matter what happened between us. My childhood was lonely," she said. "We moved a lot. We had to, because we were dodging landlords. Creditors. Always. So I might make friends at school, but it would be for a small moment. And sometimes my mother didn't even enroll me in school because we weren't in a place long enough. It was very fractured, and it was extremely uncertain."

"Tell me," he said. "What were you planning on doing? Really. You didn't tell me that you were still pregnant. You must've had a plan."

"I didn't tell you because you said you didn't want a child."

His jaw firmed and he nodded slowly. "I did. I'm not angry at you for that."

And yet there was anger in his voice. But she wondered if it was mostly directed at himself.

"Well good, if you were angry at me for that, I would have to punch you in the stomach, because you don't deserve to be angry at me for what I did to survive."

"No."

And somehow, that resonated inside of her. What she had done to survive. She looked at him, and she wondered how much of what he'd done was trying to make sure he survived.

It created sympathy where she hadn't expected to feel it.

And she wanted to continue to press him about his childhood, not allow him to derail the discussion with her own stories. But maybe he needed her stories.

"I knew I wanted to give her stability," she said. "And most of all love. Support. I was an afterthought to my mother. She dragged me along with her, and I think she often resented it. I made her life harder. I was very aware of that. I wanted… The reason that I was a virgin, Krav, is that I never wanted that life. I thought that I was smarter than her. And I met you, and I threw it all out the window. Because smart… There was no being smart. I just wanted you. And I threw everything I knew out the window for that. But when I found out that I was going to have Soriya… Well, then I knew I had to be better. I got a job in England. I decided that I would stay there. I didn't want to go back to Georgia because I didn't want to feel like I was living the same life my mother was. And maybe that was just a feeling, and something I did to make myself feel… Better. But I got a job, and it was a good one. I found a decent living situation. I was delivering baked goods when I got into my accident."

"Do you remember the accident?"

"No. I still don't. The last thing I remember is going in to work. I don't know that I'll ever remember the accident. It scares me, a little bit. That lost time. But I gained some of it back, so… Anyway, I did have a plan. But I think the most important thing wasn't the plan. It was recognizing where my mother failed. And promising in my heart that I wasn't going to let her decide my path. I want to decide it."

"You are strong," he said. "I'm grateful my daughter has such a strong mother."

"Tell me," she said. "What was it like growing up in that state?"

"It was a nightmare," he said. "Mostly, my father only had oversight with me via tutors and nannies. They were told to be hands off with me. Not coddle me. But sometimes... He was a violent man, Riot. And sometimes there was a fury in him that could only be expressed on me. But even that... I found ways to survive it.

"The worst part was knowing I'd had something different. And losing my connection to that day by day. Bit by bit. Until love wasn't even a memory, it was simply a picture in my mind, an impression of a feeling rather than the feeling itself.

"And as I moved further and further away from that... I moved further and further away from everything. It was how I survived. That distance."

"Krav..."

"They aren't pretty stories."

"No. But life isn't always pretty. And I want to know you. You can tell me. You don't have to simply make broad sweeping statements about all the things that happened. You can tell me exactly what it was."

"He once beat me so badly I thought I would die. So did my nanny. She took me to the hospital, but they had to hush up what had happened." He stared off into the distance, his eyes dark. "And I remember it. Every blow. Every kick. Over and over again. And if you cannot escape physically, you go somewhere inside of yourself. I don't know if I ever made it back out."

Survival. Everything he was, was because of what he'd done to survive.

And it broke her. Destroyed her. That this man had been through so much. That he had been so badly treated.

"I survived despite him," he said. "And when his health failed, I removed him from this house, I sent him away. I put him in a facility, and I never saw him again. There were no bedside declarations. No deathbed rants. I let him die alone. And I hope… I hope that in that moment, when hell opened up to greet him, he was as scared as I was when I was a child. As alone. As cut off from everything he cared about. His money didn't cushion him. Not in the end. And the only reason I even put him in a medical facility was so that he could live in such a reduced state." He looked at her. "Do you think me cruel?"

"Yes," she said, answering honestly. "But I don't blame you for it."

"It is interesting, isn't it. I tried very hard not to let him decide who I was. But the thing that I feel the most… The thing that I feel the most connected to is that rage that he left for me. And the cruelty. Sometimes that concerns me."

"It doesn't concern me."

"Have you ever wanted revenge on your mother?"

"No. She's too sad. She never had any power. She never had any power, so she rebelled continuously against the world around her. Against her own choices. Revenge would accomplish nothing, she was an eternal victim, and it would simply give her more things to justify herself."

"You are kinder than I am."

"I don't think I am. I'm not sure what I would've done if the opportunity presented itself."

They looked at each other, and she felt… Burdened. By all these things between them.

But she cared for him. Deeply.

And she felt less… Justified in being upset about returning to the home on the Amalfi Coast. Because he lived in the place where he had nearly been beaten to death, and he managed to deal with it. She recognized now that whatever Krav had done, it hadn't been out of cruelty.

He was just trying to survive.

He had made a bad choice in a bid for that survival.

A hurtful one.

But everything between them was fraud, and they were not going to make it through all of this without hurting each other. They would probably do it again.

It was just… It was just how things were.

There was something in the acceptance of that that made her feel calm. She couldn't explain it.

They landed at the villa, and her heart went tight.

Yes, she really had been hurt badly here.

But now there was a nursery.

And it was beautiful.

It reminded her of the bedroom that he had done for her at the estate. The bedroom she didn't sleep in anymore, because she slept with him.

"This is beautiful."

"It was important to me to have this place for her."

"You've changed," she said to him, putting her hand on his face.

"Have I?" And there was a thread of desperation behind those words, and they broke her.

"Yes," she said.

It was strange to walk around this place, this place she hadn't been for nearly a year. And where she had been… New and hopeful in her connection with him, but not deep either.

They hadn't known each other. She couldn't get him to share things about himself.

And now it was different. They were different. But there were barriers still.

And she wondered if they had the strength to get through them.

Don't lose hope.

And she had no idea where that voice came from. Because there was nothing in her life to suggest that hope meant anything.

Liar.

You're stuck thinking about your childhood. Not this life with him. There is every reason to believe that hope means something.

Hadn't they endured so much already? And they weren't apart from each other, in spite of all the things that had happened. They were still together. They were married. Krav was her husband and that had to count for something. He had told her about his childhood. About the trauma that he had endured. The abuse.

That mattered.

They had both had so many chances to walk away. And even if they had done for a while, it hadn't stayed that way.

There was hope in that.

There was hope.

And it was here that she'd said she loved him for the first time. And she'd said it again in Paris.

And each and every time something in her had been broken after.

Each and every time.

She wondered if she had the bravery to say it again. Because she did love him. She did. She had from the beginning, and learning about him had only deepened it. And now she had scars, scars from him.

She liked to think he had a few from her.

It hadn't been easy to get here.

But they had a marriage, and they had a child. And he was no longer holding himself back from Soriya. So that had to matter.

And maybe she was too attached to echoes. To rain. But she decided to plan a nice dinner for the two of them. Like that night everything had fallen apart. Because she was determined to write them a different ending. Because he was her fate. She had known it then, and she knew it just as deeply now, so perhaps what was required was trusting in that. Trusting in them.

She had the same dinner prepared, maybe she was a glutton for punishment of one kind or another. She wouldn't be surprised. She wouldn't be surprised if there were things and issues in herself she didn't fully comprehend. But here she was.

The nannies had Soriya taken care of. Tonight was about her and Krav. It was important. And necessary. Tonight was about the two of them.

Their connection, but also everything they had learned since that night. That night they'd met.

She had believed their connection had been chemistry. But it was more. Deeper. And it grew deeper every day.

When he came downstairs from his day working in his office, he was dressed in a white shirt, two buttons undone at his strong throat, the sleeves pushed up to his elbows, revealing strong forearms.

He was beautiful, and she would never tire of him. Of all that tanned, toned skin. His perfectly chiseled features. His large, strong hands and the way that they held her.

"I thought tonight was special."

"Why exactly?" he asked, looking down the table.

"I thought it was special because we were together."

"We are always together," he said, kissing her on the lips.

"I know," she said. "That makes life feel kinda special."

He pulled away from her slowly, a cautious grin on his face. "I suppose."

"I'm not going to tell you I'm pregnant."

He laughed. "That is a relief."

"Do you want more children?"

He paused for a moment. "I'm not opposed. You and I are both only children. Perhaps Soriya should have siblings."

"I think I'd like that," she said.

And maybe that was the point of the dinner. To plan for the future. It made her feel light and happy. It made her feel hopeful.

They ate in relative silence, making occasional companionable conversation.

This felt like the real connection she never had with anyone in her life.

Deep and special.

But… But something was missing. Something was missing.

She swallowed hard, committing to making it through dessert at least.

She didn't know where the disquiet inside of her was coming from.

And maybe the problem was she was being like a ferret, feeling the need to weasel at something endlessly.

But it was this one thing.

This one thing.

When they finished dessert, he held out his hand, and she stood, responding to his call. He pulled her down onto his lap, kissed her, and she could taste dark chocolate and coffee, mingled with desire.

"Krav," she whispered. And she had every intent of telling him that she loved him. She wasn't afraid to tell him. She had told him so many times.

But she stood there realizing that… They had done it before. And they needed to stop repeating things. Here she was in the middle of an echo of a night many months ago. How many echoes had there been?

But something had to change.

Something had to change.

"Do you love me?"

CHAPTER THIRTEEN

HE HAD NOT expected that. He had been awash in victory.

He had won her back.

It had become abundantly clear over these weeks. She was no longer withholding herself from him. She was happy to be with him, just as she had been in the beginning. He had her. He had her in that way that he craved. In the way he had never had another person. Not in his real true memory. She cared for him. And it had felt like victory. He was confident he had gotten to a place where she no longer hated him. That place they'd been in that dark, hideous night.

When the worst parts of him had been on display.

And she had said one of the words he had expected. But she had flipped it. And it had sent everything in him to a grinding halt.

And he found that he... That he couldn't respond. So he wrapped his hand around her head, gripped the back of it, and pulled her down to him, kissing her hard and fierce, because it made sense. Because it... Because it let him move further away from that question.

Because how many times could they do this? How many times could she pull away from him? How many times…

How many times could he run?

This isn't running. And words don't matter.

He kissed her. With all of the pent-up ferocity inside of him. And this wasn't that time out in the rain. It wasn't sweet or tender. It was fearsome. Because everything in him was. A tiger threatening to devour them both. But him most of all.

An ache inside of him blossomed, grew.

Made it all untenable.

He didn't want to feel this. Didn't want to want.

"Krav…"

"Don't speak," he said, nipping at her jawline. And he could see that tears filled her eyes as he continued to kiss her, but she didn't push him away. She didn't pull away.

And he growled, biting her on the side of her neck, and kissing down further, wrenching the straps of her dress down and exposing her breasts to his gaze.

His staff would know better than to interrupt. They knew how it was between the two of them.

Inevitable.

Dark.

Is that because of you?

He had thought the sun had gotten in. And it had. For bright moments it did.

But then there were these walls. These things. That she asked for, that life asked for, that he couldn't respond to.

That he couldn't…

He couldn't. It was impossible.

It was impossible.

And so he kissed her, because that he could do. He lowered his head and sucked her nipple into his mouth, because he knew that. Desire. He knew need. And he knew how to slake the lust that sparked between them. But he did not know how to answer this question.

He didn't know. And he wasn't a man who trafficked in uncertainty or fear, and here he was made of it. Because of her.

Always because of her. Because she had come into his life and she had demanded things of him that he didn't know how to answer. Because he had brought her here, to this very place, at this very table, this very moment, and she had told him he was going to be a father when he couldn't even think of the word father without everything inside of him turning to stone.

And he had found a way around that. He had. He held the child now. He… He cared for her. And he cared for Riot too, why must she continually demand more?

Why does it not end?

It was a foolish question, because it wasn't simply coming from her. The desire in him wouldn't end either. It didn't stop. It didn't change. There was no way to staunch the flow. The flow of this need.

It was endless. And he could not control it.

And that was what he found unacceptable. Unendurable.

Her hands went to his chest, tugging at the buttons on his shirt, and he could feel her rage. It was nothing less than rage.

She was angry about all of this. About wanting him. About the way he was responding to her question. Then yet still, she couldn't keep her hands off of him.

He made the mistake of looking into her eyes. And he could see there, a kind of desperation. A request that reached down into his heart and tugged.

And he could not find the distance that had carried him through life up until this point. Even that moment in the nursery with Soriya paled in comparison to what one simple look from Riot did to him.

He felt like his guts had been torn out. Like his heart had been grabbed and squeezed. Crushed. In the delicate palm of her hand. And only she had the power to do this. Only she could destroy him like that. And it was utter destruction.

He could not look at her. He couldn't.

He lifted her up off of his lap and pushed her up against the bar. Pressing her hands flat to the marble top. He swept her hair to the side and kissed the back of her neck and she shivered.

And he waited. To see if she would tell him to leave her. To see if she would push him away. But she didn't.

He pushed her dress up past her hips, pulling aside the silk of her underwear and pushing his fingers through her slick folds.

She was wet for him. Even now.

Just as he was hard for her. No matter that the world was burning around them.

No. There were no flames. They were all inside of him. He was a light. Tortured by this devastation raging inside of him. Tormented by her. All that she was.

He had seen her as a gift that day. Waiting at the ruins for him. Waiting to satisfy his urges, something that he could bury his grief in.

And yet, she had not helped him bury his feelings at all. Ever since he had first met Riot all she had done was call deeper feelings up to the surface. She had not been a gift. She had been a curse. This long road of attempting to recover from the death of his mother…

These things could not just go on hurting.

The world could not keep delivering endless pain. What was the purpose of it? What was the purpose of any of it? He growled, pushing two fingers inside of her and wrapping his fist around her hair, pulling it back. She arched her spine, pressing her bottom more firmly into him. Letting his fingers go deeper.

"You want me even now," he said. "I cannot give you what you want, and yet you desire this."

"You won't give me what I want," she said, looking over her shoulder, her eyes glinting.

"You don't understand," he said, working his fingers in and out of her. "I can't."

"You're a coward," she said.

He growled, freeing himself from his pants and thrusting into her in one smooth stroke.

He gripped her hips hard with one hand, held her hair with the other, and he punished them both. For needing each other like they did. For all the feelings that this created inside of them. If he could open his chest and pull his heart out, take out everything that offended him, he would.

But he could not. So here they were. Lost in this maelstrom of need.

And when his desire overtook him completely, he roared out his release, as he felt her break apart, tremble and cry out as her internal muscles pulsed around him.

"You may not love me anymore," he growled, "but you need me."

"I didn't say I didn't love you," she said.

He moved away from her.

"But you don't."

"I do. I really, really wanted to make you say it, Krav. I did. Because I have torn myself open for you time and time again. Only to have you tell me no. Only to have you look at me and tell me you don't feel things the way that I do. But I can see now that... I have to. I have to, don't I? Nobody loved me either. You don't have a monopoly on pain. On parents who are distant. Who don't care. The difference between you and me is that I want to love. I want to. I want to be loved. When I woke up from that coma, and I thought that we were in love, it was like every dream I had never even known I had had come true. And maybe that's it. I had that moment. That clarity. It was all that mattered. I couldn't remember the steps that we took to get there. I didn't care. All I cared about was that we loved each other. And everything else, all of the past pain can go to hell. I will forgive you for all of it. I will forgive my mother. I will forgive my absentee father. Whatever pain I need to let go of I will do it, so long as it doesn't stand in the way of me loving you."

"And Soriya."

"Yes," she said. "And Soriya. But to be honest it's much easier to love a baby than a full-grown man with issues and scars that run deeper than my own. But if I have to do it… If I have to cut myself open again and bleed for you then I will. I love you, Krav. I want you to love me."

"I can't," he said.

"Why not?"

"It's dangerous," he said. "Do you know… Do you know what it's like to desperately want the approval and love of the person who beats you? And to not be able to make that go away? Do you know what that's like? I wish my feelings had died the day they had taken me from my mother's arms. It would've been better. What a sick and twisted thing to pray that you can make the person whose fists leave you battered and bruised love you the way that you love them. He was all that I had. He was all that I had, and I loved him. I wanted to be like him. Until he finally beat it out of me. Only then did I stop loving him. But along with that… It's not easy. To wake up a heart that you have taught to be quiet."

"I am so sorry," she said. "I am so sorry for the way that he hurt you. And it is worse. It's worse than what happened to me. I understand that. It's why I am willing to do this again. Why I am willing to make a fool of myself for you. To consider not my own comfort here. But you have to meet me somewhere."

"No," he said.

She straightened her dress and turned fully to face him, grabbing hold of the sides of his face. "You want this. You wanted it, but you're standing on the edge, afraid to jump in. Afraid to submerse yourself. You're afraid of going all the way with this, and I get that. I do. But we are the only ones that can fix this. No one's going to do it for us. No one else cares enough. You, with all your money and power, you could've remained broken forever if you chose. I am the only one standing here telling you to fix yourself. And you are the only person… Yes, Soriya provided me with clarity. Yes, she made me want to be better. But you were the first thing when I woke up, when I remembered nothing. You were what made me want this life. She has grounded me here. And she gives me purpose. But you matter. Oh, you matter so very much. Please don't forget."

"I…"

"What can I do for you?"

"We should… I should leave you. I should leave you alone for a while. I should…"

"No," she said.

"I can't give you what you want."

"That's okay." A tear slid down her cheek. "That's okay if you can't do it right now. I want it. Please make no mistake. I want it more than I want anything else. For you to love me. No one has ever loved me. No one. Soriya will because she's my child. And you know how that is. I loved my mother. You loved your father. I am grateful for that love. But I have fought hard through the wilderness to be brave enough to love you, Krav. And I want you to love me that same way. I want you to love me enough. But… I'll be patient."

"I don't deserve your patience. I don't need it. *I don't want it.*" He paced back and forth, like a caged animal.

A cage he had built for himself.

"Because you don't know how much you need this. Because you don't understand what love is, do you?"

"I need to go."

"Where?"

"Cambodia. I need to go back there. Because it was the only place that I have her... It's the only place."

"I'll go with you."

"No. I need to go alone."

She shook her head. "We've done this. We've done separation, haven't we? You withdrew from me and I went away. Look what happened. Do you want me out of your life?"

"No."

"It's just that you don't want to love me."

"I don't think I can."

"Let me go with you."

"Damn it," he said. "Damn you to hell, Riot. Can't you just leave me? Can you let me go?"

"Why? So you can try to fix this on your own? So that you can come to all the conclusions about why you don't need to fix it? No. You were able to have me without changing. That was the gift of my amnesia, wasn't it? You could pretend that all the mistakes you made were gone. But I remember them. I know them now. I'm still standing here willing to love you. But you have to do the work. I will stand there with you while you do it. You don't have to be alone in this."

"It's not that simple..."

"It can be. If you'll let it."

"I don't love you."

"Stand in the ruins and tell me that."

And he stood there, rage burning inside of him, anger, at this woman for pushing him. Challenging him. He wanted to tell her to leave him the hell alone. But he was also terrified of what life might look like if she was gone.

Coward.

She had called him that. Even as she had taken pleasure from him.

And he just wanted… He wanted something else. Something other than what he was. Something other than what they were.

"What about the baby…"

"She was fine without me for a month. She will be okay with the nannies while we do this."

"What if it's for nothing?"

"I'm fighting for you. It will never be nothing. No matter the outcome."

They made arrangements with the staff, and got on the private jet. They barely spoke on the trip over. It was almost like she might have left him. The pain that stretched between them was palpable. The tension. This was like dying.

The only time he had ever felt this way before was after his mother's funeral, but in that case, there was nothing to be done. Nothing to change.

He didn't know what he wanted now. Whether he wanted to be right, or whether he wanted… Her to be right.

It was an endless night. Neither of them slept. They didn't speak. And when they landed in the morning, it wasn't morning there. Just another endless day. And by the time they got out to the temple ruins, the sun was setting again.

He began to walk through the columns, the endless rows of brick and climbing vines.

And he remembered asking her if she was here for a spiritual pilgrimage. As if that was laughable.

"What did you hope to find here?" He looked back at her.

"Myself."

"And you found me instead."

"Yes. But along the way I found myself. I… I thought I was the lamb being led to slaughter. But I'm not. I'm stronger than that. My question is… Are you?"

He didn't know what answers he was looking for, but as they walked through, in total silence, he stopped in front of the remnant of a goddess. And something about it flashed a memory through his mind.

They had something like this. A likeness of the same deity in his home when he was a child. He could scarcely remember. Just like he could scarcely remember his own mother. And suddenly, he could remember feeling. He could remember being in that little house. And everything being right. There was nothing to think about. He was a child, and everything had always been taken care of for him, and he believed that it always would be.

And then…

He remembered… He could remember clinging to his mother's shirt, crying. While they tried to take him away.

And she cried. She screamed, her wailing matching his own.

And they had taken him. They had taken him anyway. He couldn't understand a word they said. He couldn't understand anything. And then there was that man. His father. And he had been... Blisteringly cruel. And he had still longed for his approval. For his affection. For something. Anything.

And all those realizations seemed to pour from him. He wasn't examining them with distance. They were pouring out of him like a flood. Like bleeding.

And he had no control. None at all.

It was just pain. There had been so much pain. And he had chosen to block it out. But he couldn't do that. He couldn't do that and love her. That was the problem. That was the problem.

"I almost lost you," he said. "And you know what that would've done to me?"

"No," she said.

"I wasn't okay. When you were gone. I didn't take another woman to my bed. I didn't want anyone else. I wanted you. Then I found out you were in an accident..."

"And would your detachment have spared you?"

"Maybe. I would... I would never have even known what I felt. I..."

It wasn't raining now. The sun was setting, shining through the ruins, casting her in a glow. And he wondered if he had ever seen colors before. Quite this bright. As the sunrise glinted off her skin. "Because I could never... I could never really see before. I do now."

And it was like blinders had been ripped away. And like every wall had been torn down.

Because of her.

It was work that had started that first moment when he had seen her standing there.

And now it was… Now it was clear. All of it.

"Riot…"

"What?"

It was like seeing for the first time.

"I have lived half a life. Trying to figure out how to keep breathing. But it was only half a life."

"Oh, Krav…"

"I would've not held my child. I would never have had a child. But you. You."

And the lesson was suddenly clear.

He had met her in his weakness. In his vulnerability. When he was feeling.

"I don't think you can have beauty without pain," he said.

"I'm not sure you can either."

"That night of my mother's funeral… Everything was wrong. I was bombarded with memories that I had spent so many years trying to keep at bay. I was devastated. For all that we could never have. The years taken from us. I felt more in that time than I ever have before. And that was when I met you. And I think it might've been the only moment I ever could have. And I made mistakes. Trying to protect myself still. But I couldn't unlearn what I knew. Which was that feeling was pain. It's taken all this time for me to realize that… I was right. Feeling, loving someone, loving something... It is pain. But that's okay."

"Is it?"

"No. It's not okay. It's terrible. But you make life worth living. These feelings make life worth living."

"Krav."

And it was like that moment, but cast in sunshine. As he walked toward her, as he closed the distance between them, and lowered his head. "I love you."

She could breathe. For the first time in all these hours, she could breathe.

She had decided to hold her ground. She had decided to stand firm, stand with him. They had tried to do things apart. There had been no revelations, only accidents. Stumbling blocks.

And now... Now they were here.

Because they had fought. Because they had emerged from the fray with bloody knuckles and valiant hearts.

He loved her.

"I have all this time. I just couldn't let myself feel it."

"And now?"

"It's like rain. Washing me clean."

"I love you."

"I love you too."

"Let's go to the tree house."

And they did. They made love, and talked about the future. Talked about bringing Soriya here.

"I want to make a life so very different than the one that I lived before."

"It will be easy," she said, tracing her fingers down his chest. "Because we have love."

And he realized, right along with her, that that was the truth of it. That love was the truth of everything. It was what changed hearts, and healed pain. It was what made living worth it.

It was a riot in her soul. And she had made a new meaning for her name. And they had made a new meaning for their lives.

And she knew without a doubt, that here at Angkor Wat, she had found herself.

With him.

Riot Phillips had finally done something spontaneous, and though the road after hadn't been smooth, it had turned out very, very well.

EPILOGUE

THERE WAS NOTHING Krav loved more than watching his children run over the ruins. They were at the tree house, for the summer holidays. It was hot, but everyone was happy. They were tired after a long day spent exploring the mountains, but the children were still running at full speed.

Soriya was lounging on one of the walls, reading a book, for she was eleven and terminally unimpressed with everything.

But she did love stories.

"You know," he said. "I met your mother here."

Soriya lifted her head. "Really?"

"Yes."

"What happened?"

He exchanged a look with Riot across the space. He knew they would have to tell a heavily revised version, that didn't include the fact that they had gone to bed together moments after meeting.

"I saw him," she said. "And I knew he was my fate."

"And how did you know that?"

They exchanged another glance, this one decidedly

hot. And he knew they would be spending a long and blissful night in each other's arms. As they had ever since he'd let go of his fear to have her love instead.

"We had the blessing of the rain," he said.

And just like magic, the clouds opened up. And rain began to fall. Hard and cleansing, and perfect. Their four children scattered, and they all ran to the tree house, shivering in the living room and drinking tea, just as he and Riot had done that first night.

"Was that fate?" Soriya asked, wiping raindrops from her forehead, and shaking out her book.

Krav put his arm around Riot and held her close to him. "Yes, yes I do think so. I believe that with us, it always is."

* * * * *

WILLED TO
WED HIM

CAITLIN CREWS

MILLS & BOON

This one is for Flo, who I will be lost without!

CHAPTER ONE

ANNIKA SCHUYLER STARED across the disturbingly over-polished conference room table in disbelief.

"That's impossible," she said.

Not for the first time. Possibly not even for the tenth time, which would have embarrassed her if she wasn't so *beside herself.*

"Your father made his wishes excruciatingly clear," said the head lawyer, Stanley Something-or-other, who distinguished himself from the crowd of them who cluttered up the whole of the opposite side of the table by managing to look sorrowful. As if this turn of events had taken him, personally, by surprise.

Judging by the avid, too-shrewd expressions on all the other faces staring back at her, Annika suspected that she was the only one who was actually shocked.

"His wishes might be clear," she managed to say, "but I'm pretty sure they're not actually *legal.*"

Annika tried to settle herself, but panic and something a lot like desperation clawed at her as she sat there at the long table. Everyone else in the nosebleed-high law firm conference room, some fifty floors up from the New York streets, looked cool and corporate. The way she'd planned to look herself, because she'd expected the reading of her father's will today to be tough. It didn't matter that Bennett Schuyler, IV, had been effectively lost years before his death at the start of the month. He had still been here and now he wasn't.

She had expected this to be painful for emotional reasons. And it was, but she couldn't stop obsessing about the fact that in a room full of calmly suited white-collar warriors, she was nothing but disheveled. She could see her own reflection in the shiny tabletop and there was no getting around it. She'd thought it would be lovely—read: soothing, and Annika needed some of that these days—to walk down into midtown Manhattan from the Upper East Side for this meeting. Alas, she had overestimated the comfort of her *cool and corporate* shoes.

That situation had spiraled quickly. And so, now, her hair was disastrous, she'd had to come hobbling into the meeting while everyone else had been about *masterful strides*, and she was not entirely sure that her deodorant was up to the task of the overly hot September day outside, the shock of her father's will, and, of course, *him*.

Ranieri Furlan, who currently stood with his back to the room, hands clasped behind him, looking out at the city splayed out at his feet in the last of the summer sunshine.

He, naturally, looked as if men's fashion had been developed purely to celebrate his astonishing physique and that intensity of his that made grown men go doe-eyed when he walked in the room. To say nothing of what it did to weak-willed women.

If there was a more irritating man alive, Annika had yet to meet him. She had no desire to meet him.

She'd expected today to be her emancipation from this man. Not...

God, she couldn't even *think* it.

"Your father has not insisted that you behave in any particular way," Stanley, or maybe it was Stuart, was telling her. "That would certainly be legally questionable. Let me be clear. You can walk out of here today wholly unencumbered by your father's wishes in regard to one small fraction of his estate, as the rest will pass to you. All he has done is lay out a set of conditions regarding two specific parts of his estate and certain consequences that will accrue if particular benchmarks are not reached. If, within three months of the reading of this will, an independent review by this law firm finds that you are not married, Schuyler House will be donated to the city. If, in those three months, Mr. Furlan is not married, he will forfeit his position as CEO of the Schuyler Corporation. If you are not married to each other, there will be significant penalties. You will be barred from working at Schuyler House entirely. Mr. Furlan will be officially censured."

Annika had really hoped that she'd gone a little hysterical and had imagined the breadth and depth of the hole her father had left her in—but she had not. Her father wanted her married or he would take away Schuyler House, the museum Annika's grandparents had made from the home that had been built for her Gilded Age

ancestors. It was quirky and beautiful and filled with
art and antiquities, and Annika had loved it since she
was a child. She had gotten an Art History degree at
Wellesley for the express purpose of dedicating her life
to her family's tangible, accessible legacy, right there
on the Upper East Side in the original Schuyler family home. It was the next best thing to actually having
family, she'd often thought.

She was the last Schuyler. The museum helped her
feel less alone, surrounded by so much of her family
over the ages. Their things. Their treasures. Their por-
traits. The museum connected her to all of them.

That was the part that had made her lapse off into
a little bit of private hysteria. Now, as she forced herself to really pay attention this time, she realized it was
much worse.

There was a fine if she was not engaged within
twenty-four hours of the reading of the will. There was a
fine if she was not engaged to Ranieri. There was a
fine if she did not share a home with Ranieri, or whoever she
was engaged to, within a week. She was not only to be
married within the month, but significant financial penalties—to be taken out of the money her father had left
her—applied if she did not remain married for at least a
year. If she achieved any or all of these things, yet was
to blame for any of them failing—whether she called
off an engagement, initiated a divorce, or refused to
marry—she would lose Schuyler House. She supposed
it was meant to be some small comfort that if Ranieri—
or, presumably, whatever other fool she could coerce
into proposing to her in the next twenty-four hours, an

unlikely endeavor given she wasn't dating anyone and hadn't in ages—faced his own set of financial penalties, to be taken out of his compensation package.

Though, of course, the penalties if the groom in question *wasn't* Ranieri were less about taking things away and more about what he wouldn't be getting. No bonuses, no stock options, no bribes at all.

Thanks a lot, Dad, Annika thought darkly.

"Do you understand?" asked Stephen, or whatever he was called. And this time, she did not find the kindly look on his face at all encouraging.

"I understood the first time," Annika assured him. She attempted a smile, but didn't quite pull it off. "Until today I was under the impression my father loved me."

She realized when she said it that the army of lawyers now all thought she was terribly sad. When what she was actually struggling to keep inside was her temper.

Really, Dad, she thought then. *What were you thinking?*

Annika wasn't looking at him directly and yet still she was aware that this was the moment Ranieri decided to move. He turned back around to face the long conference room, and Annika was certainly not the only one who cringed away from the ferocity he wore as easily as that dark suit, exquisitely tailored to simply *exult* in the lean, fine lines of his powerful body.

Ranieri Furlan came from ancient Italian stock, descended from generations upon generations of northern Italians with the same dark hair, golden eyes, and height. He was out of context here, but *there*, he would be unremarkable. Or so she liked to tell herself. She'd visited Milan once or twice and she'd assured herself for years that if they were strolling around the Duomo, she would lose him in a crowd. Ranieri would simply blend. He'd be mundane and run-of-the-mill over there.

Sadly, Annika knew that wasn't true, no matter how many times she tried to convince herself otherwise. She'd wandered the whole of the north of Italy without ever clapping eyes on a man who seemed to *simmer* like Ranieri did. Somehow, he managed to *seethe* just under the surface while remaining effortlessly sophisticated all the while.

She had no idea how he did it.

He had come to the Schuyler Corporation after doing a business degree in London and then a master's at Harvard. She had been in high school when he had so impressed her father, who had been wanting to step down from his CEO duties for some time. Ranieri had been not only driven and focused, as all those who wanted a CEO position were—he had wanted to keep the family feel of the company intact. He had believed, right from the start, that the family beginnings of Schuyler Corporation were what made it uniquely positioned to succeed in a world overrun with corporations that tended toward soullessness.

He had been speaking Bennett's love language.

Teenage Annika had not been impressed with the interloper into her family's affairs, but then, her father had not offered her a vote. And in the fullness of time, even Annika could grudgingly admit that under Ranieri, the Schuyler Corporation had bloomed. He had delivered higher profits every single year since he'd started, showed no sign of slowing down, and still maintained the core values that her father had believed in so deeply.

She knew that the financial papers swooned over him. But the papers were neck and neck with all the single women in Manhattan, if not the world, who became giddy at the very mention of his name. Annika had served as her father's hostess for years after her mother died, and had also served as his date for all the endless rounds of annual New York social events, where she had gotten to watch Ranieri's effect on the average Manhattan socialite up close.

Really, she'd made a study of him.

He was beautiful, there was no denying it, but there were a lot of beautiful men in New York City. A lot of sophisticated men, too. Ranieri was different because he had that edge. There was something about the way his features came together. The dark hair, cut brutally short, as if he wanted the intense gold of his eyes to take over rooms as he entered. As if it was deliberate. She believed it was.

Ranieri knew exactly what effect he had, and used it ruthlessly. His bold nose and stark, sensual mouth were enough to make anyone's belly flutter. His dark brows were always *about* to scowl or lift into a mocking arch. He was not given much to smiling. Or laughing, unless it was a short bark of laughter, designed to intimidate. Nor did he trouble himself to make any attempt to engage in anything that could possibly be confused for small talk.

And yet, when he felt like it, he could be charming.

In his intense, urbane manner, focusing all of his considerable attention on the unwary person before him and making them *flutter*.

In a city filled with the glittery and the glamorous, Ranieri was a fierce and elegant blade—never polished enough to take away from the fact that he could kill. And easily.

He just never seemed *civilized*, was the thing.

And today it was even worse than usual.

It had been a rough five years. Her father's car accident that winter had taken everyone by surprise, perhaps Annika and Ranieri most of all. At first, everyone had imagined that Bennett Schuyler would snap back quickly. Or quickly enough. He had issued his usual commands from his hospital bed and they'd followed them, never imagining that he would slip into a coma a week after his accident.

And then linger, somewhere between death and life, for years.

Annika had imagined that the makeshift guardianship her father had insisted upon would end with his death. That Ranieri would have nothing more to do with her life, thank you very much. She was just glad that she had already graduated from college at the time of her father's accident. She wasn't so young that she would have been truly under Ranieri's thumb, and so he hadn't controlled her as much as he could have. He'd simply controlled all the money. And had taken it upon himself to act as the unwanted director of the museum, too.

You don't know what my father's wishes were for the museum, she had argued, for years.

Neither do you, Ranieri had replied in his usual obdurate fashion.

Annika had been so certain that once the will was read, she would be well shot of the man. This was not supposed to be happening.

Ranieri surveyed the room, which had fallen silent before him, as ever.

"Leave us, please," was all he said.

He didn't have to be loud. He rarely was. He simply spoke, his voice deep and rich with hints of Italy and England alike, making him sound even more intense.

The entire legal team had left the room before Annika could even process the command. And then it was just the two of them.

Ranieri gazed at her then, and the look on his face was at least familiar. It was that rather frozen look he always aimed her way, as if he couldn't quite believe that the creature he saw before him was truly the daughter of Bennett Schuyler, renowned the world over for his business acumen and social grace. Ranieri struggled with Annika's lack of either.

She knew this because he told her so, and she could see he planned to beat that dead horse a little more today, too. *Terrific.*

"You look a mess," he told her darkly, and he was correct, of course. But why did he have to *say it*? "This is how you choose to honor your father?"

"My father actually did love me." She often tried to sound as ferocious as he did, but she could never pull it off. She was always too chirpy. That was what he had called it once. Her *incessant chirping*. "He never held me up to unrealistic standards."

"Are the standards unrealistic?" His voice cut straight through her, as ever. Ranieri was worse than a cold winter wind howling down one of the New York streets. "I passed any number of women on my way into this conference room, all of whom were apparently capable of brushing their hair."

Annika glanced at her reflection in the table again and could manage little more than a rueful laugh. "I did brush my hair. Thank you for asking after my morning routine. It's just that I didn't brush it *again* after walking all the way here. I would have. I meant to. It's only that I had some shoe issues, and that made me late, and I thought you might have an aneurysm if I was seriously tardy. So really, if you want to blame someone, blame yourself."

He did that thing with his jaw that somehow made her think only of great stones, like monoliths set in lonely fields. "And yet you were, in fact, tardy."

Annika waved her hand. "Five minutes doesn't count."

"Try ten."

"You can take that long waiting for an elevator in a building like this." She shrugged. "And anyway, I don't really think the state of my hair is the issue here."

There were a great many issues, but she chose at that moment to concentrate on one of the major ones. That being his deep and historic dislike of her.

When she'd been younger, she'd thought that she was imagining things. She'd met the man when she was sixteen. And sure, she'd watched him be his own brand of brashly charming to everyone he met, except her. But she had been so awkward. So overset by the things her friends found so easy. What to wear, how to act, how to behave as if they were at least ten years older than they were. Her mother would have helped her with these things, she was sure, but she had died when Annika was small. Annika sometimes worried she remembered only the idea of her, handed down by those with real memories. And she felt lucky if she got her dress on the right way.

The effortlessly collected Ranieri had always looked at her as if she was the human, teenage version of a tornado. As if he fully expected her to take down the foundations of any building they sat in if she wasn't carefully watched.

As she'd gotten older, his dislike had only grown. He had made it abundantly clear that she was an embarrassment to the Schuyler name. She knew his argument. That he and her father were engaged in building that name, yet there Annika was, whirling about in her usual fashion, spreading embarrassment and chaos wherever she went. She was always too messy, too inappropriately dressed, too scatterbrained, too clumsy, too awkward.

Annika had, previous to Ranieri, considered that her own brand of charm. Her father had always smiled fondly and told her that her mother had been a tornado too—but he'd always said that like it was a good thing.

She wasn't actually used to people disliking her. Maybe everyone she encountered didn't *love* her, but they usually didn't dislike her. She wasn't the kind of woman who inspired strong feelings in others. She'd accepted that.

Only Ranieri made it clear that he not only didn't like her—she was an affront to his sensibilities in every way. Only this man, of all people.

The good news was that it didn't hurt her feelings anymore.

"I want Schuyler House and I assume you want to continue doing your CEO thing." She aimed a polite smile his way, because it was that or sob in horror. He would consider it a weakness, so that was out. "So what do you think? Elope?"

He studied her as if she'd suggested something tawdry. And she couldn't say she cared for the fluttery sensation that overtook her the moment she thought about tawdry things involving Ranieri Furlan. She couldn't say she liked it at all.

"Elope?" he asked, as if he was unfamiliar with the word.

Like most things, once Annika had the idea in her head, she could do nothing at all but roll with it. "It's a perfect solution," she told him gaily.

He was still looming there at the bottom of the table, which she figured was probably some kind of power game. If she was feeling charitable, she might say that Ranieri didn't *try* to play power games. Probably. He simply was that powerful.

But she didn't have to attempt to compete on that level. She swiveled her chair around, and lounged back in it, gazing at him like she was some kind of fat cat herself. So replete with her own majesty that she didn't need to stand and face him.

"I'm not sure why my father thought that matchmaking was a good use of the little time he had left," she continued. "But I think it's perfectly easy to obey the letter of the law without inconveniencing ourselves too much. We can elope easily enough. And that will instantly sort all the rest of it out. As far as living under one roof goes, that's easily done. I know you have that loft downtown. There's also the family brownstone. I'm sure both are spacious enough to allow us to live our own lives. After a year, we go our separate ways. Everyone wins."

She gazed down the table, smiling winningly.

Ranieri appeared unmoved.

Ranieri always appeared unmoved. He was a one-man Stonehenge, only less approachable.

"And how do you think this plan of yours will look?" He asked the question as if he was interrogating her. In a court of law. In which she was a known murderer or something equally distasteful. "To the casual observer?"

She stared back at him, not comprehending either the tone or his actual words. "What does it matter?"

His lips thinned. "Naturally it doesn't matter to *you*. This does not surprise me. But I have a reputation to uphold, Annika. I cannot simply hurtle about through life, heedless of the way my actions reflect on the Schuyler Corporation."

He paused, likely so she could marinate in the fact that really, he was calling her heedless. And hurtling.

But she didn't react, because what was the point when it was always the same litany from him, so he carried on. "Having to jump through hoops like these to secure a position I have already earned is insulting." That cold gold gaze of his was a slap. "It is distasteful in the extreme to imagine colleagues and rivals alike tittering over your father's stipulations. Am I ever to be taken seriously again?"

Annika had always found him about as serious as a heart attack, but refrained from saying so. "We don't have to tell anyone that these are the terms of his will if you don't want to. I don't care what anyone thinks about me."

"That is quite apparent."

She was used to his putdowns, but this one made her ears singe just that little bit. Still, she kept herself from retorting. She knew from experience that any show of temper from her produced amazement on his part that she, as ever, was so *emotional*.

"But that creates another quandary," Ranieri mused, his gaze glittering. He seemed to take pleasure in looking at her, all the way down the length of his nose as well as the table, as if going out of his way to point out to her how much better he thought he was. If this was the sort of energy he brought to his business meetings, Annika wasn't surprised that, as far she could tell, any C-suite he glanced at flung itself at his feet *en masse*. "It is entirely believable that you might wish to marry me."

"Only if you've never met me," Annika retorted, more stung by that than she really wanted to investigate.

And anyway, he was ignoring her. "No one will have

any trouble believing that you have spent your life pining away for me," he said, and the truly outrageous part was that he wasn't waiting for her response. He didn't even seem to notice her outrage. He truly believed what he was saying. She would have leaped to her feet and argued the point, because how dare he, but he skewered her with another cold glare. "But I'm afraid, Annika, that it will be impossible for anyone to believe that I would ever marry you."

And then he laughed, as if the very idea was so absurd it was funny.

Annika opened her mouth to suggest he take a flying leap out the window behind him and concentrate on forgetting about her and anything having to do with her on the way down, but shut it again, hard.

Because she'd almost forgotten what happened if he goaded her into washing her hands of this.

But she doubted very much that he had. He was a master manipulator. It was literally his job.

"Don't be silly," she said instead. "Sure, your dating history is basically a Who's Who of Fashion Week, but no one will be surprised if a man who dates supermodels exclusively ends up with a normal woman. Men like you are forever settling down with unflashy women. It's how your type signals that you're taking your marriage seriously. A time-honored rite of passage for a certain kind of tragically shallow man."

"Come now, Annika." Ranieri did something with his chin that swept over her, head to toe. "You must be realistic. It is not that you're plain. It is that I am me." He shook his head as if he shouldn't have to explain this to her. "I am a man of exacting tastes. Who will ever believe, for even a moment, that I would willingly shackle myself to a woman who takes such little care with her own appearance? Who would accept that I might sport such an unsightly disaster upon my arm?"

It took her a moment to realize that the true insult here was not that he was saying these things. But that he clearly did not even register them as insults. To him, they were simply facts, not opinions.

Annika found herself gaping at him, openmouthed. Normally he would raise his dark brows and ask her if her motor skills were impaired, but today he didn't even notice.

"It is too implausible," Ranieri continued as if he was alone. Then again, *he* probably thought he always was. "Unless we wish the entire world to think that I'm conducting my own personal charity, or suffering from a head injury, we must come up with a different reason for this."

It required all the willpower Annika had to simply sit there, close her mouth, and somehow keep herself from telling this man exactly where he could go.

"Don't be too hasty, Ranieri," she cautioned him. She made herself smile, lazily, as if this was her idea of entertainment. "The head injury can always be arranged."

CHAPTER TWO

THE INSULT OF this situation ate at him.

The indignity of it all.

He almost felt as if he'd already suffered that head injury.

"Are you threatening me?" he asked. Very mildly, because even if she was, he could not conceive of a threat with less weight. "Do you plan to hurl one of your precious statues at me?"

Annika sniffed in a dismissive manner no other being alive would dare to display in his presence. "I would hardly risk damaging a Rodin on your hard head, Ranieri."

As usual, it took only moments in her company to feel the beginnings of a headache. She didn't need to use whatever statuary she had to hand. She simply existed and was irritant enough.

Ranieri could not blame Bennett Schuyler, a man he had grown to admire deeply over the years, for these machinations on behalf of his daughter. In fact, Ranieri had long wondered what was to be done about the problem of Annika, the last of the great Schuyler family.

She was obviously a problem without any clear solution. New York was heaving with heiresses, but in Ranieri's experience, all of them were more or less the same.

Annika was most emphatically not the same, despite having attended the same schools and the same debutante balls. She had always stayed entirely *herself.* He had known the girl for how many years now? And in all that time, she had never managed to acquire the faintest bit of polish. Not even by accident.

Today she sat here on this most solemn occasion looking as if she'd come to the meeting via a wind tunnel. She'd arrived late and flustered. She'd come limping in, looking disheveled. Her cheeks were still unduly flushed and her dark hair was twisted up on the top of her head, but not well. Some of it was standing out as if making a break for the ceiling even as half of it fell down.

For a long time, he'd believed she *tried* to look like this. That this committed untidiness in all things was no accident, but a campaign. He had assumed this was some kind of game she played with her father, or something she did *at* him, attempting to get revenge on him for some or other manufactured teenage reason. The way he was told American teenagers often did, especially in her class.

In the years since Bennett's accident, Ranieri had come to understand, however reluctantly, that this was no act. This was the real Annika Schuyler. She was constitutionally incapable of pulling herself together. Ranieri had been forced to conclude that despite a hefty and generous personal trust, a world-class education, and the fact that she lived in one of the most fashionable cities on the planet, Annika would simply always look like this. Her dark brown hair was always in some state of disarray. Whatever clothing she wore, no matter the occasion, it was always unequal to the task set before it. He had seen her in casualwear as well as in formal attire, and it was always the same. He had come upon her in that museum of hers when she could not have been expecting to see anyone, and it was the same. It was always the same. No matter what she did, she always looked as if she'd only moments before rolled out of bed.

He told himself that the familiar sensation that swept through him at that thought was distaste. That was all.

"This all sounds like a terrible quandary for you," she said sweetly now. Too sweetly from a woman who usually spent her time scowling at him. Openly. "Shall we call all the lawyers in and say you've defaulted before we even start?"

Ranieri decided his head would not ache. Not even in the face of such provocation. "I think not. The Schuyler Corporation is not merely an eccentric personal project, like your museum of curiosities. Many people will suffer if I am forced to abandon it."

"Schuyler House is consistently ranked as one of the city's favorite museums, *actually*," she replied, sounding offended at the notion that her stake in this was... exactly what it was. Her odd little obsession. Not quite the same thing as a major multinational concern. "Probably because its curiosities include the odd Vermeer or two mixed in with Great-Grandmother Schuyler's childhood dolls."

"I am more familiar with the museum's exhibits than I could ever wish to be after these last five years," Ranieri growled before he thought better of it, because he knew by now that engaging with Annika was a recipe for frustration. She was the most maddening woman he had ever encountered. "Not that it matters. We have to come at this issue before us in a different way."

When he said such things in the office, battalions of underlings frothed about in a frenzied attempt to impress him with their "out of the box" thinking.

Annika, by contrast, was lounging back in her chair, looking more than a little ornery. And the real problem here was that Ranieri truly could not believe that this was happening to him.

To *him*.

He had distinguished himself by not merely wanting the best, as so many did, but having it. Always. He chose the women who graced his arm no less carefully than he chose the cars he drove. Both were picked for their fine lines and stellar performance. And the deep, rich envy they caused in anyone who looked at them.

Annika was…not in his usual categories.

So, yes, he might have understood, on some level, why Bennett Schuyler had felt he had no choice but this. How else was the old man planning to see his daughter cared for? But Ranieri was not at all certain that he could lower his standards like this. No matter what was at stake.

Don't cut off your nose to spite your face, he warned himself.

He knew full well that excessive pride had been tripping up members of his family for generations. Then again, his preferred way to deal with the ruinous Furlan pride was to create a life that supported whatever level of pride he brought to bear. His father had been stymied by the fact that while he talked a big game and could play the part, at the end of the day, he had no head for business. His grandfather, too, had been known far and wide as a too-proud man in all the worst ways— to his own detriment. Ranieri had inherited all of that.

But he had also built himself an empire.

It was not arrogance to think himself one of the most powerful men alive. It was a fact.

Ranieri preferred facts.

And now, at last, there was no other possible rival for his position. Now that Bennett Schuyler had actually died, the Schuyler Corporation was Ranieri's at last.

The penalties would be paltry to a man of his means, but still. He didn't have it in him to let it go.

Especially not because of this gray area that he'd been mired in for the past few years. Given the appearance of control but no actual control over the one remaining Schuyler family member who could challenge him, if she wished.

If, that was, she also underwent a major sea change he thought was unlikely and became the sort of serous person who could impress shareholders. Serious people did not appear at will-readings without managing to brush their hair.

He eyed Annika now. "There is only one possible reason anyone would ever believe the two of us together," he told her. When she gazed back at him blankly—insultingly blankly, in fact—he found his mouth curving. Because he knew she wouldn't like what he was about to say and he could admit he took a certain pleasure in that. "Passion."

"I beg your… *What?*"

He was not precisely *insulted* that she looked so horrified. Still, it was a further indignity. Ranieri would have to add it to the ever-growing pile.

"Sex is the only thing on this earth that would convince a man to overlook his scruples, his own long-held preferences, his reputation, and his position." He sighed, perhaps a bit more dramatically than necessary. "Though it is still quite a stretch in this case, I grant you."

"Sex," she repeated, as if he'd said a terrible curse word. "I can only assume that you are kidding."

"It explains all of this chaos," he said, warming to the subject. "Why else all this haste and hurry? If we are to be married within the month, it will cause all kinds of comment. I will let it be known that having waited respectfully these last five years in the fervent hope that your father might rouse himself from his coma, now that he is dead we can wait no longer." Ranieri was already planning out how he would launch this unlikely relationship on the world. Trying to imagine the angles, the explanations, and even the possible advantages. "It's not an elegant solution, perhaps, but I feel it will work. It gets the job done, in any case."

She stared at him in that particular way only she had. Or only she dared. Ranieri was used to vast female awe bordering on worship. He was fully aware of his effect on women.

But Annika had always been different. Always and ever *herself*. She had always looked at him as if he had just crawled out from underneath the nearest rock, and she alone could see the dirt and mud still clinging to him. It made him want to look down to see if he could see it on himself, when he knew better.

He was a Furlan. He could trace his family back to ninth-century Venice. That he recognized any American as possessing any sort of pedigree was an indulgence of the highest order.

In these recent years, when he'd had more exposure to her than before, her insolence had been worse. Or he'd been more aware of it, perhaps. It wasn't just that she looked as if she saw that mud on him. She was also notably suspicious. She always frowned at him as if she alone could see the terrible truth about him.

Until he was tempted to wonder what, in fact, that truth was. If maybe she knew something he didn't. When that was doubtful in the extreme.

Ranieri was not used to being uncomfortable. He did not appreciate that Annika alone could make him feel that way.

It was safe to say he did not appreciate Annika Schuyler at all.

But if he needed to marry her to secure, at last, what he knew he fully deserved, well. He was prepared to do that.

Even if it meant contorting himself to appear as if he might actually have found himself besotted with this creature. No matter how bizarre and out of character that seemed.

He had moved with his usual swiftness into an acceptance of what needed to happen. It only distantly occurred to him that she had not agreed to his plan.

"I just don't think that anyone will believe that or anything like that," she said now, looking at him as if he'd lapsed off into incoherence. Or as if she'd actually succeeded in providing him with that handy head injury. She looked as if she couldn't imagine any other reason he would even suggest such an absurd plan. "On any level."

"We don't really require acceptance, of course." Ranieri said that as if she'd mounted a coherent argument instead of staring at him as if he'd lost the plot. "There needs to be a rationale that people can whisper amongst themselves. They don't have to believe it so much as accept that it could exist, and then do as they normally do and gossip shamelessly about it."

He waited for her to offer the usual accolades and acceptance that his statements usually provoked in those around him. *Thank you, Ranieri, you are quite right,* she ought to say.

But this was Annika Schuyler. The only woman he had ever met who looked at him as if *he* did not make sense.

She had looked at him the same way when she was only a girl. It had only gotten worse over time.

Today she had the unmitigated gall to sit there, her hair all askew, and regard him as if he was a raving madman while she was a bastion of calm rationality.

When he could see that she had kicked off her shoes and was currently sitting in one of the most august and revered law firms in the world—priced accordingly in fifteen-minute increments—in her bare feet.

Yet her expression suggested that *he* should be embarrassed.

She wrinkled up her nose in distaste. *Distaste.* "I'm not sure that I'm interested in claiming that I'm suddenly swept away by passion for you, of all people. So suddenly and uncharacteristically swept away, in fact, that I'm suddenly flinging myself headlong into a very public marriage with the kind of man I would never, ever consider. No one who's ever met me will believe for one moment that I could possibly end up with such a man. Not one. They are far more likely to believe that I have been blackmailed into it for nefarious purposes."

It took him long moments to accept that she had actually managed to prick his temper. He normally kept it so far under wraps that he barely thought about it any longer. And yet here, beneath the baleful gaze of a messy, impertinent girl who should have been prostrate on the floor in the face of her good fortune, he could feel it surge.

He had to stand there and fight it down, like the boy he had not been in a lifetime.

And accept that while he did so, there was a part of him that thought that if she was so heedless of the dragon she poked at, perhaps she should meet him in all his glory—

But no. He chose to be civil. He alone would choose if that should end. He would not be goaded into it by a woman who, he needed to recollect, had a vested interest in making him walk away from this and leave her to it. She wanted her silly museum. It was possible she wanted the whole company, too. He would not consider her a candidate for even a low-level corporate position, but the company did bear her name. Maybe this was all another part and parcel of her sentimentality.

In any case, whatever her motivations, he did not intend to succumb to her needling, like a child might.

Ranieri comprehended in that moment that he had almost—*almost*—committed the cardinal sin of any negotiation. He had almost underestimated his opponent.

Maybe Annika Schuyler was, at heart, the disaster she appeared to be. But that didn't mean that was *all* she was. He was grateful he'd caught himself before he'd allowed her to take advantage of the five years he'd spent attempting to be careful with her. For her father's sake.

"I understand that I am not to everyone's taste." He managed to sound almost smooth. A triumph, given the growing storm in him. "Rich, devastatingly attractive, and sought after by all and sundry can be off-putting to some, I am sure. I suppose that if left to your own devices you would be far more interested in a poor, weak man who was an assault upon the eyes?"

"I don't know," she said, tilting her head, her green eyes blazing. He didn't know why he'd never noticed that her eyes were *green* before. Not hazel. Not muddy. Pure, bright *green*. "Is the poor ugly weakling arrogant? Full of himself? Suffering from delusions of grandeur?"

"My grandeur is a fact," Ranieri replied with soft menace. "Not a delusion. As I think you are well aware."

"If you say so." Annika sniffed. "Again, this is all a little too icky, thank you. I don't really care if the whole world knows that I was forced to marry you to retain my birthright. It doesn't make *me* look bad."

"I see." He regarded her for a long moment, and took pleasure in the way her cheeks heated. Because he liked making her uncomfortable in turn, he assured himself. That was all. "Are you throwing in the towel, then?"

"Not at all. I'm just…not agreeing to your modifications."

"But you already agreed." He shook his head slightly, as if he despaired of her. "Is this what your word is worth, Annika? No wonder your life is so…hapless. A person's word is their bond."

"Nice try."

Annika stood up then, with no apparent grace. The dress she was wearing, a perfectly serviceable linen sheath, was a wrinkled mess. Her hair had slid farther down the back of her head, so she looked truly bedraggled. And she winced as she stood, reminding him that she, apparently, didn't know how to walk in her shoes. Even when she wasn't wearing them.

She was a *disaster*.

He wanted to raise Bennett Schuyler from the dead so he could wring his fool neck.

"You can't actually make me do what you want just because you want it," Annika was informing him. "I don't work for you. This thundery, growly, alpha male thing probably works really well for you in your capacity as CEO of all the things. But you're not the CEO of *me*."

Ranieri had the bizarre urge to put his hands—

But no. He rejected that urge with every part of him. There would be no hands. And if, later, he found himself questioning the fact that he had imagined sinking his own deep into the bedraggled mess of her silky brown hair… Well.

That was a horror he did not intend to delve into too deeply now. Or ever. Not all questions required answers.

"It is interesting you would mention my position as CEO," he said, a bit forbiddingly. Maybe a little ruthlessly. He reminded himself that he did not have to play these games. That he was choosing to engage with Bennett Schuyler's unfathomable directions, to serve his own ends. His own appalling sentimentality, perhaps. "If I were you, Annika, I would bear in mind the difference that exists between us. As far as I'm aware, that museum of yours is the only thing that you could possibly do with yourself. Having made yourself essentially unhirable in any other capacity."

She looked unmoved by any ruthlessness or forbidding tones on his part. "That's quite a leap. I haven't actually attempted to get myself hired anywhere else. But if I did, I'm sure that I would be an excellent candidate. For any number of reasons."

"You would not be," he said shortly. "On the other hand, while I would like to keep my position at Schuyler Corporation, it is not essential. At the end of the day, Annika, I am me."

She blinked at that. And then, with no apparent understanding of the danger she was in, she rolled her eyes.

Those impossibly green eyes. Directly at him.

Ranieri ground his teeth together, but pushed on. "I can go anywhere. Most corporations would sing hosannas at my approach. I can see that you want to argue this." And it pleased him, perhaps more than it should, when her green eyes blazed but her mouth snapped shut. "But once again, that is the function of arrogance. Yours, not mine. This is reality. You want to be very, very careful here, I think."

He had the impression that she wanted to rage at him, and found himself intrigued by the notion. What would rage look like on her? She was already flushed. It made her cheeks brighter, and he found himself wondering if that flush extended all over.

Clearly, he needed a woman. Badly. It was obviously an emergency if he was lowering himself to imagining *flushes* on Annika Schuyler's body.

And maybe it was even more lowering than that, because when she pulled in a breath, he found himself tensing. Everywhere.

As if he wanted her to shift all of this into a different place. A place of anger. *Passion,* something in him whispered. *Isn't that what you wanted?*

But instead, she let that breath out again. And though he didn't see her move, he had the impression that she lengthened, somehow. Ranieri had never thought her the least bit elegant or graceful in any way, and yet she had the look of it, then. As if there was something innately graceful about her when she chose to show it. As if, when she pleased, she could posture up like any other debutante worth her salt.

He would not forget that.

"I'll need you to be very clear here," she said quietly. "I want to make sure I'm understanding you completely."

"I think you understand me just fine," he replied carelessly. Mostly to see if the tone he used brought out the red in her cheeks, and it did. "But for the sake of argument, Annika, why don't we say simply that as far as you and I are concerned, I am your CEO."

And surely he was much less of a man than he should have been, because when she sputtered at that, he enjoyed it.

Not because he'd clearly won another negotiation, so of course he liked it. He always liked winning, or he wouldn't make sure to do it so often.

But this victory felt personal.

Ranieri decided he would hold that against her, too.

CHAPTER THREE

ANNIKA DIDN'T RECALL agreeing to anything.

She knew full well she hadn't.

But her actual, verbal agreement was unnecessary, apparently. Because Ranieri took control. He looked as if he meant to laugh at her, there in that conference room where she'd so foolishly believed for a giddy moment that she might have the upper hand.

When, as far she knew when it involved this man, no one ever had the upper hand. There was a reason he was feared and loathed and revered and admired wherever he went.

"You might consider putting your shoes back on," he told her in that icy way of his, perfectly calibrated to make her feel as ashamed of herself as she had when she was a teenage girl besieged by her own hormones. What an unpleasant reminder of those dark years. "Unless, of course, it is your goal to impress upon the entirety of this law firm that you are, at heart, distressingly bohemian unto your embarrassing soul."

His expression suggested that if she took that route,

she might find herself in even less of a good position concerning her father's final wishes.

She could have argued about that. But it felt like she was aiming for nothing but a Pyrrhic victory and she wasn't in the mood for self-immolation on such a tough day. Annika bit her tongue and kept her protestations to herself. She slid her feet back into her shoes, tried to pretend they weren't the torture devices she knew they were, and then limped out after Ranieri. He merely stalked to the conference room door in his obviously handcrafted Italian shoes—likely made for him personally, with love, by teams of rapturous artisans—flung it open, and somehow summoned the entire team of lawyers to his side. Simply by appearing, she had to think. Because she would have heard him if he'd yelled, snapped his fingers, or did whatever it was he did to make them all dance to his tune.

He exists, a voice in her said glumly. *That's the beginning and the end of everything, including you.*

Annika was not a glum person, generally speaking. That was why she was good at what she did, getting people to donate money to keep the museum running smoothly with an eye toward a Schuyler-less future one day, keeping the staff happy, and making sure it remained a desirable destination in a city with museums for every mood.

Yet her father's will and his demands had her feeling pretty distinctly glum, all the same.

Ranieri barked out commands, the lawyers scuttled about taking notes and aggressively agreeing to everything he said—big surprise—and the next thing she knew, Annika was seated in the back of a gleaming limo, gliding through Manhattan traffic as if even the usual Midtown snarls did not dare keep this man waiting.

Annika didn't ask where they were going. Because she had the distinct impression that he wanted her to ask. Likely so he could have the pleasure of telling her, which would make it even more clear that he was in control of what was happening here.

She refused to play along. And she decided there and then that she did not have it in her to cater to this man's pleasures.

And then had to sit there, contemplating his pleasures, such as they were, as she thought about what that might mean for a man like him. A man who looked so *physical* in clothes that made a great many other men look like they were playing dress-up or trying to do a James Bond impression.

Ranieri looked as if he was the man all James Bonds had tried, and failed, to emulate.

More she had to wonder what *his pleasures* might mean for her, the woman who hadn't actually agreed to marry him…but was marrying him anyway.

Surely he was only talking about sex and passion in general terms, because he planned to put on this act of his. Surely he had no intention of…experimenting with such things. With Annika.

She fought, hard, to keep her expression as impassive as humanly possible. Even while her entire body seemed to burn, like she'd immolated herself after all.

Still, it was impossible not to show some hint of surprise when he stopped…at a bank.

How prosaic.

"Are you planning to fling money at the people who dare to question this unholy alliance?" she asked. "That will really get you in all the papers."

Entertaining that image in her head was a lot more amusing than the other one. The one involving pleasure and sex and *passion*.

Ranieri only slanted a dark gaze her way. Just a glance, and yet it fairly seethed with reproof. "Wait here."

His driver opened his door and he exited the back of the car without any heaving around or fighting for purchase on the back of the seat in front of him. Not Ranieri. He merely rose from within, as if he was inevitable. As if he had more power and flexibility in one toe than most mortals held in the whole of their bodies.

And there she was again, thinking about bodies.

His body, to be precise.

Alone in the back seat, she allowed herself a little breather. A little chance to check in with herself. Nothing this morning had gone as she had intended it to go. So now, by herself, she could finally accept that really, she was just a mess of too many feelings.

The very thing her father had always despaired of most in her.

Emotion is a trap, my girl, Bennett had liked to rumble at her. *Be better than that, and if you can't, do please refrain from chewing your legs off in public.*

She found herself smiling at that, even now. Even here. Because that had been her dad to a T. Gruff. Blunt. Funny.

Annika missed him dreadfully. At least while he'd been in his coma, she'd still been able to see him. To sit by his bed and tell him about her life. To hold his hand and love him.

Maybe the real truth was that despite everything she'd been told by every single doctor who had spoken to her at length about her father's condition, she had still believed that somehow, he would beat this. That despite everything, he would rise up again, take his rightful place, and these past five years would be washed away as if they'd never been.

Maybe she still hadn't quite accepted that he was really, truly dead.

The funeral hadn't helped. It had been packed full of all the sorts of people her father had enjoyed but who she always found so overwhelming. Mostly because they spent all their time speaking out of both sides of their faces at once. One side to express their condolences, and the other to sneer down their noses at her. Even in her grief, she had been keenly aware that she did not live up to expectations.

That poor, sad creature, she'd heard one of her father's friends murmur. *It's hard to imagine a less likely heir to Bennett.*

Maybe he died to escape the shame, the friend's snide female companion had tittered.

Though Annika almost laughed, sitting there in the back seat of a limousine waiting for Ranieri to return, as she imagined all the snooty people she knew and the reactions they were going to have when this got out.

When Ranieri told the world he was actually marrying the hopeless, sad, *shameful* Annika Schuyler.

For *sex*, no less.

That really did make her laugh, no matter how she tried to put her hands over her mouth and muffle the sound. And the more she tried to muffle herself, because even she knew it wasn't good manners to snort with laughter when the driver could hear her, the louder she got. The more hysterical.

Then, after she'd laughed a bit, it turned into something a little closer to sobbing, and she understood that. She understood that grief was physical in a thousand ways and much like the flu, it would come as it chose. Stay as long as it liked. And leave when it was ready, not a moment before.

Yet when Ranieri swung back into the car, she spent a few moments congratulating herself on having stopped the sobbing before his return. Then questioned herself. Why hadn't she run off? It was the principle of the thing. It wasn't as if she could run away from what was happening. She knew that. But it would have been nice to not simply…surrender to this man. And so easily.

Annika was certain that was what everyone did. She was certain he expected no less, in fact. He was the sort of man who expected that everywhere he went, mass genuflections should follow. Really, she should have walked off for the sheer joy of interrupting his arrogance for a few moments.

The way he'd reappeared had been a shock. Or maybe that was simply him. The door had opened and there was the usual assault of a New York City street. The noise, the smells, the rush of people.

But then Ranieri was in the middle of all that, somehow rougher and rawer than anything around him. Somehow more intense than the rush and whirl of Manhattan itself.

"Did they not give you your bags of money?" she asked him, because he certainly wasn't carrying any. She blew out a dramatic sort of breath. "Don't they know who you are?"

He ignored that. He thumped his hand on the roof of the car, clearly an order to his driver because sure enough, the car pulled out into traffic again.

"I'm having my people prepare the appropriate statement," he told her coolly. Maybe she ought to have been grateful that he seemed to be so focused on keeping this businesslike. Then again, that was just his personality, as long as she'd known him. All business. All power games. That was the Ranieri Furlan promise. "It will be delivered to media outlets within the hour."

"Dare I ask which statement that is?" Annika felt that uncontrollable laughter well up inside her again and did her best to stuff it back down, because she doubted he would react well to it. "Is it the one where you're the boss of me?"

He turned then, shifting his body so that he could face her across the back seat. His golden gaze slammed into her, so hard that if she hadn't been looking at him, and perfectly aware where his hands were, she might have thought that he'd pushed her back against the seat with one of them. That was how it felt.

"I hope you're enjoying these witticisms of yours," he said in that soft way of his that really wasn't soft at all. "Someone should. I will suggest to you that it would be better if you got them out of your system here in private. I doubt they will play as well on the national stage."

"Goodness," she said weakly. "Will there be a *stage*?"

"Our engagement will be news, Annika. I am news. And so, I suppose, are you. In your way."

"That almost feels like it was supposed to be a compliment." She shook her head at him. "And yet you couldn't quite commit to it, could you?"

He looked at her in that manner of his that she'd experienced entirely too many times over the past five years when he'd been the guardian she neither wanted nor needed. As if he found being in her presence required so much patience, *so much*, that it nearly wrecked him as he struggled to provide it. As if even gazing at her required a level of forbearance most men could not possibly achieve.

There were times she found it amusing. Today was not one of those times.

"My grandmother, like most of the women in my family, had an innate elegance and exquisite style." He bit off those words as if they were bullets, but not necessarily aimed at her. "She consulted the finest jewelers in Paris for this ring, which I bestow upon you in the hope that you will rise to meet it, and it is not so much…"

Something in her curled around and around, a little too much like the sort of shame ruthlessly curated women at funerals thought she ought to feel. The kind of shame that made her angry, because it wasn't hers. *She* liked herself. Annika clung to that anger, that red-hot burst of something like defiance, because it was better than the alternative.

"Pearls before swine?" she threw at him. "Is that what you meant to say?"

Ranieri's mouth went grim. He reached into his pocket and pulled out a small velvet box, then flipped it open.

And Annika was no stranger to beautiful jewelry. The museum was full of it. Her sweet mother had left Annika all of hers, and she treasured every piece. She told herself stories about the various jewels, and had, when she was younger, excavated every known photograph of her mother so she could wear her jewelry in the same manner. But it wasn't only her mother's jewelry. As the last in her family, she had been handed down beautiful heirlooms from every side. Wearing them, or even gazing at them, made her feel closer to all the women who had gone before her.

But the ring in that small box Ranieri held was in another category altogether.

For one thing, it was mammoth.

"Is that a ring or a life preserver?" she breathed.

"It is a one of a kind, sixteen-carat Asscher-cut diamond without peer," he growled at her.

Annika had the strangest notion that she'd offended him, and then he was reaching over and taking her hand, notably without his usual patience, tried however sorely. And she knew what he was doing. There was only one thing he could be doing. Still, something inside her shivered with a certain wild anticipation that suggested she actually thought—

But of course she didn't. *Of course* she didn't think anything of the kind. She knew he wasn't *holding her hand*, just as she knew this wasn't real. He wasn't *actually* proposing to her.

Most importantly, she didn't *want* him to touch her. She'd never wanted that.

Annika felt the cool touch of the platinum band as he slid it over her knuckle, then into place. As *into place* as anything could be when the stone attached to the band was the size of a golf ball. It was obscene. It was outrageous.

It was really very beautiful, she thought in the next moment, almost against her will. It seemed to float over her hand, catching all the September light and making flares out of it. The diamond itself was cut to look like a hall of mirrors. As if she could simply sink into it and disappear forever...

And then both she and Ranieri seemed to notice, in the same moment, that the ring fit her perfectly. Almost as if it had been made for her.

Annika's gaze flew to his, and just like that, it was as if they were somewhere else. No longer in this car, careening through the New York streets. They were somewhere else, a place where there was only her hand in his, that ring on her finger huge enough to take out an eye, and yet all she could concentrate on was the gold looking back at her. The gold that seemed to spear straight through her, filling her up, *changing* her—

"Congratulations," Ranieri bit out, breaking the spell.

His voice dark. Grim, even. A sensation that matched moved through her, a deep shudder. A dark knowing. A foreboding, she was sure. "We are now engaged."

As if he was handing down a prison sentence.

Ten momentous days later, Annika made her way through yet another depressingly well-heeled crowd, all too aware that she had been to more parties in the past week and a half than in the entire previous five years.

She had discovered many things. That she did not, in fact, enjoy New York society parties, for example. This one had taken over the whole of an industrial loft that, as far she could tell, existed entirely for its floor-to-ceiling windows with lazy views all around. Sometimes, she was given to understand, there were art shows here. But tonight it was all the same sort of people doing the same sort of thing.

New York's finest and brightest and snobbiest, too, raising money for some or other cause célèbre.

Annika had gotten her fill of them quickly. By the time Ranieri had dropped her home the afternoon of their engagement, such as it was, it seemed that all of New York had heard the news. Her phone had been ringing off the hook, and her phone never rang off the hook. It barely rang at all. Mostly because her friends knew that she preferred a text. Still, she'd locked herself away in the sprawling family apartment on Fifth Avenue that rambled over three floors, felt like a house, and was an excellent place to take refuge from the world.

She'd left her phone on the hall table so it couldn't bug her and if it weren't for the incredible piece of hard-

ware on her hand, she might have been able to convince
herself that nothing had happened.

Except the next day, far too early, there had been an
impatient hammering on her door. Not the door to the
apartment, the door to her bedroom.

When she'd opened it, expecting one of her father's
staff members to inform her that the ceiling had caved
in or some such emergency, it was instead Ranieri.

What are you...? she'd started to ask him, bewildered
and so beside herself that she'd barely even noticed that
while *he* was completely dressed in another one of those
suits of his that really should have been against the law,
she was not dressed at all. She wore a giant, shapeless
T-shirt that came down almost to her knees.

Our first event as an engaged couple is tonight, he
had informed her, his golden eyes glittering. *You'll understand that I must insist steps are taken to make you
presentable.*

Annika liked to look back on that moment and tell
herself it was because she was still half-asleep—and
not entirely understanding why he was in her apartment in the first place—that she'd simply taken that
at face value.

Because what had followed was one humiliation after
another. It made the sight she must have presented to
him—hair doing God only knew what and that sad tent
of a T-shirt—fade into insignificance. What she would
give now to fume about the fact the doorman should
never have let him in. Even though she knew that wasn't
entirely fair. Throughout her father's long convales-

cence, Ranieri had been a near-daily visitor. Of course they had let him in.

Her phone had been ringing when she'd come home, but she'd ignored it. So it hadn't been until she'd walked out of the apartment building on Fifth Avenue the following morning, in Ranieri's company, that she got a taste of how everything had changed.

It was awful.

Annika was now engaged to the most eligible man in…maybe anywhere. And she hated it. There were cameras everywhere. Flashbulbs and unpleasant men shouting her name. The ring itself caused a commotion. Almost as much of a commotion as Ranieri had caused inside when he'd discovered that she had not slept with it on.

I never sleep in my jewelry, she'd told him, scowling at him when she'd finally had enough coffee—and had found enough actual clothes—to deal with him.

I suggest you learn, he had retorted. *Quickly.*

In that way he had that wasn't a suggestion at all.

He had dragged her off and delivered her to what appeared to be a pleasant brownstone not far from the neighborhood where she'd grown up. Except it turned out it was far more pernicious than that. It was no family home, it was the modern New York version of the modiste. Ranieri steered her to one of the house's salons, and then—after conferring for some time—left her to the tender mercies of the women who worked there, all of them dressed in black and possessed of the kind of sharp gazes that suggested they existed entirely on cigarettes and spite.

What they did was provide her with an appropriate wardrobe. That was the word they had kept using. *Appropriate.*

I already have clothes, she had complained before he'd left. *Lots of clothes, actually.*

Ranieri had not rolled his eyes, though he had done something that she could only describe as the Italian version of *almost* rolling his eyes, but not quite. *My woman will be held to a different standard, obviously. It is the* kind *of clothes. Not just anything will do. And if we're lucky, the clothes themselves will lend you an air of elegance.*

It had taken her a while to work out that when he said that, he meant the sort of elegance she did not possess already. And she wanted to be angry about that. She did.

But after ten days with the paparazzi in her face, she was forced to contend with the realities of her life. Like the fact she was so klutzy. Clumsy, even. Then there were all the ways she was incapable of doing her hair in the way people who contended with the paparazzi needed to. She kept falling over her own two feet, her hair a mess, the way she always did. And it was disconcerting to suddenly have an audience.

An audience that liked to take pictures of her looking foolish, not that it was hard.

Meanwhile, Ranieri kept dragging her to events. And it had been one thing when she was her father's hostess or date. People had been a little more indulgent, not that she had entirely recognized that indulgence at the time. Back then, she would make idle conversation with her father's acquaintances, but when he decided to start talking business, she would excuse herself.

And not so she could mingle with the sorts of people who attended these parties. Perish the thought. Her actual friends did not attend New York City social events. If they did, they wouldn't be her friends. At such events Annika preferred to wander off on her own. She had befriended a great many caterers and actors that way, which meant, over time, she got into the best restaurants and went backstage at the best shows. She'd also seen a number of unexpected views, from unique angles. She'd also seen a lot of people doing things they probably shouldn't have been doing, but anyway, none of that mattered now, because being with Ranieri was like being in the spotlight.

A glaring, endless spotlight that was as blinding as it was hot.

It was bad enough that she could never pull off looking sophisticated, while he oozed it with his usual edgy effortlessness. There were other hazards. Most of them of the feminine variety.

There were entirely too many sophisticated, not-a-hair-out-of-place type women who circled her like sharks at these things. All of them seemed to take her engagement to Ranieri personally. Especially because he'd made no secret of the fact that they intended to wed at the end of the month. Within two weeks, now. She assumed that was why all of them tried, in various ways, to mean girl her whenever they saw her.

No one, in or out of a tabloid, could believe that Ranieri Furlan was marrying *her*.

Most people suspected she was pregnant.

But being assumed pregnant usually meant that people had accepted the notion that she and Ranieri had something between them. That they'd actually had sex. There were a lot of others who couldn't quite get there.

Tonight, for example, Annika had been caught against her will in a tedious conversation with three debutantes she wished she could pretend she didn't know. But she did. They'd all gone to private school together. One was on her fifth engagement. Another was on her second husband, having rid herself of the first when he was stripped of his royal title—though she let it be known that she was already in the market for her third. The other debutante—really more of a socialite, since they weren't eighteen any longer—spent more time in the tabloids than some actual Hollywood celebrities. And what they'd wanted to talk about was how much they'd desperately wanted to be her friend all these years.

Lies, of course. Which she'd known even before the much-engaged one felt the need to make a few pointed comments about the rock on Annika's hand.

I've always preferred a classic style myself, she'd said, though the look in her face was one of pure envy. *But I suppose that if I'd managed to land Ranieri Furlan, I'd also want evidence of my triumph to beam out into outer space.*

What Annika wished she could have said was that she didn't particularly *want* to be engaged to Ranieri in the first place, and certainly didn't view it as a triumph. What she'd done was hold out her left hand and gaze down at the enormous stone as if she'd never seen it before, then had glanced at the "classic" stone on the other woman's hand.

Which, she realized only after she'd done it, might possibly have been seen as some kind of…flex.

The reality was that Annika was no good at these games. She didn't like playing them. Especially because Ranieri had gone and told anyone who would listen that their engagement so soon after her father's death was all about passion.

He actually kept saying that, repeatedly. *Passion.*

She'd heard him talking about it some more tonight, though she had attempted to give him a wide berth as she'd headed out of the main loft space. *At a certain point, passion can no longer be denied,* she'd heard him say. *Mea culpa.*

The man was terrifyingly focused. It wasn't enough that he'd taken it upon himself to *My Fair Lady* her. It wasn't enough that he'd followed that up by hiring her a personal stylist that she didn't want, so that now she had to contend with being followed around by the steel-eyed Marissa, who was always trying to *do things* with eye pencils and *foundation*, whatever that was.

I will have your things moved into my loft in Tribeca, he had told her that first day, after she'd spent entirely too long being measured and then forced to try on clothes and prance about in them. At least she hadn't had to do it in front of him, and then he hadn't even looked up from whatever it was he was doing on his laptop when he'd collected her. She shouldn't have cared. *Tomorrow, I think.*

I have a much better idea, she had retorted, feeling stung. And maybe something like overwhelmed, though she had chosen not to ask herself why, exactly, that was. *Why don't you move into my apartment, which has the added benefit of numerous floors we can put between us?*

His golden gaze had swept over her and left her feeling... Not shaken, not really. It was more a quivering, deep inside. *I think not. That would not give off the right impression at all. You will move in with me.*

She had, because she knew as well as he did that any refusal to cooperate with him could be leveraged against her. And with everything around her changing so rapidly, and so against her will, she couldn't lose Schuyler House.

It was the only thing she had left.

Which was why she'd reacted the way she did to Ranieri's nightly round of ultimatums tonight.

The wedding will take place a week from Sunday, he had informed her on the way to tonight's fundraiser. Looking as bored as ever. *I have already had your dress made.*

Of course you have. She had stared out the window, toying with the ring on her hand and making it flash against passing cabs like a beacon. Possibly a cry for help. *No need to consult me. I'm only the bride.*

He had ignored that the way he ignored most of the things she said. Sometimes she thought that if he had his way, she would stay tucked away in the guest room in his loft where he'd installed her. It had exposed brick and a sumptuous bathtub, a killer view, and every night she went to sleep and dreamed of him.

It was not ideal.

But then, none of this was.

I'm thinking we should just run down to City Hall and be done with it, she'd told him earlier. *No muss, no fuss.*

And, bonus, it wouldn't feel like a real wedding.

Absolutely not, he had replied. He'd looked up then, that gaze of his far too steady. *We will get married here in New York City. Where both of us are known so well. We will not get married at City Hall. I'm thinking your beloved Schuyler House will do.*

She'd sat bolt upright. *No. That's out of the question.*

It is not a request, Annika, he had replied in that dark, stirring way of his. *For one thing, there are very few appropriate venues on such short notice. For another, it is no secret that it is a place you love. What else could possibly lend this enterprise the patina of truth?*

Truth does not have a patina, she had tossed back at him, surprised at the rush of red-hot temper inside her. Surprised, but not enough to tamp it down or hide it. *Truth is truth, no patina required. Why am I unsurprised that you don't know that?*

That's very earnest, I am sure. And very naive. He'd shaken his head. *There are lingering whispers about us, as I'm sure you know. Getting married in a place that has such resonance can only put those to rest. That and a honeymoon.*

We're not having a honeymoon, *Ranieri,* she had yelped. She had actually *yelped* at him. *Honeymoons are for people who need to loll about on beaches and have marital relations. That is not us.*

She'd regretted that, instantly. It was bad enough when he traipsed around Manhattan, speaking endlessly about *passion* to all and sundry. They did not speak of it themselves. That seemed... like adding fuel to the fire, at the very least. Foolish, in other words.

And then, in the back seat of a limousine, it seemed something far worse, far more dangerous, than simply foolish.

It almost seemed like a dare. Or like arson. Annika couldn't breathe.

She'd never in her life been so happy to arrive at a party she already knew she would dislike. And now, having managed to slip away from the main room of the party, she made her way out to one of the balconies. This one looked north, and she took a moment to sigh a bit and look at this marvelous, magical city she'd called home her whole life. New York was unknowable and familiar at the same time. New York always rose, no matter how it fell.

Staring out at the city, she felt something stir inside her.

She'd been going about this all wrong. She'd been so surprised by Ranieri's ferocity and command since the reading of the will, especially after the milder guardianship years, and he was pressing his advantage, wasn't he?

But then, she should have expected he would. That was who he was.

The stark reality was that she had only a little bit of

time left to get him to break this engagement. If he was the one to break it off, he would lose the company and she would lose nothing. More importantly, she would be free.

She'd been so busy letting him trot her about from stylist to fashion house to party, each stop more soul killing than the last. And she'd gone along with it, because implicit in every ultimatum he handed her was the fact that if she refused, he could report that she wasn't playing along. He could make the case that she was not abiding by the rules her own father had set out.

But there were levels of compliance.

And two could play this game.

She stood there, looking out at the gleaming, glittering city. Always so many bright lights, from red brake lights on the streets below to all the thousands of lit-up windows, so many people and so many lives piled on top and around each other.

Surely there was no passion greater than this.

But that word echoed around inside her differently now. Maybe because she'd heard Ranieri use it so many times. Maybe because she finally felt as if her head was a little bit more clear, at last. Out here in the cool air of a late September night.

Because he wanted to get married at Schuyler House and she wanted to keep Schuyler House as it had always been. Hers, alone. Not marked by him the way everything else in her life was. And yes, maybe she'd thought that it might be nice to get married there someday, but not to him.

Never to *him*.

But if she didn't want this to happen, she had only one path forward.

Passion, she thought to herself.

Maybe it was time that she gave Ranieri some of that passion he kept going on about. A lot of passion. More passion than he could handle—and none of it violating the terms of her father's will. Or involving sex, no matter what she dreamed about, curled up in his guest room in Tribeca.

All these people in his glittering, shallow world already treated her like she was some kind of loon.

Annika smiled at her beloved city. Why not act the part?

She couldn't think of a better way to get him to end their engagement, so she could keep Schuyler House to herself.

And free her from him, once and for all.

CHAPTER FOUR

RANIERI WAS AN hour into an important, if somewhat tedious, meeting when the conference room door burst open. His immediate assumption was that the building was on fire, for there could be no other reason his people would disturb him. They knew better.

It took him long moments of staring down the length of the conference table, over the laptops and stacks of documents everywhere, to make sense of the fact that the person who stood there in the open door was not his long-suffering personal assistant, the competent Gregory, though he could see Gregory himself out in the hall, looking horrified.

The person who had tossed the door open was, improbably, Annika.

"I don't want to interrupt," she trilled, while doing exactly that.

And Ranieri was not one to countenance acts of defiance. He insisted on respect and reasonable obedience in all things and, when he received both, he was perhaps a demanding boss, but fair. Always fair.

But what was *fair* when it came to this woman who

had been foisted upon him? The truth was, he had no earthly idea what to do with Annika.

He had spent a significant amount of money outfitting her appropriately. He'd had a number of stylists convene upon her, taking the raw materials she presented and working their magic. And he had to admit it had been worth it. Gone was her typical bedraggled look. Ranieri had been quietly pleased to find that while she would never be knocking anyone off the cover of *Vogue*, Bennett Schuyler's daughter was, in fact, capable of looking reasonably put together. And that was a relief. It made it slightly less inconceivable that she had somehow captured his interest.

Yet she was still Annika.

Today she wore a dress in a shade of teal he would normally have considered loud, but it flattered her. It flattered her too much, perhaps. He hadn't expected that. The first night he'd picked her up after the stylists had taken their liberties with her, he'd been...surprised. That was the word, surely. He'd been *surprised* to discover that beneath the careless hair, the wrinkled linens, and the voluminous cardigans she liked to drape all over herself in the colder months, Annika actually possessed a figure.

He told himself he was noticing such things for strategic purposes, nothing more.

Today, for example, he was merely noticing that the teal dress was expertly tailored to flatter her surprisingly generous breasts as well as the tiny waist he hadn't realized she possessed. The flare of her hips below was another surprise, and one he had revisited—privately—a few too many times since she'd moved into his loft.

In his head, that was.

Her hair was twisted back this morning, not falling down this way and that. She still wore what he supposed was a version of one of her ratty cardigans, but at least this version whispered of quiet sophistication as it draped behind her like a cape.

And yet he realized that all the usual disheveled energy came directly from her. Even when, objectively speaking, he could find no specific fault with her appearance, she gave off the distinct impression that there was at least one.

Then again, perhaps the problem was that she was bearing before her a potted plant with raucously pink flowers.

Ranieri blinked, certain he was imagining that—but no.

His newly minted fiancée was indeed charging into his conference room, holding before her a large, potted plant. The pot itself appeared to be wrapped in something, a kind of foil perhaps, but it was magenta. Which matched the oversize bow wrapped around it. And yet those pinks were a different pink from that of the exuberant, round flowers.

Ranieri had never been in an actual fistfight, despite the many years he'd spent training in martial arts like Brazilian jujitsu. He had never *actually* been attacked. And yet this moment felt the closest he'd ever been to an all-out assault.

He did not dare look around the table at his col-

leagues and business associates. The strained silence
in the room told him all he needed to know about their
reactions. It was obvious they matched his own.

"I just wanted to take this opportunity to bring you
this plant," Annika was saying brightly. She swept to the
head of the table and stopped before him, then smiled.

Fatuously, to his mind.

"Our passion cannot be contained," she said, that
smile widening, her voice almost certainly loud enough
to carry down the length of the hall outside. "How I've
longed these last years to tell the whole world what we
mean to each other!"

"I am delighted," Ranieri managed to say, without
sounding *entirely* as if he had glass in his mouth. "But
as you can see, I'm also rather busy."

Annika responded by thunking down the pot before
him, a little too close to his laptop for his liking.

"I saw it and I knew you had to have it," she told him,
an intensity in her voice that he had never heard before.
Probably because she was putting it on. This close, he
could see the cool amusement in her green gaze. Then
she frowned slightly as she looked around the table.
"Pink flowers symbolize love, of course."

It was a table filled with titans of industry and the
sharpest business minds around, yet they all nodded as
if they had come here today to immerse themselves in
bloody floriography. Ranieri might have laughed, it was
so absurd, except Annika swung her gaze back to him.

"I know how important your job is to you," she said.
Intensely. "And as the woman who loves you best and

most, I want to support you while you toil away, making money and then making more money, ha-ha-ha."

He stared at her in stark astonishment as she really dug into that fake laugh.

That had to be the end of it—but no. She wasn't done.

"But of course, my sweet Ranieri Berry," she said, and he was certain he was dreaming then. Because there was no possibility that this woman had just lapsed into baby talk in the middle of the delicate negotiation. There was no possibility that she had just called him by a pet name so saccharine and nauseating that he was not entirely certain how it was the entire conference table hadn't lapsed into a sugar coma. He wished he had. "*Of course* I miss you so much while you're here. So I found you this wonderful dahlia that will bloom, pink and bright, like our love."

Because, yes, there was a darker place. A lower level of horror.

"It will bloom here at the office and you'll think of our love. You will care for it and tend to it while we are parted." Then the ghastly woman had the gall to beam at him. "Won't you?"

Ranieri stared at the explosion of pink before him. Then he lifted his gaze and glared around the table, daring anyone seated at it to so much as smirk in his direction.

As one, every person there dropped their gaze.

"You don't like it," Annika breathed, as if she had, just that very moment, watched him kick a puppy. Her puppy, when he knew full well she did not have one. Then as he gazed at her in his continued appalled astonishment, she stuck out her lower lip like a child. And if he wasn't mistaken, set it to trembling. "You hate it, and that must mean you hate me. And what does that say about our love, Ranieri?"

Her voice grew shriller with every word. And Ranieri could see her intentions all over her face. The quivering lip. That look in her eyes, like she was fully prepared to go for broke.

He honestly had no idea what he would do if she broke down and sobbed.

Which he could tell she had every intention of doing.

Ranieri stood then, briskly enough that it made his oh-so-charming fiancée blink and take a step back, which was the first reasonable thing she'd done since arriving here today.

"*Amore*, you are overset," he murmured in a low voice, and then, moving quickly, he scooped up the ridiculous pink plant in one arm while adroitly maneuvering his other arm around Annika's shoulders.

Then he made what he hoped was a soothing sort of noise as he walked her—marched her—out of the conference room.

And this was not the time to notice what it felt like to have her that close to him. He didn't touch her, as a rule. Especially not since he'd been bludgeoned by the hourglass figure she'd apparently been hiding all this time behind shapeless clothing. But it was impossible not to notice a few too many things about her as he swiftly escorted her from the room. That delicate scent that he tried to tell himself was hair product of some kind, but he knew better. It was a lotion she put on her skin when she was alone, perhaps, or maybe it was just her—a faint hint of something sweeter and better than the finest vanilla.

Out in the hall, Ranieri kept moving, striding with her toward his office, where he could deal with her without so many eyes on them. He kept his arm clamped around her shoulders, because he was passing too many curious underlings—all of whom pretended not to be studying them with avid interest.

He caught a glimpse of the spectacle they made as he marched them past one of the glossy interior walls, and gritted his teeth at the absurdity of it all. He felt like a dancing bear at the circus, which he assumed was her intent. But he was fairly certain she caught that same glimpse of their ungainly procession, because her delicate shoulders began to shake.

And when he ushered her into his office and then released her, he could see that she was laughing after all. Ranieri told himself that was marginally better than if she was crying.

This time, he wasn't surprised when his temper swept through him, but he still had no intention of giving in to it. He left her by the door, because he needed to stop touching her, and stalked across the long, stark room that was built to be a clean, cool antidote to the busy city outside his windows. Then he set the infernal plant down on his desk with a thud.

And he took his time turning back to face her, because he could hear the little noises she was making, as if trying to stifle her laughter with her hands.

When he finally turned, that was exactly what she

was doing. And for moment, he stopped and stared. Because she was so outrageous, he told himself.

But he knew it was something else. The teal dress and her hair swept back, though a dark tendril had worked its way free. In contrast to her usual messy-hair moments, this actually looked…inviting. Or maybe it was the fact that she was laughing, that she had bent over a little with one arm wrapped around her waist, which only seemed to call more attention to that astonishing figure of hers.

He really needed to get a hold of himself. It was not part of his plan to be attracted to Annika. He intended to marry her, not pant about after her.

The thought of panting after anyone was egregious enough that it sobered him. Quickly. He was Ranieri Furlan. He did not *pant*.

"Do you have any idea what that display will likely cost me?" he asked her, his voice wintry enough that she ought to have checked for snow.

She straightened, still laughing, and did not appear overly moved by his question. Or concerned about a sudden interior snowfall. Instead, she wiped at her eyes, still laughing softly. "Good thing, then, that you have more money than God."

"I cannot imagine what could possibly have possessed you," he began again, even more furious.

This time, when her green eyes met his from across the length of his office, they were shrewd. "Are you embarrassed? Angry, outraged, any or all of the above? Whatever will you do, Ranieri?" Her lips curved. "Or should I call you, Ranieri Berry?"

"If I ever hear that sickening phrase uttered aloud again, I will not be responsible for my actions, Annika. I hope you are hearing me."

"I'll be certain to say it in front of the paparazzi, then." And she only smiled deeper when he tensed. "Is it too much for you yet? Are you ready to say uncle?"

Ranieri was familiar with that odd North American saying, though he would never have used it himself. Particularly not when his own uncles had embodied the very worst of the Furlan pride and all that entailed. It had gotten one of them killed. The other was currently a shell of a man, shuffling about in the tatters of his former glory somewhere outside Firenze.

But the meaning wasn't lost on him.

"Do you think embarrassing yourself in my office will lead me to surrender?" He didn't quite laugh. Not quite. "Oh, Annika. You don't know me very well, do you?"

Her green eyes gleamed. But all she did was nod toward the pink monstrosity now cluttering up his glass desk.

"Enjoy the embodiment of our love," she said softly. "And don't let me keep you from the rest of your very important meeting. *Amore.*"

And he had no choice but to stay where he was as she turned around and sauntered out of his office. Actually *sauntered*, with entirely too much confidence for a woman who had once limped into the reading of her father's will.

He had no choice because he knew that if he went after her he would put his hands on her. And once that happened, he was not certain what would come next. And this was his place of business. It was as close to a cathedral as he got.

Because he could tell himself that what was storming around inside him was temper. Sheer outrage. That he was tensed up and ready to fight, that was all. But in all his years of martial arts training to prepare for such moments, one part of him had never been tense. And yet somehow, it was his sex that felt the neediest in the wake of Annika's performance.

All of that required him to stay where he was, seething and furious, until he got a hold of himself.

Only then could he go back into the conference room and attempt to salvage his meeting from her pink-planted wreckage.

When he got back to Tribeca that evening, Ranieri's mood was precarious. He'd managed to negotiate the deal he wanted, but with a bit more in the way of concessions than he normally allowed.

It was entirely Annika's fault.

He nodded at the doorman, then strode to his private elevator and tried to prepare himself for the woman who had not simply disrupted his morning meeting—in an epic fashion—but had haunted him the rest of the day. He'd kept thinking he could smell that faint scent, all hers. He'd kept remembering the feel of her body so close to his when he'd had that arm wrapped around her.

Ranieri had been distracted. He was never distracted.

At least he could take some solace in the fact that she was in no way comfortable in his home. Or so he assumed from the stiff way she moved around in it, always acting as if it was a great sacrifice on her part to live in one of the most sought-after addresses in the city.

She'd lived here a week exactly now, he thought as the elevator rose at its sedate pace, when he had never intended to cohabitate with anyone. In the past it had always been clear to him that was necessary to cut ties with his various mistresses when they'd made too many noises about wanting to move in, stay over, clear a little space for their things, and other such slippery slopes that led straight to all the places he did not wish to go.

But Bennett Schuyler had wanted them living together within a week, so here they were.

He could admit, when he got past the enduring fury of the plant incident earlier, that Annika had thus far been a perfectly reasonable roommate. He only saw her, generally speaking, in the evenings when there was an event. Usually it was her stylist he saw first, coming out of the guest suite looking militant. Annika came shortly after, always looking wary when she approached him. Though she always turned in a circle when he bid her do so, usually by spinning his finger in the air.

I certainly hope my latest outfit meets with your approval, she had said the night before, the mildness of her voice belied by the look in her eyes.

You would be no doubt about it if I did not, he had replied.

She either kept to herself or went out of her way to avoid him. He didn't know which it was, and in truth, did not care. His staff kept him informed of her whereabouts and whatever they did not know, the tabloids were all over. Between the two sources, he knew that

Annika had to battle a scrum of cameras every time she left his loft and every time she made her way back up to the Upper East Side to that museum of hers. Where she spent all day doing whatever it was she did, before returning to the loft in time for the evening event they normally had to attend.

If all marriages were so convenient and undemanding, perhaps Ranieri would not be so opposed to the very idea of the institution.

But he knew better. Marriage was not a good bet in his family. Not a one that he could think of in generations had lasted. His grandparents had remained married until their deaths, but had spent the bulk of their years living apart. *The secret to happiness,* his grandfather had told him, laughing uproariously, as prideful as ever.

Ranieri was cursed with the same pride as the rest of them. But he liked to win. Left to his own devices, he never would have married. It was a bad bet. He never would have started something he was reasonably certain would end badly. That had always seemed to him the very opposite of winning.

Annika made him want, a little too badly, to stop caring about things like pride, winning, and everything that wasn't that better-than-vanilla scent.

He thought he might be more furious about that than the dahlia.

Tonight they had no events to attend. He hoped that would mean that Annika had locked herself away, as well she should. If he were her, he would be trembling in fear about what he might do to her here. Far, far away from any outside eyes.

The elevator doors opened up directly into his loft, and he had only taken a few steps inside before he stopped short. And realized that Annika had not taken the wiser course, complete with piteous trembling, as she should have done.

He looked around, trying to make sense of what he saw. But he couldn't. There were…*things* everywhere. Disrupting the clean, stark modern lines he preferred. He moved toward the nearest one, and picked it up, scowling down at it as he held it in his palm.

He was not mistaken.

The infernal woman had covered almost every surface in his home with these…figurines.

His mind did not want to make sense of them.

They were egregious examples of ceramics gone wrong, some of them plump and round, others lean and hooved. But what they all had in common were the colors. Obnoxiously bright pinks. Offensive purples. Golds and pinks.

She had infested his house with bloody *unicorns*.

Still gripping the plump figurine his hand, Ranieri tossed his briefcase aside and stalked off to find her.

She wasn't in the guest room, or barricaded away in the guest bathroom, the way she would have been if she was at all wise. Though he did notice that the guest room, which had never smelled like much of anything, now held that same damned scent that had been haunting him all day.

He was already growling to himself when he climbed

the spiral stair to the rooftop garden that transformed the top of the building into an oasis in the middle of this concrete city. His little taste of the Italian countryside, so far from home. Ranieri usually found it soothing.

But there was no possibility of being soothed tonight.

He found her in the bathhouse that contained the hot tub and sauna and small sitting area that he had never used. She was curled up on the sofa with a colorful throw blanket over her legs, a tray of charcuterie on the ottoman, and a thick hardcover book open on her lap.

Annika glanced up when he slammed open the door, but did not otherwise react to his presence. Then, as he watched, she very calmly picked up a bit of hard salami and cheese and popped them into her mouth, gazing back at him as if he was the unhinged one here.

What Ranieri did not understand was how it was possible that he, widely renowned to have ice water in his veins, actually *felt* unhinged in her presence. But the figurine in his hand was an excellent reminder.

"Do you think you can hide up here?" he demanded, his voice a kind of rasp.

"If I was hiding," she said in the sort of overtly patient voice that suggested that she, for one, felt he was grossly overreacting, "I would be hiding. Instead of sitting here, easily found, and making no attempt whatsoever to spirit myself away."

Ranieri felt coiled tight. Too tight. And once again, he felt that disturbing heaviness in his sex. Once again, he found himself entirely too aware of her.

As a woman.

She was no longer wearing that teal dress. Her hair

was down, spilling over her shoulders, and in this little bathhouse, festooned with strands of lights overhead, she seemed to *glow*. It hit him then, like a kick to the chest that she was unquestionably pretty.

How had he never before noticed how *pretty* she was?

She was lounging on that couch, the throw half kicked off, so he could see that she wore a cozy-looking sweater in a copper shade and what he believed were called lounging pants in an understated neutral shade of oatmeal. Both in what looked very much like cashmere.

He should have approved, as it was a serious upgrade from that deplorable T-shirt he'd seen her in that first morning. But what caught his attention instead was that the sweater had ridden up, so that all he could seem to focus on before him was that swathe of skin. A ribbon of delicate ivory, just above her hips.

Ranieri had the nearly ungovernable impulse to set his mouth to that ribbon, then taste every bit of it.

Somehow, he held himself in check. He was not sure how.

When he moved forward, all he did was place the unicorn figurine in the center of her charcuterie platter.

Then he straightened, waiting.

Annika looked at the unicorn and then she lifted her gaze to his.

"My unicorn collection is very important to me," she told him, even though he could see the unholy amusement in her dancing green gaze. "Obviously, anywhere I live, I need all of them around me like magical guardians. It's the only way I can feel at home."

He could have pointed out that he'd spent an inordinate amount of time in the Fifth Avenue apartment she had shared with her father and had never seen even one unicorn. Really, he did not understand why he refrained.

Because she knows full well that you know that she's lying, he scolded himself. *The lying is the point.*

"Today the unwanted delivery of a dahlia and an army of unicorn figurines." He didn't sound like himself. He had the scent of her in his nose again and he was hard and ready, even though this was Annika Schuyler, for God's sake. "What is next, I wonder?"

She had disrupted a meeting, which was sacrosanct to Ranieri and would have gotten anyone who worked for him fired. And yet he had ordered Gregory to keep the damned plant watered. She had absolutely destroyed the sanctuary that was his home, with a rainbow of hideous unicorn tat as far as the eye could see. And still, he did nothing.

Annika very clearly saw her advantage. She sat up, looking entirely too pleased with herself.

"The possibilities are endless," she told him. "After all, as you pointed out to me before, I'm already known to be a disaster. Why not an emotional disaster? I know you care about very little as much as you care about your reputation. And it occurred to me that I don't have a reputation."

"Oh, you do. Be assured of that."

She only laughed. "I don't have a reputation I care about. That's the difference. So really, Ranieri. The sky's the limit."

He scowled at her, and she laughed.

She laughed and she kept right on laughing. She laughed so much that the offensively bright unicorn before her seemed to laugh with her. The lights were too bright, and she was too pretty, and his sex pulsed as if he'd been some kind of monk—possibly for years— and then he was moving.

Without thought, when he never acted without thinking it through.

Never—but then he was reaching down and wrapping his hands around the tops of her arms.

And then he thought a lot about the way she stopped laughing, her green eyes going wide, and that sensual mouth of hers dropping open. Especially when she made the sweetest little sound.

Ranieri lifted her up, letting the throw fall aside and the book she'd been reading crash to the floor.

He hauled her up and then, as if he'd been longing to do nothing else for the whole of his existence, Ranieri—who had never been carried away by passion in his life—slammed his mouth to Annika's at last.

And drank her in, deep.

CHAPTER FIVE

She wasn't prepared.

It was the only thought that scrolled through her head, because everything else was him.

Ranieri. The press of his lips, the rough heat of his tongue.

She felt shivery and strange. And swollen with a new heat, because he tasted forbidden, somehow beautiful, and she could feel him everywhere.

Every time his tongue touched hers, she could feel an answering wildfire ignite between her legs. She felt slippery, outside herself, and yet more *in* herself than ever before, because she could feel…*everything.*

Annika was suddenly, unbearably *aware* of her breasts. They felt too large, too tender, and her nipples ached. He shifted so that she was pressed against him and there was something about the pressure that made her want to squirm wildly. But not to get away.

He kissed her the way he did everything. Fully. Masterfully.

She did not have to be an expert in kissing to know that he had perfected the form. It was something about his ferocity. It translated all too well to this. All that grimness, all that starkness, all the maddening things about this man were distilled into the way his tongue slid against hers. The way he angled his head so he could go deeper, so he could take more of her, so that the blistering heat of this could wash over her, changing her.

As if wanting him, tasting him, made her new.

Her hands dug into his shoulders, and she could hardly sift through all the new information she was taking on board. All the immediate, tactile knowledge of too many things she had previously not allowed herself to consider.

How those muscles of his felt to the touch, for example. What it was like to have her breasts flattened against the wall of his chest. How it felt to let her hands discover how hot his skin was, there in that complicated dance of smooth muscle between his neck, his shoulders, and his arms.

She wanted to kiss him forever.

It was as if he heard that thought, because he made a low noise—she could taste it, and more, she could feel it *inside her*—and set her aside.

Annika staggered back, catching herself before she collapsed back down on the sofa. And not because he let go of her harshly. Or pushed her. But because her legs no longer seemed to function the way they had only moments before.

Or maybe it hadn't been moments. Maybe he'd been kissing her for a lifetime.

She could hear her own breath between them, harsh and loud.

Yet what astonished her was that she could hear his breath, too.

And maybe on some level she imagined his kiss was a punishment. For her version of the unicorn invasion. It was a punishment she couldn't quite decide if she'd loved or not, because she was fairly certain it had broken something in her—

But he was breathing heavily, too.

As if he was just as affected as she was here.

And for a moment there was only the sound of their breath, and all that jangly, wild, too-hot sensation spinning around between them.

Everything is different now.

The words echoed in Annika's head, but she shoved them aside because she didn't want that to be true. Yet what she wanted didn't seem to matter when the way his gaze raked over her was new. She could see the heat in it. And more, she could see some kind of echo of that kiss they'd shared. The passion between them. She could feel all that gold as if it was inside her.

As if it swirled around and around, centering itself in all the places she ached the most.

"I will expect to find every last one of those unicorns removed," he gritted out at her.

But he didn't sound like...*him*. Or not like any version of him she'd heard before. His voice was too rough. An edgy velvet that made her nipples nearly hurt.

"I expect to wake up every day and find myself the Queen of England," Annika replied, and she supposed she didn't sound any better. His eyes seemed to darken when he heard her. She promptly cleared her throat. "It looks like neither one of us is going to get what we want."

"On the contrary."

And Annika had been looking at Ranieri Furlan for years. She had cataloged him as if he were an artifact in her museum. She'd made no secret of the fact that she'd studied him thoroughly. And still, it was as if she'd never seen him before tonight.

Because now she knew how he tasted.

Now she knew what it was like to have passion punch through her in an instant, igniting…everything.

Now she knew.

"What a surprise you would find a way to be contrary in all things," she said, fighting hard to make herself sound dry and amused, because surely that was safer than all this *aching*.

"I intend to get exactly what I want, Annika," he said, his voice clipped. "I always do. You would do well to remember that."

And she wanted to offer some smart remark in return. Something quippy at the very least. She wanted to stand her ground and show that she was tougher than him.

But she didn't feel tough at the moment. She felt… slippery. Everywhere. And the gold of his eyes was like a molten hot liquid and she was filled with it. Near to bursting, she was very much afraid.

Worse, she suspected he knew it.

His mouth moved into something just this side of grim, but it was all the more sensual because she knew how deliciously hard that mouth felt against her lips.

And, God help her, she would have done almost anything for more just then.

When he turned and slammed his way out of the bathhouse, she told herself that she should have been grateful.

She really should have been.

But gratitude didn't really top her list as she stayed there, sinking down onto the couch again, her fingers to her lips. Even though she pressed hard, to remind herself.

Or maybe to relive it.

Annika stayed there well into the night, her body still wild and her head still spinning.

She expected Ranieri to greet her the following morning with more grim demands, or lists of tasks he wanted her to perform, but he was nowhere to be found. She found the staff guiltily removing the last of the unicorn figurines from the common areas, though they had left several in her room. As if they were concerned that she really might love them as much as she'd said she did.

Or as if he was concerned.

But she couldn't let herself think things like that. It made everything inside her feel…delicate. Instead, she decided to take the absence of the figurines as a sign she needed to come up with something better to break him.

Because surely that was what she'd seen in him last night. That he was *that close* to breaking. And if he broke, she won.

Annika assured herself, repeatedly, that she wanted that more than anything.

A few nights later, she thought she had her chance.

Fall had come in hard over the past few days, with blustery weather and the kind of wind that got into her bones. Marissa dressed her for the night's benefit gala, going for a gown in a deep, lustrous jewel-toned velvet, accessorizing everything with the soft gleam of rose gold.

"We'll stay away from extraneous jewels," the stylist told her briskly. "Your engagement is so new and your wedding is so soon. Best to highlight the ring. It's all anyone is looking at anyway."

And because Ranieri wasn't waiting for her out in the loft's main living space the way he normally was when she was finally ready, Annika had the opportunity to study that ring herself.

It was an eyesore, there was no getting around it, but it was also outrageously beautiful. And oddly enough, it sat easily on her hand. She wanted to complain about it. She wanted to pretend it dragged her hand down and was giving her some kind of ostentation-caused arthritis, but it wasn't. When she studied the ring in the light, it was hard to pretend she didn't find herself seduced by it. She gazed into it and disappeared there, as one facet after the next seemed to draw her deep into the heart of the stone—

"Everyone falls under the spell of that ring eventually," came Ranieri's dark, forbidding voice. "Even you, it seems. Careful, Annika. It might well enchant you."

She looked up to find him wearing formal attire, which instantly made her mouth go dry. Dressed all in black, his gold eyes seemed to glow. With malice, she tried to tell herself. Or maybe it was mockery. Whatever it was, it seemed to hum inside her.

Because she had the terrible suspicion that the only enchantment around here was him.

"I was just wondering how many lives could have been made better for the price of this ring," she blurted out, because she had to say something and his golden gaze was scalding her. She could feel it there between her legs, where she was already too soft and too hot.

"You are known to be one of the foremost champions of sustainability," he replied, his tone deeply sardonic. She bristled, but he didn't wait for her to shoot something back at him. "That is, naturally, why I didn't buy you a new ring. I thought you would appreciate that it is an heirloom. I thought that was your stock-in-trade?"

He didn't wait for her to respond to that, either. He nodded off to the side and staff appeared at once to present them with coats to ward off the brooding autumn night outside.

It took her the whole way down in the elevator, fuming, to remind herself that she only had a few days left before the wedding. There had to be a way to get him to break this off before it got that far. She hoped that tonight's gala would provide her with the perfect opportunity to nudge him in that direction.

Annika didn't necessarily enjoy making a fool out of herself. But since she managed to do it all the time without meaning to, why not do it on purpose? She daydreamed about simply…having her life back. Endless, easy days in the museum. Retreating into her apartment.

The odd meal out with friends without the assault of flashing cameras everywhere she turned.

It sounded lovely, that life she'd lost.

Out in front of his building, Ranieri helped her into the car, then climbed in after her. And then there they sat, cocooned together in the warm, plush darkness.

She could feel her pulse take her over, as if she was about to have a heart attack. Annika thought that sounded like a lovely reprieve, given what was actually happening to her.

"It was never my intention to remain faithful to a bride I did not choose for myself and, indeed, never would have chosen at all," Ranieri announced.

Almost conversationally.

And it was the oddest thing. Annika had given absolutely no thought to fidelity in this relationship at all. Mostly because she didn't accept that they were in a relationship, that kiss notwithstanding. And as much as she might have thought, in a gauzy sort of fashion, that should she ever find herself married she would require an appropriate level of faithfulness...she still couldn't quite believe she was going to have to marry this man.

Is the problem that you have to *marry him?* a voice inside her asked, too knowingly. *Or that there is no small part of you that thinks, just maybe, it wouldn't be the worst thing in the world?*

She shoved that thought away, feeling betrayed. By herself.

All of that raced through her head in the wake of his statement.

Followed by a searing burst of outrage that he had

thought about all of those things himself and had decided that he would stray.

She couldn't make sense of it.

"Thank you so much for informing me," she murmured. Stiffly.

"I'm out of the habit of engaging sexually with women of your…" He turned his head and she was speared, suddenly, by all that gold.

"Education?" she supplied. A bit crisply. "Self-confidence? Disinterest in you?"

"But now I think perhaps that was unduly hasty."

And once again, she found her throat had gone bone-dry.

"I would be perfectly happy if you would remain faithless," she told him, even though something in her turned over in dismay as the words came out of her mouth. "That you pride yourself on being the master of all things yet would find it impossible to keep your wedding vows seems emblematic of you as a person, Ranieri. I wouldn't want that ruined."

His mouth curved slightly, acknowledging the jab. "I always keep my promises," he told her. "I would have made it clear to you what I was and was not promising. I would not have snuck around, though any dalliances would never have been something you would need to confront during the course of our union. But the truth is, Annika, I think perhaps that you can meet my needs after all."

"Your *needs*," she repeated.

But she could hardly hear herself speak. Her pulse was a mad roar in her head. And a danger everywhere else.

And as if he knew it, Ranieri smiled, that little crook in the corner of his mouth. And then, making her pulse go wild inside her, he reached over and took her chin between his thumb and two fingers.

All he did was tilt her head toward him. But it felt to her like a clamp of impossible heat, not merely localized to her chin, but taking over the rest of her.

She couldn't understand it.

But understanding did not appear to be required, not when he was holding her like that, so that the two of them were practically huddled together there in the back seat.

Close enough that if he'd wanted to, he could have taken her mouth once more, and pleased them both—

Stop that, she snapped at herself. *This is not about pleasure. You're supposed to be coming up with ways to shake this man.*

Oddly, none came to mind.

"As in many arenas," he said after a moment, that same gold light so hot inside her it nearly hurt, "I'm drawn to quality. But I also have certain requirements when it comes to quantity."

"Are you… Are you talking about sex?"

And maybe the racket in her pulse was shorting out her brain, because she could have sworn she saw a different expression in those golden eyes of his then. It spread across his face. He looked very nearly…amused?

She didn't dare think the word *affectionate*.

"I see no reason why our marriage of convenience cannot be even more convenient, for us both," he said as if he was simply making a rational observation. As if he wasn't talking about sex—and with his hand on her. "It was obvious that there was some chemistry here the other night. As much as I wish to disbelieve it, I find I cannot deny it."

Her heart was knocking much too hard against her ribs, and she was finding it difficult to sit still.

"It's the compliments, really," she managed to say. She tugged her chin back to break his grasp—but he didn't let go. Just for a moment. Just to show her that he could have held her fast if he'd wanted to. But then he released her, and she felt a rush of something she told herself sternly was relief. Even if it felt a whole lot more like regret. "They go straight to my head. It's overwhelming, Ranieri. It's almost as if they might be fake, you shower them upon me with such abandon."

"Because you have always been such a particular fan of mine?" He shook his head, but his mouth was still crooked in that corner. "But then, it will not be the first time in history that enemies become lovers, will it?"

He was talking as if it was all a foregone conclusion and she felt the heat of that assumption as if she'd poured molten gold all over her. She could feel it at the back of her eyes. She could feel it carving its way deep into the center of her, that place where she was hungriest.

More hungry than she had ever been before—but she didn't want to focus on that. It was too dangerous. That was clear to her, no matter how new and sharp and breathtaking that hunger was.

"I think you're overlooking an important point here," she told him, trying to sound stern and only coming off a bit wispy. She cleared her throat, but that only made his eyes gleam the brighter. "I have no desire to… Um. Consummate this relationship."

"Do you not?"

"I do not. I *certainly* do not."

But she knew they could both hear that undercurrent of longing in her voice.

"We will see." Ranieri settled back against his seat as if it was all the same to him, this casual talk of sexual needs and *lovers*. "It will be difficult otherwise. Not to find a willing woman, you understand. But to find the sort of regularity I prefer while making certain that the woman in question does not come away with any ideas about what I might offer her. That is always the most difficult part."

"Yes, I'm certain it's very hard to be you," she managed to say.

What she was thinking about instead was regular sex. Did he mean daily? Nightly? More than that?

Contemplating the possibilities made her feel lightheaded.

She was still feeling dizzy when they arrived at the gala. So dizzy and gold-drunk as they stepped onto the red carpet to face the gauntlet of reporters that she almost let Ranieri hurry her along inside. She almost passed up this opportunity.

Because she was too busy thinking about sex, multiple times a day, with this man and his *needs*.

But then she remembered that she didn't want any part of that. That what she wanted was her very own, perfectly happy life of artifacts and old trinkets and beautiful pieces of art. And that wasn't going to happen unless she *did something*.

She looked up at Ranieri as he took her arm and then she took a deep, full breath, because she fully intended to project the nickname he hated so loudly that it bounced up and down the entire island of Manhattan.

That breath gave her away.

Because Ranieri tugged her to him, then gripped her waist. He pulled her close, as if they were dancing.

And then suddenly, before she knew what was happening, he was tilting her down over his arm in a parody of a grand dip.

"What on earth…?" she began.

"This is romantic," he growled, not even bothering to smile, his mouth close to hers. "Ask anyone."

Then he kissed her again, right there, while the flashbulbs put on a light show.

A kiss so thorough that it made her too giddy to mind. And when he finally set her upright again, inclined his head toward the paparazzi, and ushered her into the gala, she had completely forgotten that she'd intended to call him out to the tabloids as *Ranieri Berry* in the first place.

The following morning, she saw that picture—that kiss—plastered everywhere. And what she'd taken as a grim, hard expression on his face looked like…intensity. Passion. An almost unendurable need.

While she looked…

It made that shivering thing inside her go wild to look at herself. Because she looked absolutely transported.

Very much like a woman who was marrying the love of her life in a matter of days.

It's possible, that same voice inside her chimed in, clearly not impressed with any sense of betrayal she might feel, *that this has all been you protesting a bit too much. Isn't it?*

And she tried her best to nip this all in the bud, truly she did, because she was all too aware of the truth of things. No matter how he tasted.

Every time they went anywhere together, she tried again.

But Ranieri cut her off with a kiss here, a deeper kiss there. Always in front of people. Always in front of cameras. Because any venue that she could try to use to embarrass him was the same sort of situation that he could turn against her.

Which he did.

Proving to all the world that the great passion between them was real, after all.

Maybe proving it to you, too, came that voice, inevitably.

Damn him.

And that was how she woke up on the morning of her wedding day, surely and totally doomed, because she hadn't made any headway at all in getting him to call this off.

But as she looked at the set of photographs splashed across the usual papers from the night before—because they hadn't bothered with a rehearsal dinner when there was an art show to attend and no rehearsal necessary for a forced travesty—she didn't see a woman who was one short, fitful sleep away from being married off to appease her late father.

Annika saw herself looking bright and flushed.

She looked like she was well and truly his.

And though she should have been distraught today, *doomed* was not how she felt at all.

CHAPTER SIX

THE WEDDING WENT precisely as Ranieri had planned.

It was true that the Schuyler House museum baffled him. There it sat on a side street on Upper East Side, lost, to his mind, between the flashier museums that littered the area. The Metropolitan. The Guggenheim. The Frick.

But there was no denying that using Schuyler House leant this wedding of his a certain extra glow.

Even the weather dared not defy him. It was a spectacular afternoon. The deep blue of the sky was a color only possible here in the fall, and yet this first Saturday in October was neither chilly nor overly warm. As if the skies above approved of the outdoor venue he had chosen.

The house was built in that old Gilded Age style, and rather than rearrange the museum—and contend with Annika's potential reaction to that—Ranieri had decided that the back courtyard was more appropriate. He had found the best event planners the city, offered them enough money to make this last-minute high society wedding a prospect too appealing to turn down, and today he found himself pleased with the results.

Perhaps he was particular. But *particular* got results.

He had several fortunes to prove it.

Ranieri stood at the head of the aisle the event planners had constructed there in the walled stone courtyard. He waited for his bride while a select number of the world's and New York City's wealthiest—as well as Annika's close friends—filled the few rows of chairs. And when Annika finally appeared, a single violin began to play.

She caught his gaze and stood there a moment, and he wondered—not quite idly—if she might attempt to play one of her tricks here. But instead, she gripped the bouquet she held before her a little tighter and then she started down the wide stone steps at the back of the old house.

And then she headed straight for him.

Ranieri had planned every part of this wedding. Including the dress she wore now, because he'd known that its elegant sweep would highlight her beauty perfectly. He was pleased to see it did. She looked graceful and ethereal, a vision in white.

He had slowly come to terms with the reality of Annika over the past few weeks. Perhaps it was simply that once he'd kissed her, all the blinders he'd kept firmly in place for years had come crashing down.

Annika was a beautiful woman. Full stop. What she was not, he had found, was overly concerned with maintaining and showing off that beauty. He doubted she thought much about it at all. Just as she did not care overmuch about fashion the way everyone did—including him—because it was considered a calling card in these circles.

She had never been interested in calling cards. If she was, she would not have secreted herself away in this funny old museum.

And Ranieri knew this: if she had truly been as embarrassing and awkward as she and everyone around her pretended, she would not have inspired the kind of snide commentary that forever followed in her wake. That sort of thing only came about when jealousy was involved.

It made sense. A beautiful woman so unselfconscious could only be considered a threat to some.

Not that this explained his long-term aversion to her and what he liked to think of as her bedraggled state. Kissing her had brought other memories back, too. He could recall his first introduction to her. She'd been standing there in the stunning foyer of her apartment, beneath the Baccarat chandelier with her father, and he had taken a quick initial impression of her. He'd seen the long, silky hair. Her lovely oval of a face. An hourglass figure in a lovely dress. He'd noticed, because of course he noticed, how pretty she was—

And in the next moment she had been introduced to him as Bennett Schuyler's daughter and he had shut all of that off. So completely that it was as if he hadn't truly seen her again until now.

But it made sense to him why her sartorial choices had always irritated him so deeply. Why he had only been able to see the careless hair, the oddball choices of dress. If asked, he would have banged on about the stain upon the Schuyler name, which affected him personally in his position. He often had, at length.

Now he rather thought the truth of it was, deep down, that he'd always known exactly how pretty she was. And it offended him, connoisseur of all things beautiful, that her loveliness was obscured. When all it would take was a little work on her part to showcase it.

Today, he'd done the showcasing himself.

And he had done it well.

What he hadn't been prepared for was the punch to the gut he felt when he laid eyes on her for the first time in the dress he'd picked out for her, walking toward him as if she'd chosen this.

As if she'd chosen him.

It was as if that violin was scratching out the bridal march inside him.

Annika had opted to walk down the aisle herself. And though Ranieri knew she'd done it because she thought that somehow made what was happening less real, he thought she'd miscalculated. It didn't make her look removed from the proceedings, but the opposite. She could not have made her father more present here in any other way.

All anyone could possibly see as she walked was his absence. The afternoon shadows almost seemed to make it possible to imagine him walking proudly beside her as she made it down the aisle and faced Ranieri at last.

And he felt everything far too keenly, though he told himself it was the sweetness of his victory here, nothing more.

He reminded himself of that victory when she took his hands. When he said his vows and her green eyes darkened. When she repeated them, her voice gone ever so slightly scratchy on those old words that he knew she would say did not apply to them.

Love. Honor. Cherish.

Then it was done, so Ranieri hooked a hand around her neck and pulled her close to kiss her. Once more for a crowd.

They were getting good at it, this kissing thing. He had staved off God only knew how many humiliations this way, and now was done. The marriage her father had demanded, sealed with a kiss.

Now if either one of them wanted to walk away, it would take a divorce.

The reception kicked into gear as they walked back down the aisle and posed for a few pictures, because not doing so would look strange. When the photographer had snapped what must have been hundreds of shots, Annika murmured something about tending to the guests, and excused herself.

Ran away from him, more like, but Ranieri could allow it. There was nowhere for her to go, after all. He did his own rounds of the party, checking in with the usual heavy hitters he always found himself talking to at parties like this. He liked that the caterers Annika had recommended were deft and seemed functionally psychic, replacing a drink the very moment a guest noticed it was empty. Or producing a plate of appetizers to choose from at the very moment someone *almost* felt hungry.

He was tempted to imagine that if they wished, the two of them could do well together. Stuck as they were with each other for the year. Today, it seemed less a bitter fate than before.

The events coordinator oversaw the removal of all the chairs from the ceremony and swiftly set up the single long table down the length of the courtyard as the sun began to set. The courtyard was lit all around with lanterns, a bright glow against the October evening, with heat lamps placed every few feet to keep the warmth of the day. Schuyler House stood there before them, its old walls surrounded them, and Ranieri almost thought he understood Annika's connection to the place now. It was beautiful, in its way. A slice of old New York and, having grown up in so many old places himself, Ranieri felt drawn to it.

When really, he should've been basking in his triumph. His complete and utter victory, despite much provocation from Annika herself. Despite the pink monstrosity that was still overtaking his desk and *unicorn figurines*.

But in truth, all he could think about was the honeymoon. About getting away from all these *people* at last and taking her somewhere that there would be no eyes on her at all, save his.

The violinist was joined by three other musicians to form a proper string quartet, and they played classical standards as the party was called to dinner. Ranieri wasn't hungry. Not for food. But what he liked was that it gave him a good excuse to do what he wanted to do anyway. He found his way to his bride's side, intending to take her hand and tug her away from the conversation she was having with the group of women he knew were the college friends she sometimes spoke of. Not to him, but to the staff when she thought he wasn't paying attention.

She had not yet learned that he always paid attention.

"There you are," he said as he came up beside her. As if he might have lost track of her in the small crowd. Or ever.

Then he found himself smiling slightly as her friends all turned the same sort of steely, assessing looks upon him.

"Do you not have a family?" one of them asked. "Is that why none of them are here?"

"Or are you estranged from your family?" asked another.

His brand-new wife frowned at her friends, but her smile was apologetic when she aimed it at him. "They're very nosy and wholly ungovernable," she told him. "I told them to leave it alone, but you see how well that went."

"We can't be contained," said the third friend with a shrug. "But it is interesting…" She lingered over that word as if it was the clue they'd all been looking for, and perhaps it was "…that your side of the aisle was all business associates, isn't it?"

Ranieri acknowledged her with the barest lift of his brow. "I admire this support for your friend. But I must steal her away."

And then, he steered Annika away with him, giving her no choice but to follow him—unless she wished to make a scene. He rather thought her appetite for scenes had diminished these past few days. Maybe it was because she viewed the wedding as a setback, having failed to make him call it off. Or possibly it was because he kept responding to each attempt on her part to make a scene with a kiss.

Either way, though he braced himself for her to struggle with him now, she didn't.

He led her over to the center of the long table and seated her, then took the chair beside her. All around them, the guests filled in the empty seats, and then the caterers outdid themselves as they began to serve the simple, but exquisitely prepared meal that Ranieri had chosen.

Yet he could barely taste it.

Beside him, Annika only picked at the food on her plate. And Ranieri almost laughed, because to all appearances, it must have looked as if they were consumed with the sort of wedding nerves normally reserved for people in love. That or virgins, tremulously expecting the unknown on their wedding night.

"If you wish to ask me questions about my personal life, you should simply ask," he said, sitting back in his seat and looping his arm on the back of her chair, because he could. Because she was his wife. And possibly also because she didn't sit up straight to get away from him, so his fingers could graze the delicate strap of her dress, the tempting line of her shoulder blade.

"I don't know what makes you think I have the faintest interest in your personal life," she said, but she didn't say such things the way she had at first. Her voice was warm. And the look she shot him was green and bright.

"It must be your friends, then, who are so interested. Such that they feel it reasonable to interrogate me at my own wedding."

Annika shifted around in her seat to look at him then. And it should not have surprised him as much as it did, the way the rest of the reception seemed to fall away. As if it was only the two of them out here in the Manhattan night.

He would have sworn they were entirely alone.

"I'm the very last of my family. And there's not a lot I wouldn't do to bring them back, if I could." Annika glanced away briefly, her eyes moving over the museum and then returning to him. Almost shyly, he thought, or perhaps that was a trick of the lantern light. "It's not really a surprise that I've chosen to spend my life immersed in all this family history. It's the closest I can get to the real thing."

Ranieri felt very nearly…unsettled, and that was a new sensation. He had to fight the urge to rub his free hand over his chest.

"This seems unduly introspective," he said, but softly. Very softly, and not, for once, because he wished to score any points. "But it is not surprising. Weddings can be very emotional."

He would not have thought so, previously. They had always been networking opportunities to him. But in this moment of sudden, bracing honesty, here in this private little bubble between them despite the fact they were surrounded on all sides, he found it was easy to admit it.

Alarmingly easy, as though it took nothing from him. He had to consider that its own sort of win, he supposed.

"Everything happened so fast," Annika told him, almost gravely. "It wasn't until I walked down the aisle that it really hit me. My father isn't here. I actually got married without him."

Her green eyes were too bright, for a moment. She lowered her gaze. And he had to fight not to reach over and pull her to him. He didn't know why it occurred to him to try. When had he last offered anyone comfort? But this was Annika.

He allowed his hand to move, rising until he could wrap his palm over the nape of her neck. It wasn't enough, he felt certain. But it was something.

She looked at him again and took a steadying sort of breath, and he wasn't sure if the warmth he felt in his hand was hers or his. Perhaps it was both of theirs.

"I think I've decided to be grateful that I didn't have to anticipate the loss," she said in the same grave tone. "I didn't spend years having to imagine walking down a wedding aisle without him. It happened so fast that it's already done."

"I'm delighted that could be a part of this…expediency."

That should have come out sardonic. Hadn't he meant it to? But instead, he said it with the same weight and gravity she had used.

And more astounding, Ranieri found he meant it.

Her gaze rose to meet his again and they were not

kissing. Not now. Yet somehow, that was what this moment felt like anyway. There was heat, intensity. There was that breathlessness. He wasn't sure that he had ever felt connected like this to anyone.

The closest he had ever come had been when he'd been deep inside a woman, and he would not compare the experiences. This felt…sacred.

It occurred to him to pay attention to where he was. The clink of the glasses around them, the sparkling conversations. The eyes on them, everywhere, even as Annika quietly took him apart.

He assured himself that all of this was about sex. Sex and the year ahead, that was all.

That was all it ever could be.

As the dinner wore on, Annika lost that hint of melancholy. Or emotion, of whatever stripe. She got up from her seat and walked around the table, talking to whoever stopped her, and Ranieri learned some more things about her then. That she was not, perhaps, as awkward as she always appeared at galas and the like. That here, with her friends nearby and only a few close business associates to contend with, she bloomed.

He wasn't sure how it had never occurred to him that the secret of Annika Schuyler was simply that she was shy. Ranieri tried to tell himself that she was putting on an act here the same way she did elsewhere, but he couldn't quite make himself believe it. He'd seen the genuine emotion in her gaze. More than that, he had tasted her now.

And a person could fake a great many things, but a kiss was not one of them.

Not the way Annika kissed him, as if she might die if she stopped.

Act or not, the result was the same. She had invited her friends. He had made strategic choices for the guest list and he knew full well that all of them would tell tales about Annika Schuyler Furlan's easy, elegant hospitality for years to come.

He would have set about congratulating himself, but he had far more pressing things on his mind.

Like the marital relations she had seemed so shocked to discover he wanted.

Ranieri might have been shocked too, but he wanted her too badly. And while he had never been led around by the hardest part of him in his life, he hadn't been married before, either. All bets appeared well and truly off.

After dinner was done, the string quartet began to play dancing music. Ranieri gritted his teeth and got to it.

Because that was the most expedient way to fast-forward to the part he was actually interested in. He strode over to Annika, involved in another deep discussion with her college cohort, and drew her away once more.

This time without an interrogation.

"That was rude," she told him, looking over her shoulder at her friends.

"This is not a reunion, *amore*," he told her, loud enough that her friends were not the only ones who could hear the endearment he used. "You are the bride. You have certain duties, and one of them, I am afraid, is that you must dance with your husband."

He was suddenly overtly aware of the platinum band on his finger. And the slender, matching band Annika now wore, because she hadn't wanted more diamonds. She had felt the single one she wore was more than enough. She had said as much, repeatedly, waving his family heirloom around as if she would have liked it if it flew off and shattered the nearest window.

Ranieri drew her out into the middle of the courtyard that been set aside as a dance floor, and pulled her into his arms at last. Where she fit too well and he was a little too invested in that.

He told himself that, too, was about sex.

The truth was he couldn't recall the last time he had been required to wait.

The strings played, singing out an ancient song of love, and he whirled her around, again and again.

And while the music played, Ranieri did not think of winning or losing. He did not calculate the advantages here or plot out his next move. He only held her in his arms, this woman who had become his wife, gazed down at her, and lost himself in all that marvelous green.

Grave again, as if she could see the deepest parts of him. The things no one ever saw.

Finally, when the dancing was done, he drew her with him as he climbed the steps of the museum.

"Are you planning to make a speech?" she asked as they went. "What a good host you are, Ranieri. I doubt anyone saw that coming."

He liked that dry little bit of teasing in her voice. It made him feel like himself again. It chased away all

the unexpected weight of this odd emotion he couldn't
seem to dispel.

"Only in a manner of speaking," he told her. "My ferocious reputation will remain spotless, I promise you."

And then, while their assembled guests watched and
applauded—or in the case of her friends, frowned—
he bent slightly, then swept her into his arms. Ranieri
held her there for a moment, so the whole of the wedding reception could see them. So the photographers
could be certain to take the last picture for some time.

Then he turned without another word and bore her
into the museum.

Ranieri did not put her down. He carried her straight
through the museum, then out the front door, and de-
posited her in his waiting car.

"I think this counts as a kidnapping," she said, but
she did not sound unduly concerned at the prospect.

"I would not be surprised to discover that many a
honeymoon started off the same way," he replied, un-
repentantly.

And then, finally, Ranieri kissed her the way he
wanted to.

He feasted on her as the car pulled away from the
curb, carrying them off to the jet that waited for them
in a private airfield.

She surged against him, tasting of the same hunger that burned so hot and wild within him. He kissed
her and he kissed her, and this time, they were safely
ensconced in the back of a moving car. There were no
watching eyes. No cameras.

No acts to perform.

He could indulge himself.

And so, at last, that was what he did.

Ranieri succumbed to the temptation of her mouth, angling his head as he took the kiss deeper. And while he was at it, he let his hands explore the glory of that figure of hers she had so long kept concealed.

He wanted to take that as some kind of evidence of her perfidy, even now, but he couldn't get past the notion of her shyness. Her disinterest in the games so many in her set played.

And the possibility that it had never occurred to her that her figure was a gift.

One he did not intend to share.

He bent his head to press his mouth to the graceful line of her neck, then followed it down. He lavished attention on the sweet, rounded mounds that rose above the bodice of her gown.

But he wanted more. He wanted some proof that he was not alone in this wanting. This need that had taken him over, little as he wished to admit it.

He pulled her voluminous skirts up with him, still kissing her. And he reveled in every noise she made. Because she sounded greedy and half-mad, just as he felt.

And because he could taste the sounds she made, and that made him even harder.

He found the garter she wore, and he moved his fingers up higher. Then still higher, until he found the soft heat of her at last.

"Ranieri…" she whispered brokenly.

But her hips rose as she said his name. And she

opened herself beneath his hands, giving herself over to him that easily.

As if this was no surrender, but an invitation.

He traced the shape of her, learning the soft, hot contours of her femininity. The scent of her was wilder now, but still that same sweetness that was only hers. And only when she was shuddering in his arms, her head thrown back and her back arched as if offering herself to him on the altar of his choosing, did he test the tight clasp of her heat.

Then, following an urge that felt like a drumbeat within him, he tested her heat with one finger, then another. She sighed, and opened herself even farther as he set a slow, unhurried pace, twisting his hand around to let his thumb press hard against the center of her need.

Now, finally, she was his.

Ranieri gazed down at her, her face flushed, her head thrown back, the very picture of grace and greed.

He had never wanted a woman more.

In point of fact, he could no longer recall if any other women existed.

After only a few thrusts, Annika bucked all around him, flooding his hands with her sweet heat.

Ranieri forced himself to sit back. He rearranged her skirts, and found himself smiling as he pulled her up from where she'd gone limp against the seat, arranging her so that she looked a proper bride and not the debauched creature he'd made her.

That she was both of those things, and both were his, pleased him deeply.

It took her some time to open her eyes and when

she did, the green of her eyes seemed to pierce him straight through.

"But… Don't you want to…?"

"Amore," he said with a certain intensity, and did not choose to ask himself why he was using that particular endearment when there was no one but her to hear it, "you are a Furlan now. And I am taking you to my ancestral home, such as it is. Where I will sample you as is only good and proper and civilized, in an actual bed. Not in the back of a car as if we are nothing but overwrought teenagers."

If she didn't matter to you, you wouldn't bother to wait, a voice inside him whispered.

He ignored it.

Annika stared at him for a long moment. Then a smile took over her face. And this was not the kind of smile he'd grown used to from her. This one seemed to crack her wide open, until all he could see was sunlight, and no matter that outside the car the October night was dark and deep.

"Yes, dear," she said, almost diffidently, and then her smile widened. "Isn't that the appropriate, subservient mode of address? Is that what we're looking for here?"

And Ranieri had to shift on the seat before he forgot his good intentions and had her here and now—

But he was taking her home. And he would wait until he got her there, or really, he could count himself no better than animal. Something he was certain he would have to remind himself of during the flight ahead of them.

If she didn't matter to you…

Ranieri took her hand and played with his grandmother's ring, sitting so snugly on her finger. "I'm glad you're taking your wifely duties so seriously, Annika," he said, and found himself smiling again at her laughter. "See that it continues."

Then he allowed himself one more kiss.

But only the one.

CHAPTER SEVEN

To Annika's tremendous disappointment, Ranieri meant what he said.

And he could not be moved.

There was that lovely interlude in the car, and that was it. They boarded the jet waiting for them and he ushered her to one of the rooms on the plane, gruffly suggesting that she take the opportunity to change out of her wedding gown. She might have wanted to argue about that, or suggest he stay with her in the stateroom, but Marissa appeared and bustled into the room with her. Because, it occurred to her only after Ranieri left her there, she could not get out of her wedding gown on her own. It had taken a handful of attendants to get her into it earlier.

And when she was finally changed and comfortably ensconced in the sort of lounging clothing that Marissa approved of—all cashmere and merino wool, which were not exactly a hardship to wear, though she hated to admit it—she wandered out into the main part of the plane to see if she could find Ranieri again.

He wasn't hard to locate. He was in his own stateroom but he was seated at a desk with his laptop open and his briefcase beside him, talking gruffly in what sounded like German. Annika supposed she could have disrupted whatever meeting he was conducting on his wedding day, but she didn't. She was still floating on the remains of the day they'd had—and what had gone on in the back of that limousine.

She was still flashing too hot, thinking about *his hand*.

How had she let it happen?

But she knew the answer to that. They had been alone as they had not been since that kiss up on his roof. And all the kisses in between, parceled out to the paparazzi as little punishments for her attempts to shame him, had stoked a greedy, breathless fire within her. The wedding had made it worse. Walking down that aisle to him. Dancing with him.

Being swept up in his arms and carried off.

There with Schuyler House looking on like the benevolent relatives she missed so dearly.

She had lost herself. There was no other way to describe it. And she should have been barricading herself away from him now, but she couldn't quite get there. She didn't *want* to get there.

Because there was that fire in her and there had been his *hand*, and now she no longer wanted to deny it. To fight it with dahlias and unicorns and nicknames. Now she wanted to know where it went.

She wanted to chase that fire, not run away from it.

He had talked about needs. It turned out she had some, too. Why shouldn't they both get what they

wanted out of this situation? She felt wildly sophisticated as she thought that—like the woman she looked
like in the mirror now, the woman he dressed her to be
these days. Theirs was a temporary arrangement, so
why not enjoy it?

If he could do it, why couldn't she?

Why not *choose* to burn?

All she had to do was take care of her heart, she
thought, as it beat too hard. Much too hard, there in her
chest. She just needed to make sure this all stayed sophisticated. And that she didn't get too…silly about this.
About him. Because these were games people played all
the time, and that meant she could, too. She was sure
she could, no matter how dangerously attractive he was.

That in mind, Annika made her way back to her
room and, without meaning to, curled up beneath the
blanket on the bed and fell asleep.

Something she was only aware of when she woke up
as the plane began its descent.

This time, when she walked out into the main cabin,
Ranieri beckoned her into the seat beside him. And
maybe she should have worried about how eager she
was to take the place he offered her. Maybe she should
have questioned why it was that the wedding she hadn't
even wanted had turned her around this much. It was
only a wedding, after all. Not even one she'd had a
hand in planning. She knew it was practically fashionable these days to have any number of weddings, follow them up with divorces, and treat it all like a series
of amusing parties.

But Annika wasn't that woman. She wasn't sure, as

she sat there next to Ranieri feeling a little bit silly and entirely too giddy, that she even wanted to be that kind of woman. She hadn't expected to find her wedding moving, but she had. She couldn't see rushing to have another one.

Still, what she really kept thinking about was the limousine afterward, his hand beneath her skirt, his clever fingers moving through her wet heat—

Or maybe, came a voice inside her, *it's the sex part you don't know how to handle.*

She blew out a breath. And dived into a related topic she really had no interest whatsoever in discussing. The innocence she'd held on to all this time, without even meaning to. Not really. The innocence she was suddenly horrified to imagine was the reason he had always looked at her with such disdain—since it was the very opposite of the sort of sophistication he was known for, wasn't it?

"Is the reason you didn't touch me again after what happened in the back of the car because..." Annika could feel embarrassment coil, hard and hot, deep inside her. "Is it because you could tell?"

He took his time turning his head so he could gaze upon her and she remembered, in a distant way, that she'd used to think that he looked brutal. That was how masculine he was. That was how intense he looked, always.

But these days all she saw was the stark beauty of the man. As if one taste of him had made it impossible for her to see anything else.

As if she'd imprinted on him.

Even when he raised those dark brows of his as if he couldn't believe what he was hearing. An expression he wore often in her presence, but it was amazing how differently she felt about it now. When she could still feel the press of his mouth to hers. When she could still feel his hard fingers, deep inside her.

"Let me hasten to assure you, Annika, that I have been perfectly able to discern a woman's pleasure for some time." His voice was icy, but his golden gaze was hot. "In my opinion, a man cannot call himself a man unless he is capable of making a woman happy. It is my understanding that American men…" Ranieri shrugged. "Perhaps they do not deserve to use the term."

That lined up with a great many things she'd heard over the years, particularly from her college friends.

But, "That isn't what I meant," she said. "Although it is interesting."

Fascinating, more like it. She was still slippery at the very thought of the pleasure he'd given her, and there was a part of her that simply wanted to beg him to do it again. To keep doing it. To make her feel things she'd had no idea could be like that. His hand wasn't like hers. It was so big. His fingers blunt and long.

He'd put them *inside* her.

She had to fight back a shudder, though she could feel goose bumps all over her anyway.

"What did you mean, then?" he asked, in that way he had that made her think he knew the location of each and every goose bump on her body. "What do you think I could tell besides the fact you came apart in my hands? And so beautifully?"

Annika would have to add that to the list of things she'd had no idea people could just…talk about. She'd read a lot of books, certainly, but it hadn't occurred to her that in real life, a man might actually say such things to a woman. Just sit here and *say* them.

And she realized she'd been too busy thinking it all through when those relentless gold eyes of his seemed to soften and he reached over to run his knuckles over her cheek.

That was also when she realized that she was blushing. A lot.

But she needed to take this seriously regardless of whether or not she was bright red, because she felt she had to make this declaration. She'd talked it over with her friends. There had been votes for and against. Some thought, given the realities of their relationship, that she wasn't required to tell him anything. She could simply…see how it all went. Others were convinced that Annika, personally, would like it better if there were no surprises. Though she wasn't sure she believed anything they said, because all of her friends seemed to think that Ranieri, renowned the world over for his many love affairs, would not react well to the news anyway.

I'm not sure that man has ever met another virgin in his life, one of her friends had said.

But then, Annika rather thought her friends wanted him to react badly and keep his distance as a result. They had all been united on one thing: that the man who had been such a thorn in her side these last few years didn't deserve her.

Annika felt compelled to tell him anyway. Even if her friends were right that he would hate it.

Even if that means he never touches you again? a voice inside her asked.

It would be easy enough. Now was the time, before things…progressed. All she had to do was say it. *I'm a virgin.* Easy and to the point.

And she couldn't quite bring herself to open her mouth and do it.

"We are about to land," he told her, and for some reason, he sounded deeply amused. Possibly because he was the one who could *see* how she was blushing. "And we will have a bit of a drive. If you require more time to tell me whatever it is you wish to tell me, you have it." He ran that knuckle down her cheek again, then over her lips. "I cannot promise that I will be in a talking mood once we reach our destination. What I can promise you is that you will enjoy it, whatever happens."

"I don't have a lot of experience," she told him in a rush.

And then felt as if she might break into a sweat. Or possibly start crying. Maybe she already had.

He considered her for long moments, with that steady intensity that made everything within her seem to constrict. "And it was perhaps not so great, the little experience you have had."

She regarded him solemnly. "That is…not incorrect."

Ranieri looked down, then took her hand in his. "Annika. Hear me on this. I want you."

And that, too, astounded her. That he could simply…
say such a thing. So baldly. And with such certainty.

More, he sounded as if it was normal. Run-of-the-
mill. As if maybe a discussion of his needs was simply
par for the course with him. She admired it. Maybe she
was even the smallest bit jealous of it.

Annika felt her heart kick at her. So hard she was
surprised it wasn't catapulting straight from her chest.

"This is not what we might have chosen, you and I,"
he said, in that low, stirring way he had. "But here we
are. I already know that you want me, too. Handily, we
are married to each other, like it or not. It seems to me
that there are a great many ways that we might spend
this year together. One of them is to enjoy each other
as much as possible. What do you think?"

It was a variation of what he'd said to her before, but
everything was so different now. She'd had much the
same thought herself, hadn't she? More, she had walked
down an aisle and made vows to him, in front of people she cared about. He had put his mouth against her
neck and let his fingers find their way inside her. He
had made her sob and writhe in his arms.

He had touched her face gently and looked at her as
if even then, given his way, he would have preferred
to devour her.

And now she found herself thinking too many things
at once—

But mostly, she really, truly wanted to know what
enjoying him might entail.

She wanted to know that with such intensity that it
made her shake.

"I would like that," Annika told him quietly.

Because she loved her museum, but she wasn't an exhibit in it. She was alive. She would never have chosen any of this, but it was happening. It had already happened. He was her husband and she wanted to experience that in every possible way she could, for as long as she could. No matter what came next. And no matter how much she'd loathed him all these years.

The look he gave her then reminded her of the same expression he'd worn as he'd said his own vows. That intensity. That gravity.

As if all of that ruthlessness he wore so easily he would bring to bear here, too.

Something in her shook and shook at that notion.

Because even now, even though he'd had his hand between her legs and he'd spoken of things like *coming apart beautifully*, she still couldn't imagine—no matter how she tried—what it would truly be like to lie naked with this man, to feel him all over her, to welcome him deep inside her body. Only not his fingers this time.

Ranieri's eyes lit with a deep heat, and he laughed. And Annika knew then that he could read her every thought, all over her face.

"Steady on, *amore*," he murmured. "We have a little way to go yet."

But for Annika, everything shifted into a kind of overbright, sweet syrup of need and longing. And threaded through it all was a humming sort of anticipation. It seemed to take her over. She could feel it in her bones.

They landed in an airfield high in the hills. Outside, the air was crisp and the sky was a deep, moody blue, the last gasp of a fall night. Ranieri was the one who swung into the driver's seat of one of the vehicles that waited there. It was a smaller sort of SUV, the kind they liked in Europe, and Annika was not surprised to find that he drove it the way he did everything else. With that singular focus. That intense competence.

She thought she'd be perfectly happy to sit beside him forever and let him drive her wherever he wished them to go.

Because all she could think about was that growing hunger inside her. The fire was indistinguishable now from that ache, making her feel trembly. Everywhere.

And the terrible wanting that left her too close to breathless, like that was all that was left of her.

"I am not close to my family," he told her, unbidden, as the new day began to stir outside. She knew they were somewhere north of Milan as he drove her into the hills without consulting a map, moving swiftly along winding mountain roads he seemed to know the way he knew everything. As if the whole of the world was etched there on the back of his hand.

Even the valleys she glimpsed seemed a part of his singular magic—vineyards stretching toward the rising sun, medieval castles standing guard.

She was beginning to think she was a part of it, too.

"You don't have to talk about it," she said quietly. "Families can be complicated."

"Perhaps that is so. But I have always felt that mine was more complicated than most—or perhaps less inclined to pretend otherwise. My parents divorced long ago. And both of them are entirely too proud to admit that they might have borne any fault in the split. Then again, as their only child, I have long been entirely too proud myself and more, unwilling to admit that anything they did with their personal lives bothered me in the slightest."

She glanced over at him, then returned her gaze to the hills all around them, gleaming gold in the morning light. "You do know what they say about pride."

"I do indeed. And it has precipitated many a fall in my family, I assure you. I tell you this because we have come here and it is entirely possible that my parents will take it upon themselves to turn up. And if they do so together, well." He shrugged in that supremely Italian way of his that was mesmerizing enough in New York. Here, it seemed a part of the very landscape. "Anything might happen."

The roads grew more twisting and steep. Annika held fast to the door handle beside her and let what he'd said sink in.

"I don't suppose that your interest in proper behavior has anything to do with your parents, does it?" she asked quietly. "It doesn't sound as if you find them appropriate, either."

Ranieri let out a bark of laughter that seemed to surprise him as much as it did her. He took a sharp turn, the SUV seeming to hug the narrow road. "My grandmother was all that was graceful and refined. My mother and father, not so much. I think you already know where I fall."

And he sounded the way he always did. Assured. Arrogant. Ranieri, through and through. And yet…

Annika didn't know how she dared, but she reached across and put her hand on his leg. Then felt the heat of him, of all that rock-hard strength. It seemed to flood her palm, making her want to do something more, like lean down and explore him. Possibly with her mouth, though surely that would kill them both on a road like this—

Focus, she ordered herself.

"Don't worry," she told him, sounding throatier than was wise, surely. "I would happily embarrass you in front of the entirety of New York City. But I would never do such a thing in front of your parents."

The sun was up now, so she could see with perfect clarity the faintly arrested expression on his face. He glanced over at her briefly, then dropped his gaze to where her hand rested on his leg.

She felt very nearly scalded as she went to pull her hand away.

But he stopped her easily enough by placing his hand over hers, trapping her there.

Annika told herself at once that she wasn't to torture herself with questions about what this might mean. She told herself to simply enjoy the heat of his thigh below her palm and the hard press of his palm against the back of her hand, too.

And she could not have said how long it was that they drove like that. She was lost in the motion of the car, the Italian countryside all around. The fact she was *touching* him. Eventually, he took a road that wound down into a charming valley. There was a river that cut through it, a lake at the center. And everywhere else there were fields turned golden, vineyards winding down into autumn, sturdy cypress trees like sentinels, and there, nestled in the middle of carpets of wildflowers, an old house.

It was built of ancient stone with a red roof and charming shutters. And it was not the sort of castle or fortress they'd seen along the way. It was prettier, as if someone had taken the old stones and determinedly made them over into a home. Yet it still had the feel of something suitably medieval as they drove closer, and Ranieri finally pulled to a stop in the pebbled courtyard in front.

"This is my grandmother's cottage," he told her, his voice gone rough. He turned to her, still holding her hand beneath his. "She left it to me when she passed."

"It's beautiful," Annika whispered.

It was more than beautiful. It looked like a fairy tale. It made her wish she believed that fairy tales could be real. It made her wish—

But no. She stopped herself there. It wasn't safe to lose herself in all these *wishes* when there was only a year. Only one, solitary year.

"I have come here many times," Ranieri told her in that same gruff way, as if he didn't know how to say these things. As if they were torn from within him. "I cannot always be in cities, you understand. But what I need you to know, Annika, is that I have never brought another woman here. Ever. You're the first." Something seemed to swell between them, then. "The only."

And she could feel that fluttery beat inside her. Her pulse. Her heart. Her relentless longing. All of her, lost somewhere between a shudder and a sob, no matter how dangerous it was.

She understood, very distinctly, that this was an offering. His wedding gift, perhaps. That he could not give her innocence. He could not erase her father's demands that had brought them here. He could not give her anything other than what he was—all that he was.

But he could bring her here.

To this far-off valley that meant something to him. To this old, beloved house, nestled in fields of flowers and flanked by ancient columns of cypress. She could see that this made him vulnerable, though she knew better than to use that word. For men like him, it could only be taken as an insult. Even now, when he had done this deliberately.

Still, she knew. She could feel it in the heat of his hand, the hard stone of his thigh. She could see it in his gaze, gold and intense.

And she knew with a deep, feminine certainty that she would walk through the doors of this enchanted place, give herself to this man, and be forever changed.

In this moment, gazing into his rich, golden eyes as a beautiful Italian morning danced all around them, that felt like a bargain.

"Ranieri," she whispered. "I want you."

And when he laughed, it was a dark, thrilling sound.

If there was vulnerability in him then, she did not see it any longer. He slammed out of the car and rounded the front of it, opening her door and pulling her out with so much obvious, leashed strength that it only made her aware of how in control of himself he'd been all this time.

How in control he always was.

Her feet hardly touched the ground before he swept her into his arms again, and then he was striding forward, shouldering his way into the house and carrying her over the threshold.

She clung to him, having no idea how she could focus on the details of the house as he moved through it so swiftly. He carried her up a set of stairs and down another corridor, but all she could really see was the stark sensuality in his expression. A certain kind of grimness that translated directly into a bright heat inside her, spiraling all around until she ached even more, there between her legs.

And then, suddenly, she was in the air. Then bouncing on a mattress, and she couldn't help but laugh.

Ranieri followed her down, and then there was no more room for laughter. Everything crystallized into that blistering heat.

Finally, she thought. Maybe she said it.

Her clothes came off easily, soft cashmere and smooth wool no match for his touch, for the cleverness of his fingers. His mouth was on hers, then on her neck, and then he followed the curves of her body, pausing as he liked to taste her, to tempt her.

But before he could settle into any one of the places that longed for him, Annika was pushing against him. She made him sit up and then, however inexpertly, she set about pulling his clothes from his body until he laughed, pushed her away, and handled it himself.

Annika knelt there, gaping as he was finally revealed to her.

On some level, she had expected the perfection of his chest. The dark hair dusted over the impossible glory of his chest, his ridged abdomen. She'd expected that, yes—but she hadn't really understood *how* perfect he was.

Or how the act of looking at him could make her whole body quiver with excitement.

Especially when her gaze was drawn to that male part of him, heavy and low between his legs. It made her feel something like drunk. And when she lifted her gaze to his again, he wore a grin that reminded her of nothing so much as a wolf.

"I intended to finesse this," he told her in a low voice. "We will have time for that. Later."

"I want you," Annika said again, because she understood, now, the power in those words. The beauty in them. Their stark, simple truth.

Ranieri made a low, deep sound that seemed ripped from inside him. And then he was crawling over her, kissing her everywhere, his hands touching, taunting, tearing her into pieces, each touch making her want him more than the last.

She wrapped herself around him, and experimented with pressing her greedy breasts against his chest, rubbing them a little this way, then that, to feel his hard, hair-roughened muscles against them.

And she shuddered so hard at the sensation that she almost thought—

"Wait for me," he ordered her, there against her mouth.

Annika was dimly aware of it when he reached for protection, and rolled it on, but everything was a clamoring riot within her now. Everything was so sharp, so hungry.

He reached down, guiding himself through her heat, a hard grin glimmering on his face when he made her moan. When he made her buck up against him, and try to force him to...*do something*. Because she knew there was something. Something more—

But then he thrust deep inside her, and everything shattered—

And she knew.

She finally knew.

Ranieri gathered her against him and held her there as he worked himself deep inside her, again and again.

And she couldn't tell what *finesse* could have added to this, because it was everything he was—and more.

It was so raw. It was so *male*. It was a glorious ferocity and she felt its glorious teeth inside her. It was a cresting wave that never quite broke, or always broke, and made her want to do animal things, like dig her nails into his skin. Bite his shoulder.

And when she did those things, following some deep, inner feminine savagery, he made deep noises of approval, and thrust harder. Deeper.

Annika sobbed out his name, a terrible, wonderful

wave rolling over her. She arched up against him, and he laughed.

Then did it again.

And again.

Until everything inside her became a storm and when she flew apart, she heard him call out her name.

Then follow her, straight into all that sweet fury, as if it was who they'd been all along.

As if he'd known who they were from the start.

Annika took a long while to come back into her own body, there in a bed in a strange room, far away from New York and the life that she'd known.

And no longer the innocent she'd been.

No longer innocent at all… And she had expected such a momentous thing to feel complicated. She had heard so many terrible stories. Even some supposedly good stories that had lingered over the mechanical issues of the act. She had expected tears, and a great deal of *I'm a woman now*, but all she felt was…*wonderful*.

She could barely rouse herself. She wasn't sure she ever wanted to move again. And then when she did, she found Ranieri gazing back at her. Gold eyes and dark hair, and a possessive look on his sensual face.

And as she watched, a slow, hot sort of smile spread across his mouth.

"I think we can say we have well and truly taken the edge off," he said, his voice a low rasp.

Then he was crawling over her, pulling her with him. And to her utter shock, Annika felt those same wildfires burn bright in her anew.

"Now," Ranieri said in his sternest voice, kissing

his way down the length of her body and settling himself between her legs, only looking up to flash a bit of that gold at her before returning his attention to the part of her that wanted him most, "why don't we do this properly."

CHAPTER EIGHT

NOTHING COULD HAVE prepared Annika for her honeymoon.

The days were warm, golden bright, and perfect. The nights were cool and called for fires in the grate and long walks in the vineyards, her head tipped back to take in the sky sloppy with stars. He had brought his trusted staff with him from New York and they managed to be both efficient and mostly invisible. It was at mealtimes that she was most grateful that they were here, heaping the bounty of this enchanted valley before them, so that there was no part of her day or night that was not a feast.

If this was the marriage her father had wanted for her, she was only astonished that he hadn't hurried her into it sooner. Had he known all along? She hoped so.

Because this was magic.

Ranieri was magic.

Annika couldn't get enough of him. No matter how many times he took her in the night, she woke up starving for more. No matter how he spread her before him, letting the golden light dance all over her naked body, she wanted to give him more.

There was nothing she wouldn't give him, she thought after a week had passed, a soft, hot rush of sensation and delight. She only grew more voracious. She only wanted more. There was no sensual banquet she wasn't prepared to share with him.

Their days took on an easy routine. They tended to wake at the first hint of light, turning to each other in that wide bed they'd claimed as theirs. It sat at the back of the house, so that sometimes Annika imagined that she could hear her own cries echo back to her from the hills beyond. And no matter how wild or adventurous they'd gotten the night before, their mornings were always about fire. Need.

As if, she sometimes thought, neither one of them could believe that this was real.

Ranieri usually left her to spend his morning in the cottage's study, tending to his empire from afar. But Italian mornings were early in New York, so Annika allowed herself to be lazy. Sometimes she got up when Ranieri did, but more often she turned over and dozed.

She would have been the first to say that she'd led too privileged a life to have earned her idleness, and some mornings, the guilt of that had her charging out of bed. But as the days passed, she felt less and less guilty. She couldn't remember losing her mother, yet the loss had marked her whole life. Losing her father had been two terrible days, with five years of a slower, more pervasive grief in between. The day of his accident and the day of his death had been unbearable in their own ways, especially because she'd had all that time in the middle to let herself imagine that things might be different. So much time that his death had been a shock, when perhaps she should have seen it as a blessing.

Because he was free now.

It was only here, across the ocean in Italy, on a honeymoon with the least likely man alive, that Annika found the space to let herself mourn.

Maybe it was because she wasn't fighting it here. Maybe it was because she simply let whatever emotions came up wash over her in this place of golden ease. It was grief, but it was sweeter, somehow, than it might have been otherwise.

When she finally rose in the mornings, she took her time in the bath, or in the shower. Often, she would find herself staring out the windows until the beauty of the small, perfect valley overwhelmed her and she would feel drawn to take long walks through the fields.

And as she walked, she thought about…everything. Her lost mother she hoped she resembled in as many ways as possible. Her father, who had loved her so. His confounding will, which seemed to refute that. The past month and a half. And Ranieri, who was so tangled up in all of it.

Some days he would come and find her out in the fields when it was getting toward midday. He would grin at her, that dark, fierce face of his set in such bold lines. He would tumble her down into the sweet grass or the soft earth, and teach her new ways to cry out. To hold that beauty in her hands and chase the wildness that was only theirs.

Other times she wandered back to the house, and would take a light lunch with him on the patio outside his study, if the weather was fine. Or inside near the fire if it was cool. And they would talk. The way they never had in all the years they'd known each other, stretching back to when she'd been a teenager. Not necessarily of big, emotional things, but all the rest of it. Small stories. Observations. The connective tissue that held all the big things together, she liked to think.

Like they were just people. Not enemies making the best of things.

Over lunch one day, she made some comment about needing to find more ways to teach him a lesson or two. Ranieri gazed at her with laughter all over his face and his eyes bright. And no matter how many times she saw it these days, it never failed to make her breath catch.

"I'm happy to teach you jujitsu," he said after a moment. "Though I cannot promise that I will teach you to be any good at it."

"I've actually taken a jujitsu class before." Annika wrinkled up her nose. "It seemed like a whole lot of very dramatic cuddling."

He stared across the brightly tiled table at her, looking as outraged as he did astonished. *"Cuddling,"* he repeated.

"All that clenching together. And then writhing about everywhere. You know, it all seemed like a lot of *thighs*." She shook her head. "And then quite a bit of heaving about. It was off-putting, I have to say."

Ranieri continued to stare at her for a moment. Then

he reached over, plucking her out of her chair and pulling her over his lap.

"Perhaps you need another lesson," he murmured, nipping at her chin and making her shiver.

But what he taught her then, carrying her into the study and laying her down on the thick rug like an offering, was not jujitsu. Or any martial art Annika had ever heard of.

It was glorious all the same.

In the afternoons, she liked to check in with the museum back at home. Then she usually found a book and curled up with it, loving the afternoons when Ranieri ignored his own work, sought her out, and took her back to bed. But loving just as much the peaceful hours she got to spend in her favorite chair, sometimes dozing, sometimes unable to turn the pages fast enough.

And always, at some point, thinking back to when he'd brought up sex and she'd wondered what *regular sex* might even look like.

They dressed for dinner every night, and the dressing itself sometimes took longer than necessary. Because Ranieri's "help" always ended the same way—with him surging deep inside her as they both took their pleasure, because the real magic was the way they fit together.

That friction. That heat.

His hardness so deep in her softness, his mouth ravaging her neck, her breasts. Her nails leaving marks on his shoulders, his back.

It only seemed to get worse, this need. This endless wanting.

Sometimes they had their dinner outside, taking advantage of the last of the mild nights. When it was colder—and it kept getting colder—they sat in the cottage's pleasant dining room, or took trays before the fire of their choice. And always there was the sensual delight of the food they ate. Every night it was a feast of local fare, prepared to perfection. But for Annika, the real treat was the opportunity to get to know this man who had cast his shadow over her life for so long.

She knew better than to say out loud some of the conclusions she'd come to during her lazy mornings or out on her long walks. She knew better than to say that clearly, her father had known what he was doing here. That he'd been on to something. That he'd seen something in them that neither one of them would ever have come to on their own.

After all, Ranieri had only signed up for a year. Annika might already be hoping that they would last longer than that, but she wasn't foolish enough to say that. She didn't want to ruin the year he was willing to give her.

Because she wanted every greedy, glorious moment of it.

"Tell me about your grandmother," she said one night, when one week had turned into two, and kept rolling on. "She's the one you speak of most often."

Tonight they were seated not in the cottage's formal dining room, but one of the smaller sitting rooms. Like everything else in this lovely house, it was furnished in light, pleasing shades. The fire in the grate seemed to dance lovingly over the carefully placed objects that graced the tables, the precisely arranged stacks of books, and the quietly impressive art that was hung haphazardly over each wall.

Like every other room in this house, the elegance of the surroundings never took away from the room's comfort. Even if the previous owner hadn't been Ranieri's grandmother, Annika would have been curious how anyone had managed to pull that off. She assured herself it was a professional interest, given she was the one responsible for staging the exhibits at the museum.

Ranieri sat back in his chair, the last of the night's meal before them. They had eaten at a small round table that allowed them to sit closer to each other and he had fed her morsels throughout from his fingers, adding a glimmering undercurrent of fire to every bite she took.

And now that fire was banked, though still in his gaze as he held his wineglass and swirled it in his hand, taking a moment to glance around the room.

"Everyone told my grandmother that she was making a bad bet on one of those Furlans," he said after a moment or two passed. "That it would all end in tears. But she defied them and did it anyway, to her sorrow."

"Are you all so bad, then?" Annika smiled when his gaze moved back to hers, even though he looked remote again. "I thought it was only you."

She was used to him smiling more these days. There was that crook in the corner of his mouth, but it went beyond that, too. Sometimes he grinned widely, the autumn sun pouring all over him as if the grin had summoned it. He laughed more and more as the days went by, usually a wicked, sensual sound, there against her skin.

The world might have been spinning them into another winter's darkness, but between them, the light only grew.

Yet she was reminded that he was still Ranieri Furlan as he gazed back across the table now, his expression taking on that grave, grim coldness she knew so well. Even if she hadn't seen it since they'd left New York.

And maybe it told her everything she needed to know about herself that seeing it now only made her shiver with delight. It made her want him, as if she had never had him at all.

It made her wonder why, exactly, she had told herself she hated him all these years. All these long years when he had always looked at her this way. When he had always been so inaccessible, so remote.

And all the while, there'd been this hunger deep inside her, just waiting for him to feed it.

But she had asked him a question and he was answering it. She tried to squirm in her chair unobtrusively.

"It is not that we are bad in the ways you might imagine," he told her, his gaze dark. "On the contrary, we usually do quite well for ourselves. But sooner or later, we are presented with choices. And almost without exception, we choose our own pride over everything else."

"You have to give me examples, Ranieri." He had mentioned *pride* before, she was certain. But… "Pride can mean anything."

She thought she saw his jaw tense. Or maybe she only wanted the excuse to reach over and touch him, to soothe him… But she kept herself from it, curling her fingers around the delicate stem of her own wineglass instead. Though she hardly needed intoxicants when she was in his presence.

"Take my grandfather," Ranieri said, sounding distressingly cold and sober. "My grandmother was descended from Florentine nobility. She could have chosen anyone, yet she had eyes only for him. And this was a different time, you understand. So no matter their affection for each other, it was accepted practice that a man of my grandfather's station would secure the family line, then seek his pleasures where he chose."

"Mistresses," Annika said, though the word tasted bitter on her tongue. "You can just say the word."

Ranieri's eyes gleamed in a way that sent a cold shiver down the length of her spine. "My grandfather had only one mistress then. By all accounts, she was magnificent. The toast of Italy. There was not a man alive who did not want her."

Ranieri returned his attention to the room. More specifically, to the mantel above the fireplace. She followed his darkening gaze to a set of framed photographs and took the moment to study them. The dark-haired woman, laughing in one photo but too serious in the next.

Annika could see Ranieri in her face.

She felt a strange little tickle then, a kind of foreboding, and wanted almost desperately to stop this conversation. She knew how she would do it. She could launch herself across the table, then sink to her knees and take him in her mouth the way he'd taught her.

It would be a distraction, perhaps. But it would also

make them both happy. She knew that as well as she knew her own name.

But she didn't dare do it. She didn't quite dare.

He was opening up to her, and no matter how being naked with him moved her, no matter what it showed her about the both of them, Annika understood that this was real vulnerability. That him telling her stories could never be dismissed as *just sex*.

A stray memory moved in her then, of her reaction when he'd told her that he had not initially intended to be faithful in this marriage. How outraged she'd been at the very idea, and that had been long before she'd developed this unhealthy, possessive fixation on his body.

On *him*.

She did not want to be married to any man who kept a mistress. And she specifically did not want to share Ranieri with anyone.

But she did not need to risk saying those things out loud, because she already knew she had no right to feel them. That was not what this was. That was not what they'd agreed. This one, miraculous year.

She cleared her throat. "I take it your grandmother was not pleased with this arrangement," she said instead.

"My grandmother was raised to accept these things as all women of her class did," Ranieri said, his voice seeming to grow darker and more forbidding by the word. "At first, it did not occur to her to object to what was common practice. But then she made the critical error of falling in love."

"With your grandfather?" Annika asked, hesitantly.

"He was in love with her, too," Ranieri said, but he sounded almost bitter. "She bore him a son, then two more. Both of them always said that those were happy years. Who knows how long that could have continued? But instead, my grandmother asked my grandfather to give up this mistress of his."

"That doesn't seem unreasonable."

Ranieri let out a laugh, too dark to be anything like amusement, and she knew the difference now. "Perhaps not. But then, my grandfather was a Furlan. There was no question that he loved my grandmother. He said so at the time. He loved his sons as well. But he would not be told by his wife that he should give up anything. He would not permit my grandmother to dictate his behavior. So they lived apart until they died, as he would not divorce her. And he not only kept his mistress, he took others to prove he could. He wasted a fortune on each, leaving my grandmother to fend for herself. Leaving her to raise his sons with the money she had brought into the marriage. He felt he could do as he liked, and so he did. What is that if not egregious pride? And how many lives marred because of it?"

Annika's heart was kicking at her, as if this was perilous, this conversation. She could not see how, seeing as they were speaking of people long dead. But she could feel the danger. She felt as if she was standing on the edge of a steep cliff and the wind was high.

"Still, my grandfather is not the best example of the Furlan pride," Ranieri continued. "His sins were only ever of a personal nature. There are far too many others who made certain that their stumbles ruined more than their marriages and families."

"With all these cautionary tales, you must have spent your life doing your best to rid yourself of this pride," Annika said.

Perhaps too hopefully.

His dark brows rose. "Quite the opposite. I am so proud, Annika, that I refuse to accept that I will lose anything I wish to keep. My father has lost at least three fortunes by my reckoning. One of my uncles lost his life, too proud to admit he made a mistake and too proud to recognize that he was on the wrong side of the wrong kind of people. My other uncle considers himself too good to do what he ought to do to better his situation, an abominable display of misplaced pride if ever there was one. But as for me?" He did something with his glass of wine that seemed to take in the whole of the room, the cottage, perhaps the world. Certainly her. "I have made so many fortunes that it cannot matter if I lose three. Or even ten. Call it insurance if you will."

But he did not sound pleased by this. He sounded wrecked, and she hated it.

"Ranieri," she whispered. "Surely you must know—"

"I will show you what I know best," he told her then, his voice dark and grave.

But when he moved, coming to pull her out of her chair, his kiss lit them both on fire.

And he made love to her like a man possessed that night. First there on the couch in that sitting room. Then he carried her upstairs, spent some time with her in the spacious bath, and then ripped her to shreds in their bed.

Again and again.

Annika thrilled to it all.

He was ruthless and demanding, and she felt as if she'd been made for this. Made for him, to meet his need, his hunger. To match his ruthlessness with her own.

To make certain that both of them burned bright and long, together.

And in the morning, she woke as he surged inside her once more, framing her face with his big, restless hands, his gaze pinning her to the mattress in the early morning light.

Usually their mornings were flash fires, bold and bright and fast-moving, but today was different.

He moved slow, setting them both to smoldering. So slow that every thrust took forever, and every retreat felt like a loss.

Still, he held her gaze. Still, he held her face in his hands.

With every deep, beautiful thrust, he broke her heart.

And when it was done, Annika lay in the bed and understood that she was already repeating the mistake his grandmother had made.

She was in love with him. Irrevocably, unpardonably, and not at all *temporarily* in love.

And looking back, she thought as she sat in the bath again—sinking down until her whole body was submerged by the warm water, save her face—it was possible she always had been.

More than possible. Likely.

This morning's lovemaking had stripped away the last of her defenses, and she could see everything so clearly now. She had met him when she was barely sixteen and had hated the very sight of him—but what use could she possibly have had for silly boys after a sight of Ranieri? She'd gone on to college, where so many of her friends had experimented with passion and longing, crushes and relationships, but never Annika.

Some part of her must have known all along that she could settle for no substitutes. Even though she'd continued to despise him. Even though she'd considered him the bane of her existence.

Maybe there had been something in her that had sensed the kind of fire they would kindle together, all along.

"It's all right," she assured herself as she rose from the bath and got dressed in her walking clothes, an easy pair of soft overalls, a chambray shirt, a wide-brimmed hat. "It's all going to be all right."

Because it was clear to her that last night's storytelling had indeed been a cautionary tale—but for her, not him.

She stopped by the portrait of his grandmother that hung in the hall outside their bedroom. "I will not make the same mistake you did," she promised this woman long gone, who had been punished for her heart. "I won't tell him."

Though she understood why the other woman had made the choice she had. Annika could feel her heart beating too fast. She could *feel* her own heart. And she knew that there was nothing more she wanted to tell Ranieri than the truth.

Even though she knew he wouldn't take it well.

She would hold it inside. She would keep it sacred, and hers. And as long as she didn't say it, she didn't see why she couldn't have this year of theirs.

And maybe more than this year, a voice in her whispered, because in everything concerning this man, she was so greedy. So interminably greedy. *If you play your cards right.*

Annika almost laughed at that as she made her way down the stairs, heading toward Ranieri's study on autopilot. Because when had she ever been even remotely good at cards?

Well, she would have to learn. And in the meantime, she would take all these new, unwieldy feelings and keep them where they belonged. Deep inside her. Hidden away, like treasures too precious to be taken out in the light.

She could do it, she was sure.

Or in any event, she *would* do it.

But when she pushed open the door to Ranieri's study, she didn't have to worry that he might see her love for him all over her face.

Because he wasn't alone.

And she was certain she knew exactly who the two older people were who sat there on the couch of the study, neither one of them looking pleased. If she looked closely, she was certain she could see the man she loved in both of them.

Her gaze flew to Ranieri as he stood there at the mantel, looking…cold and cruel.

As distant as if none of these sweet honeymoon days had ever happened.

"*Buongiorno*, Annika," he said, but not in the way he normally said her name. Not with that dark delight she'd come to depend on. "How kind of you to join us. May I present my parents. It appears they have invited themselves along on our honeymoon."

CHAPTER NINE

RANIERI TOLD HIMSELF he was grateful.

Grateful that he had not spoken this morning, so deep inside Annika's body that he had somehow felt that he was turned inside out. He had not said the things he knew he shouldn't. He had fought back all those strange and terrible feelings that had broken loose after their conversation the night before. When he had never wished to speak to her of *pride* at all.

That was not the word he wanted to use, not when he came to Annika. This woman who took everything he threw at her, wrapped it up in endless delight, and then asked for more.

In his whole life, Ranieri had never met anyone who did not grow weary of his intensity. He had never spent this amount of unrestricted time with a woman. Or with anyone. He had learned long ago that he was better— more effective, even—in small doses. He had come to think of that as a virtue.

But then there was Annika, who had all but lived in his skin for weeks now, and showed no signs at all of wanting or needing a break.

If anything, she seemed to want more.

She was a wonder.

And he had nearly opened his mouth and said the kinds of things he couldn't take back.

The kind of things that would ruin them.

So really, all things considered, he found himself profoundly grateful that his parents had arrived, unannounced, this morning of all mornings.

His mother, the perpetually dissatisfied Paola, did not openly sneer at her new, American daughter-in-law. Instead, she only treated Annika to a slow perusal, from head to toe and back again, making it clear that she was not impressed with what she saw. "I see that you've taken to country life with enthusiasm," she said.

Ranieri wanted to take his mother apart for that snide tone. But before he could find a way to do that without also showing how much he cared about Annika—information his mother would only use as ammunition, which he could not allow—Annika herself laughed.

"You must forgive me," she said, her voice warm and something like merry. "I'm on my way to my morning walk out in the fields. I had no idea Ranieri was entertaining or I would have changed into something more appropriate."

She glanced down at her clothes as if she'd been off rolling around in the dirt when she looked the way she always did. Beautiful. Natural and unstudied, and Ranieri thought that Paola, with her penciled-on brows and dark grooves of disappointment bracketing her lips, would do well to take a page from Annika's book.

"Your mother has apparently come here to make uncivil remarks," said his father. "I did not."

Giuseppe Furlan looked more like his only son than Ranieri cared to acknowledge. Because looking at his father was always like looking into a kind of fun house mirror. It was a view of the future, but a future that required that Ranieri make a certain set of unpalatable choices. To be embittered, always. To make the same mistakes again and again. And to blame others instead of himself, forever. If he took care to do those things then Ranieri was sure to find himself with those same stooped shoulders and his father's indignant chin.

A fate worse than death, Ranieri had long believed.

Giuseppe barely even glanced at Annika, its own insult. "I have a very important investment opportunity I need to speak to you about, Ranieri. This is a business call."

Ranieri offered what he hoped passed for some kind of a smile, though it felt far too harsh. "Perhaps you both missed the news," he said, a deep chill in his voice. "I am on my honeymoon. This is my wife. You appear to have forgotten to offer us your felicitations. An oversight, I am certain."

"I had no idea you were even getting married," his mother said querulously, but with enough heat that he suspected he'd hit upon her true reason for coming here today. "How do you think that made me look? You didn't even think to invite your own *mother*!"

There were a great many things Ranieri could have said to that, all of them unkind. But instead, Annika went and sat next to his mother on the couch, reminding him that despite the way high society New York liked to talk about Bennett Schuyler's supposedly shameful daughter, she was, in fact, the consummate hostess. Her manners were exquisite. Here, when it counted, not out there in public where everything most people did was a bid for status and points.

"It happened so quickly," Annika was saying. "And it's all my fault. My father died so suddenly, you see. He'd been in a coma for a long while, and then there at the end…well. I didn't see it coming." She kept smiling in that engaging way of hers, despite the sour expression Paola offered her in return. "Our wedding was very quick and very small. But you must forgive Ranieri. I'm sure that he wanted to wait until his whole family was there, but it wasn't possible."

Ranieri stood there, battling warring urges within him. He wanted to throw his parents out. But then, he always did. He wanted to protect Annika, even though he knew if he did that, his parents would focus on her in a way he knew he *really* wouldn't like.

And beneath all of that, he wanted to live in the version of their story that Annika was telling. Where everything between them was clean and new and theirs. No wills, no games of one-upmanship. Only a man and a woman who had rushed to marry because they wanted each other that badly.

What did it say about him that he wanted that to be real?

It should have shaken him that here in this cottage, so far away from reality, he had almost convinced himself that it was.

"Congratulations on your union," Giuseppe said grudgingly. His cold eyes moved over Annika, then dismissed her. Another insult Ranieri would have dearly liked to address, but that was the trouble with his parents. Calling attention to their behavior only made it worse. "I'm certain the wedding was charming. How nice. But I would really like to talk to you about this investment. This one is a sure thing."

Ranieri stood there, frozen at the mantel. His parents were playing their usual games, here in this cottage that was all things elegant and graceful but was still nothing more than a monument his grandmother had built to her own loneliness.

And he felt nothing but dirty.

He might thunder on about the Furlan pride, but pride wasn't what he felt when he was around these people. It was this other thing.

They were a stain and he had never been able to wash it clean.

And he might have tried to conceal that stain with money, businesses, properties, too many women. He might have found ways to pretend.

But at the end of the day, it always came down to this. His mother's inability to think of anyone or anything but herself. His father's obvious feeling of entitlement to his son's hard-earned and long-kept wealth. When he'd been young, the details might have been different but the end result had always been the same. Anything he did was an insult to his mother, if she chose to take it that way, and whatever it was had to be scrutinized to see if it might be an opportunity for his father to leverage his own interests.

They had never cared about anything else. He knew that despite their divorce the two of them met regularly to discuss all the ways Ranieri had let them down and what they could do to force him into line. This cottage was his favorite place on the planet, but he only used it sparingly, because they had their spies in this valley and they always descended upon him here.

He would have said he'd grown immune to them.

But today, in the middle of the same old story sat Annika. His Annika, looking fresh and pretty and entirely his.

And she did not belong here, with them, where they could get that stain on her, too. The certainty of that was like concrete, falling through him like so much stone.

Yet he understood it now, what had happened last night. What he'd almost said this morning. Annika made him feel clean. She made him imagine that there was something more to him than his father's grift and his mother's complaints. Of all the women he had ever been with, Annika was the one who should have wanted him least. And she was the one who'd asked him for nothing.

It was no wonder at all that she was the only one he wanted. The only one he could not be without.

For it was clear to him now, standing in this study while his parents began to bicker and Annika sat between them looking serene, that there was no reason he should have adhered to even one of the stipulations attached to that will. It might have been inconvenient to start over, but as he'd told Annika already, that was what he excelled at. That was what he did.

He didn't need the Schuyler Corporation at all.

But he was very much afraid he might need her.

And it was not lost on him that acknowledging this now, with his sordid past on excruciating display, was as good as not acknowledging it at all. And no matter that the admission made everything inside him seem to slide off the side of the planet, even if he made it only to himself.

"You always do this," his mother was saying shrilly to his father. "You always try to cut me out. I won't let you do it this time."

"I owe you nothing, woman," Giuseppe retorted, with a snort of laughter. "You've already sucked me dry."

He remembered Annika telling him what he was sure he already knew on some level, but could see with such unfortunate clarity now. That obviously this display was why he put such stock in good breeding, good manners, and the trappings of civility. Like proper dress, as if allowing so much as a tendril to break free from a chignon signaled the end of civilization.

Because, after all, that was what he knew. Anything could set either one of them off, and then they were here again. In this swamp of accusation and threat, insult and anger.

His childhood in a nutshell.

"Ranieri," his father all but bellowed. "You really must give me a few moments of your attention. Have you no head for business?"

"Ranieri," shrieked his mother, not to be outdone, "what kind of unnatural son are you, to hate your own mother so much that you would not only bar me from your wedding, but ignore me in your own home?"

And he felt something inside him, like a cracking. Maybe it was a shattering.

Whatever it was, it was as clarifying as it was unpleasant.

Across from him, it was as if Annika could read what was happening. As if she alone could read *him*, when he would have sworn no one could. She stood, smiling at Paola and Giuseppe in turn.

"How wonderful that you could come to catch up," she said smoothly, as if that was something either one of them would ever think to do. "I'll have a light lunch put together, so we can all enjoy each other's company." She nodded at Giuseppe. "Why don't you stay here and have a little chat with Ranieri. This is the perfect time." Then she smiled encouragingly at Paola. "I'm not ashamed to say this is a bit overwhelming for me. Maybe you can come and show me how it's done?"

His mother looked back and forth between them, as if deciding whether or not she was winding up to pitch a larger fit. But her sense of her own magnificence won out, as it usually did. Because she enjoyed nothing more than telling others how they were doing things wrong. He imagined she would enjoy it even more than usual, here in his house.

Ranieri wanted to pull Annika to him. He wanted to kiss her mouth again and lose himself there, because he had the sinking feeling that kisses like that were lim-

ited. More limited than he might have imagined before
his parents had turned up here today.

Instead he had to settle for her smile as she led Paola
away.

He had to watch her leave him, looking wholly at
her ease, as if she could think of nothing better to do
than spend time with a woman so toxic that Ranieri had
never known her to have a single friend. Not one. If he
had not seen the photographs of his mother when she
was young and almost ethereally beautiful, he would
have assumed that she'd somehow blackmailed his father into marriage.

The truth, he knew, was worse. They had been mad
for each other, but all that heat had turned into hatred.

It was a lesson Ranieri had no desire to learn.

After the door closed behind the women, his father
launched into his latest ridiculous pitch, but all Ranieri
could think about was Annika.

Because he understood now that he had no choice.
He needed to end this.

It had already gone too far.

Later that evening, he waited for her in the small sitting room off their bedroom, a bright sanctuary he remembered from his childhood. This cottage had been
his refuge. Here, his grandmother was an interested yet
soothing authority figure—a far cry from his parents.
His grandmother had liked to sit here to catch the afternoon light on her needlework and he'd always joined
her, when he was still small enough to lie before her on
the floor, or pretend to read his own book at her side.

I wish I could live here forever, he had said, more than once.

But she had always responded the same way. *It is true that home is where you make it,* she'd replied. *But sometimes we are drawn to places because they permit us to hide.* And she had looked at him, her brown eyes so wise. *But we are Furlans, you and I, for good or ill. Much as we might wish to hide forever, we know we can't.*

Ranieri had remembered those words his whole life. He had used them as a guide.

He hid from nothing. He faced everything head-on, always.

Or he had, until Annika.

So there was no one he could blame this on but him.

Perhaps that made him colder when Annika finally came upstairs after the interminable dinner with his mother was finally done, and Paola had been packed off to a car that he hoped would take her far, far away from here.

His father had left in a rage much earlier, after Ranieri's typical, inevitable refusal to invest in anything he brought to the table. The good news about that was that it had left one fewer parent to remind Ranieri of his own shortcomings. The bad news was that the remaining parent was Paola.

And even though he could have recited her many litanies of victimization by heart, every word she'd uttered had seemed like a nail in the coffin of Ranieri's marriage. One after the next, all evening long. Because his mother managed to pollute a place as impossibly graceful as his grandmother's house with her usual poison. He didn't think she had even been trying all that hard. It was that easy for her.

What made him think that he wouldn't do the same thing, given time?

How could he imagine that he could hold on to something as clean and bright as Annika? He knew what would happen if he did. He would be the one to get his grubby fingerprints all over her. He would be the one to turn her around, taking all that bright defiance and greedy need and turning it sour.

He did not think he could bear it.

"You're never in here," came her happy voice from behind him, and when he turned, she was smiling at him.

So artlessly. So easily. The wedding at her museum had changed everything. Before that, he knew she'd been desperate to embarrass him enough that he'd break it off. After that, she'd been his.

Maybe that museum of hers was enchanted after all.

But the trouble was, Ranieri did not believe in enchantments. He believed in evidence. And he had a preponderance of that, all of it pointing in the same direction.

That still didn't mean he wanted to do this.

"Why are you looking at me like that?" Annika asked, her voice soft even as a frown gathered between her eyes.

He waited. She blinked, then looked around the sitting room. And he knew the precise moment she saw her own bags, packed and waiting. She sucked in a breath.

"Are we going on a trip?" she asked.

Ranieri was known for never hesitating. For always shooting to kill, never waiting to see what might happen first. But he knew that there would always be a *before* and *after* this moment. And he wasn't ready to be done with the before.

If he'd known that this morning would be the end this thing between them, he wouldn't have changed a thing. But perhaps he would have savored it even more.

"I'm going to Shanghai," he told her, sounding too dark. Too stiff. "You're going to New York."

Her frowned deepened. She threaded her fingers together before her and he knew, by now, how that little gesture betrayed her unease. A month ago, he wouldn't have cared. Tonight, it moved in him like anguish. But it changed nothing.

"I always knew this couldn't last forever, Ranieri." Her voice was calm. Smooth. It was precisely why he had to do this now, before she couldn't maintain her composure in his presence. Before they were no better than Giuseppe and Paola, so committed to their own misery they didn't care who witnessed it. "But why are you announcing the end of our honeymoon like this?"

"It has been nearly three weeks. I think we both know that there was only so long I can continue to ignore my responsibilities."

That furrow between her brows deepened. "I have responsibilities, too. Not that it's a competition. But the point of a honeymoon is to take a break from them."

"You leave within the hour," he told her shortly. "I

will have a driver take you to the airfield. You'll be back in New York before you know it."

Her green eyes narrowed slightly. "You say that as if more than our honeymoon is ending."

And he'd known she wouldn't be satisfied. He'd known she would ask. There was no possibility that she was ever going to get on that plane without demanding to know his feelings—even if she would never ask about his feelings directly.

Ranieri had come to know this woman entirely too well. That was part of the problem.

"We've already stayed here too long," he said, in forbidding tones. "My parents have little to recommend them, but neither one of them has ever cared much for this house. I understand them completely. It seeps into the bones and slows you down. Stay here too long and you will almost certainly lose your edge."

"Indeed," Annika said dryly. "I believe that's called *relaxing.*"

And he was not accustomed to acting against his own self-interest. He could not recall the last time he had wanted something and denied himself.

Only this woman could have inspired such a choice.

He tried to concentrate on that. "You were a virgin, Annika, were you not."

It wasn't a question. And he didn't need an answer. He already knew, but even if he hadn't, he would have gotten the truth from the scalding-hot flush that took over her face. It wouldn't stop there. It would be all over her now, that bright heat sweeping down between her breasts—

She stood taller, as if she wasn't overheating right in front of him. "I feel certain that cannot possibly be relevant to this conversation."

"But you did not tell me, which suggests it was meaningful to you."

"What it was or wasn't hardly matters now."

"You asked me if I could tell." His voice was quiet.

She blanched as if he'd shouted. "You put great stock in *sophistication*, Ranieri. I hated to disappoint. And in any case, you didn't ask me. I didn't think it mattered."

He knew that was not at all what she had thought. And he was beginning to understand exactly why he preferred not to get this close to anyone. Why he preferred to know less, not more, about the women in his life.

This was painful.

Yet he pushed on. "You did not choose to tell me, Annika. It is not the same thing. But it does not matter. I will tell you this. Sex can be powerful. When it's done well, it can feel life altering. You know this now, yes? Yet these are all just feelings. Yours are likely to be more intense, as they are new."

"Wait." She shook her head as if there was too much noise in there for her to concentrate. Or as if he was the noise. "Are you, of all people, lecturing me on *feelings*?"

Ranieri couldn't say he liked the way she asked that. And he liked even less how it landed in him, but he shoved it aside. "I admired your father," he told her, his voice clipped. "I was fond of him. I know that worry over you, and what might become of you, consumed him in those last days before his coma. It pleases me that I've been able to help you on his behalf."

She let out a soft sound that he would not quite call a laugh. "How kind of you. You are known for your kindness, of course." Annika shook her head. "Do you really believe that Bennett Schuyler's dearest wish for his only daughter involved her being sent back home in the middle of her honeymoon?"

He was clenching his jaw and he forced himself to release it. "The fault is mine." At least that part was true. Ranieri inclined his head. "I should have known that making such demands of a virgin might create problems. You don't have the perspective necessary to handle my appetites in full. I should have gone with my first instinct."

And it killed him that as he spoke, she changed. The light in her eyes dimmed. She still clutched her hands before her, but her body—so supple, so soft—had gone rigid.

"I should have gone with mine," she said, and her voice was too cold. Too unlike her. He almost reached out, but he remembered himself in the last moment, and there was nothing to do with her brittle smile but endure it. "I was only sixteen. You came to our front door like a storm cloud and I said to myself, *That man is the devil.* I was right."

"It seems that we were both right," Ranieri gritted out. "All the more reason to stop pretending otherwise, do you not agree?"

And he would never know how long it was they stood

there, staring at each other, neither one of them saying a word.

Neither one of them reaching out.

Ranieri told himself this was a good thing. Or if not good, it was the right thing. And that would have to do.

He thought they could have stood there for a lifetime or two, but then the headlights of the car he'd called for her swept through the darkness outside the window, and the spell was broken.

The staff came to get her bags. And she stood there a moment longer, still looking at him with that imploring expression as if she thought that could reach him. As if she was debating whether or not she should throw herself into his arms—

And Ranieri knew that if she did, he would catch her. He wouldn't be able to help himself. But she didn't.

Instead, Annika turned and walked away, and took all the light in the world behind her.

CHAPTER TEN

IT WAS A long and bitter fall.

Back in New York, Annika immersed herself in the life she'd left behind and called herself lucky that it was still there, waiting for her to wake up from the dream she'd been in and remember herself.

Even if she felt a deep well of embarrassment within her because she knew how little she'd wanted to do anything but lose herself in Italy—and in Ranieri—forever.

Well. She liked to call it *embarrassment*, but she knew it was something far deeper than that. It was the way her heart beat now, and the hurt in it. It was the way the world seemed changed all around her. Darker, dimmer. Even in this city that seemed too bright to her after the soft, sultry Italian dark.

When she first landed in New York, she'd almost asked that the car drop her off at her father's old apartment, but bit back the request. Like it or not, she had married Ranieri.

That meant that if he wanted her to move out, he would have to say so and if he did, she would win.

And that was all she had left. Winning this thing.

Ranieri did not come back to New York for three long weeks. And when he did, he was a different man. Or rather, he was the man she'd always thought he was before all of this. Grim. Disapproving. Unimpressed with her in every possible way.

There were no cozy lunches. There were no intimate dinners.

There was no waking up to find him so deep inside her that she was shattering into bright, hot pieces before she'd fully come out of her dreams.

That she cried about these losses, alone in her room at night, was something she would deny if asked. But he never asked. That she had missed him—and still missed him—so horribly that it was like a flu, was something she thought she would rather die than admit.

"Is it already happening?" she asked him one night as they returned from one of the social events he insisted they attend. Because his appearance was always necessary. He left her to handle whatever social niceties were called for and closed business deals over drinks. It would have felt like a partnership, she supposed, if he didn't treat her like a questionable employee. And if she didn't have this regrettable need to torture herself like this, dashing herself against the sullen stone of his new indifference to her. "Are you already cheating on me?"

"I would not consider it cheating if I were," he replied from the other side of the car, his voice sounding gravelly. She glanced at him, watching the lights from the Manhattan street outside the windows wash over his hard face. Harder these days. "You were as blackmailed into this marriage as I was. There was nothing in your father's will about fidelity, Annika. I think you know this."

"Yes or no?"

"And if I say yes?"

It cost her something to shrug then, with such unconcern. Such blasé sophistication. That was what she'd learned, night after night, out swimming with these sharks she liked so little. That was what he wanted, wasn't it?

And it wasn't truly killing her. It only felt like it might.

"Then I will congratulate you and wish you well. The tabloids are certain to make sure the whole world knows if you're cheating, and that would reflect badly on both of us. I was hoping you and I could come to an arrangement before that happens, but not if there's already other women in the mix. That seems entirely too unsavory."

She felt the heat of his gaze on the side of her face. "An arrangement?"

"You're not the only one with needs, Ranieri."

He sighed, managing to make it sound withering. "*Amore.* Please. You are only embarrassing yourself."

She wanted to hurt him then. She actually felt *bloodthirsty.* But she wanted this more. Even if he kept calling her *amore*, which seemed more mocking and pointed each time.

Annika was sure he meant it to feel that way, like a blade beneath her skin. Because he was banking on the possibility that he could win that way.

Because that was the game. Hadn't she thought of it

as a game, long ago? And now there was nothing left but to play it.

"I don't feel the slightest bit embarrassed," she told him, still managing to keep her voice cool. "You introduced me to sex. I'd like more of it. If we decide that stepping outside the marriage isn't cheating, then I suppose that opens doors. It just sounds a bit inconvenient, that's all."

And she would never know how she sounded so bored. All the many polished and poisonous society events she'd been forced to attend had finally paid off, apparently. Because she sounded like the rest of them now.

Ranieri let out another one of those sighs. "Forgive me, Annika, but surely what happened in Italy has proven that you cannot handle having sex with me. You become too emotional. You want it to mean things that it cannot."

Yes, she thought balefully. *I am the emotional one here.*

"We live together, I like orgasms, and I thought you could help," she said, impatiently. "But believe me, this conversation makes me wish I was dead. So by all means, find yourself the emotionless mistress of your dreams. I will handle my own needs however I see fit."

He didn't say anything, but when they stepped into his elevator, she was sure she could feel a kind of edgy heat emanating from him. And when the doors opened and let them into his apartment, she'd taken all of three angry strides when he was on her.

And it wasn't like Italy. It wasn't languorous. It

wasn't an endless, rolling delight, or feeling as if the two of them were one.

It was hot. Furious. He lifted her up, dug beneath her dress, and dragged her legs around his waist. Then he held her there, pressing her back against the nearest wall, as he reached between them to free himself, ripped off her panties, then plunged deep.

It was a mad gallop to a blistering finish, and when he was done, when she was limp and wheezing, he stepped back and fixed himself while she clung to the wall and pretended she really believed her legs could hold her.

"Sleep well, *amore*," he said, his voice dark, then he left her there.

And for some time in those darkest days of the year, that was what it was like between them. They lived separate lives. They came together for the usual social events. And there was sex, but it was always about the goal, not the journey.

There was nothing wrong with that, necessarily. It was still mind-blowing. It was still Ranieri.

But she knew the shift was deliberate.

And, yes, when it was done she would sob out her love, her loneliness into her shower, but surely as long as no one knew that but her it didn't count. It swirled its way down the drain and was gone again by morning.

Annika just kept telling herself that she could live with it. One way or another, she *would* live with it.

Not because you want to win this, that voice would whisper as she lay in her bed, alone, her eyes swollen from tears. *But because you cannot bear to leave him, even now.*

It was obvious to her that she'd missed something that day with his parents. Not everybody was lucky enough to have family they admired, the way she had admired and loved her father, and the memories of her mother. Not everyone had even a family they liked. If anything, meeting Ranieri's parents had made her love who he'd made himself even more.

Because they'd certainly given him no guidance. In anything. That much was clear.

She knew that he'd decided to end what had been happening between the two of them because of that day even though she'd thought they'd handled the situation about as well as it could have been handled.

The real truth, that she could admit only late, late at night when her heart ached for him, was that Annika persisted in believing that if she could just hold on, he would come back to her.

But as the long, cold fall wore on, Ranieri showed no signs of blinking.

It was coming on the middle of December when she caught up with one of her college friends one evening. It was a chilly night, though outside, the city was festive. She had become adept at avoiding the paparazzi these days, or perhaps they'd finally grown bored with her. Either way, she had no photographers on her tail when she slipped into a quiet booth in the sort of restaurant Ranieri would never frequent, looking forward to an evening of nostalgia and laughter in thankfully unpretentious surroundings.

But her friend was looking at her mobile phone when Annika sat down, and smiled oddly when she looked up again. "Congratulations, Annika. It looks like you won."

"I won?" Annika shook her head, not understanding. "What did I win?"

Her friend swiveled the screen of her phone around and showed it to Annika. "It says it right here. Ranieri Furlan is leaving the Schuyler Corporation. Annika. *You did it.*"

And later, her friend would tell her that it was as if Annika had been hit in the head. She had stared back at that phone for far too long. She didn't respond when her friend tried to speak to her.

Then she'd simply stood and walked out.

Annika wasn't aware of any of that. She had a vague impression of running down a side street on the Upper West Side, then angrily hailing a taxi out on Columbus. Then she sat in the back of the cab and stared out blankly at storefronts and bodegas done up in holiday splendor, crowds on the street, and the usual outraged honking from too many vehicles trying to make their way around Manhattan.

She suffered through the slowest elevator in the history of the universe at Ranieri's loft down in Tribeca, but when it finally opened on his floor, he wasn't home. She even checked up on the roof, though she knew he rarely ventured there.

But he was nowhere to be found, so she headed to the only other place she knew he was likely to be, even in the wake of his announcement.

And just like the last time she'd marched into the

Schuyler Corporation offices bearing a potted plant, the reception desk was no match for her.

"You can't just walk back there," the poor woman tried to tell her.

Annika smiled. "Do you know who I am?" she asked. Nicely, she thought.

Wide-eyed, the woman nodded.

"Wonderful, then you know my name."

"Yes, Mrs. Furlan." The woman bit the name off, not that Annika could blame her. "I know who you are and your name, but—"

"That's Annika *Schuyler* Furlan," Annika corrected her, jabbing her finger toward the logo on the wall behind the woman's head. "That's my name right there. I think I can go where I want, don't you?"

She didn't get the impression the woman did think that. But Annika knew she wouldn't stop her. And it felt like déjà vu to march down these halls again, this time unencumbered by a pot of dahlias. But weighed down all the same, this time by what she wished was a righteous fury—but she was fairly certain it was fear.

Just sheer terror that he was really leaving the company, and therefore her.

He wasn't in his office, so she turned and marched along the same hall he'd once escorted her down with his arm around her shoulders. And that silly plant held before him.

And it felt not only right, but good to throw open the doors of his conference room and march in once again.

This time, Ranieri was the only one inside. He sat at the head of the table, surrounded by what appeared to be even more stacks of paper, file folders, and not one but two laptops.

"Hello, Annika," he said, with only a brief glance up her way. He managed to make that withering, too. "I take it you've heard the news."

She only realized now that she'd been running around this whole time—through the city, through his loft, through this office—because it was difficult to catch her breath. But she made herself slow down and try, because she could tell by the way he was deliberately not looking at her that he was trying to get under her skin. He expected her to fly off the handle.

And she understood that though this felt like one more round of their same game, the stakes tonight were higher.

The stakes tonight were everything.

As if he hadn't already conceded.

Oddly enough, that made her think she still had a chance to change his mind.

And she had been waiting all this time for just this. Just one chance.

"I went into your office before I came here," she said, a strange sort of calm washing through her despite the hurry and rush and worry that had propelled her here. She studied him. "I see you still have our plant. The embodiment of our love."

He threw his pen onto the pad before him and sat back in his chair, then took a moment to make a meal out of arranging his features into something suggesting an attempt at patience more than patience itself. "I cannot claim to have a green thumb, of course. That would be my assistant. Gregory can make anything grow, apparently."

Even your silly plant, was the obvious next line, though he didn't say it.

"I only have one question for you," Annika said, instead of chasing down the things he hadn't said.

And she wished that she'd known what this night would bring. She would have dressed the way he liked best. That sophistication, that hint of glamour. Because he'd taught her the language of fine clothing and she was fluent in it now. Instead, she'd spent the day in the museum and had dressed for that, followed by a dinner with an old college friend. She was wearing her usual uniform of jeans tucked into boots and a cozy sweater to keep the chill off. But if she was right—and she had to be right, or she didn't know what she would do with herself, or how she would possibly survive this—none of that actually mattered.

She moved farther into the room, peeling off her coat and tossing it on the conference room table. Then she kept going until she could take the seat catty-corner to him, pulling it in close so she was right there. Right next to him.

Then it was her turn to put on a little show of resting her chin on her hands and gazing at him as if her whole life hung in the balance here.

Because it did.

"Whatever you're about to do or say, don't," Ranieri said, his voice forbidding. Not so much withering as gruff. "No round of rainbow unicorns is going to change anything. There is nothing that requires changing, in any case. I have simply come to the conclusion that the inconvenience of looking for another company to run pales in comparison to the inconvenience of being married."

"You don't actually mean *married*, though," Annika corrected him, and though it was a fight to keep her voice even, she managed it. "You mean married to *me*. Because you take your grandfather's position on this one, don't you? You should be allowed to do whatever you want, without question. Isn't that right?"

His eyes blazed, and that stark mouth of his thinned.

"Yes," he said, though his jaw looked tight enough to shatter. "Precisely."

She could have pointed out how little he thought of his grandfather's pride, but she didn't. She could have asked him if he thought that his own father's behavior, not to mention his marriage, perhaps followed on directly from the choices his grandfather had made. It seemed like a straight line to her. But she didn't ask him that, either.

Because all of that was noise.

Last night had been a rare night without an event, so she'd gone up to the roof to sit in the hot tub for a while. Then she'd stood out in the cold until it made her shake before going into the hot water again.

She called it therapy.

When she'd come back down into the loft, Ranieri had been finishing a call. He'd tossed his cell phone aside as he came in the kitchen. One look at her, her hair piled on top of her head, wearing nothing but a robe, his golden eyes had gone molten.

And the next thing she'd known, Annika had been flat on her back in his bed and he had been pounding into her in another scalding, blistering rush to that beautiful finish.

But when she'd made as if to roll away, to gather her robe and make her way back to her room—lest she get any ideas that might turn into emotions, the horror—he had pulled her back into place beside him.

He had taken her again and again that night.

The last time, so late at night it had become early the next morning, it had been like that final morning in Italy.

Slow. Intense.

Shattering, inside and out.

When she'd woken up hours later to find herself still in his bed, he'd been gone.

But she understood now.

She reached over and gripped his hands in hers, holding tight because she expected him to pull away.

"Ranieri." Annika said his name softly, like some kind of prayer. "When did you decide that you were doomed, no matter what you did?"

CHAPTER ELEVEN

HER WORDS WENT through him like a thunderclap.

Ranieri jerked back, and only some distant hint of self-preservation kept him from leaping out of his chair and doing something he would never have forgiven himself for—like plastering himself to the far wall.

As if he was some kind of excitable feline.

His heart careened about inside his chest anyway. Surely he didn't have to *show* it.

He regarded her for a long, tense moment.

"I don't know what you mean," he gritted out.

But Annika didn't look as if she was trying to fight with him. It was far worse than that. She looked…compassionate.

It was unbearable.

"This is exactly what I was afraid of," he seethed at her. "This indiscriminate emotion just flung about. This is a conference room. We are in an office building. This is no place—"

"I love you," Annika said, and could not have silenced him in any more effective manner. And then she made it worse by smiling. "Though I think you know that. Or you wouldn't be reacting this way."

This time, Ranieri did push back from the table. He stood, though he still did not cling to the wall. He stalked to the bank of windows and tried to orient himself in the ever-shifting, ever-changing city at his feet.

Manhattan seemed infinitely easier to take on than the woman behind him.

The woman he couldn't seem to escape—even when she wasn't in the same room. She had haunted him across the planet. Even now, he was sure he could catch the hint of her scent in the air, that perfect vanilla, yet better.

Much better.

"But it's even worse than that, isn't it?" she asked from behind him. "It's far worse."

And how could he have guessed, all those years ago, that this woman would be the end of him? That the daughter of a business associate he had only ever noticed to criticize could wreck him so easily?

Because he knew what she was going to say. Every muscle in his body tensed.

"You love me, too, Ranieri."

He turned back around to face her then, everything inside him a frenzy of heat and need and feeling and *her*.

"And what a gift that will be for you," he all but snarled at her. "The love of a Furlan. Where would you like to isolate yourself, *amore*? Tell me, where do you think you would most like to hide away your broken heart while I betray you again and again and again? Because I will. We always do."

"I'm not your grandmother," she replied.

She stood up from the table then, coming around the end of it and heading straight for him.

Ranieri could not imagine how he had ever thought that this woman was plain. That she was anything but what he saw before him now.

Fierce and glorious with it. Carelessly sophisticated.

So beautiful it hurt.

That was the trouble. That was what he couldn't seem to get around. This woman *hurt* him. He looked at her and he hurt. He touched her and he hurt.

He had built himself an entire life to avoid hurt. He had walled himself off in a fortress of money and power. And none of that had mattered at all.

Annika Schuyler had walked right past his defenses and insinuated herself so deep inside him that now when he was without her, that hurt, too.

Ranieri didn't know what to *do* about her—and that was a new sensation for him. He always knew what to do.

"Not only am I not your grandmother," she was saying as she came toward him, "you'll notice that I haven't given you any ultimatums. I haven't asked you to give up anything at all. That must be very frustrating for you, Ranieri. Because that was clearly your brilliant plan."

He made a low noise, something too close to a growl. "I don't understand how you could put up with a husband who treats you as I do. What does that say about you?"

But she laughed. That silky brown hair spilled all around her, and she laughed.

"It says that I'm in love with an idiot," she replied, still coming closer to him, so that he had to worry that he might not keep his hands to himself. That he might give in to that fire in him all over again. "And I've been waiting him out."

He wanted to order her to keep her distance, but he couldn't do it.

And he had brought this upon himself. He should never have allowed her to convince him that they should bring sex back into their marriage. He'd known better.

But the truth was, he had spent three gruesome weeks alone in Shanghai and had been weak with longing. Weak for her.

Always and only for her.

And at first, Ranieri had been confident he could keep himself under control. Treating sex between them like it was no more than scratching an itch couldn't last. He'd expected that she would object. It would be too much for her. He was certain she would break down one of these nights and demand more. Demand better.

But he'd been the one who'd broken last night. He'd happened upon her in the kitchen, rosy from the hot tub's heat, wrapped in nothing but a soft robe, like a fantasy he hadn't known he'd had. He had kept her in his bed, making love to her again and again. Until this morning, when he'd realized there was no part of him that wanted to leave her in that bed.

There was no part of him that wanted to leave her at all.

That was when he'd understood, in the starkest possible terms, the magnitude of his mistake.

There had only been one possible thing left to do. Only one out, and he'd taken it. And had then spent the day in crisis talks with the Schuyler Corporation's Board of Directors.

And yet the only thing he could seem to think about was Annika.

Who'd been waiting him out all this time.

"I love you, Ranieri," she said again, her voice that much fiercer now that she was closer. Her green eyes ablaze.

And she didn't stop when she reached him. She kept right on going until she rested her palms on his chest.

He reached up to pull her hands away from him, because touching led nowhere manageable. He'd tried that. But he found himself holding her hands instead. Cradled in his, as if this was a proposal instead of him ending what should never have been started.

Not that Annika seemed to be getting the message.

"I think I've loved you as long as I've known you," she told him, her words seeming to collide with all the places he *hurt* inside. "It's not an accident that you're the only man I've been with. You *are* the only man, Ranieri. The only man I ever thought about in all my life, so how could it ever have been anyone but you?"

And even now, when he should know better, there was that current of deep male satisfaction deep inside him. Because he couldn't help liking that she thought such things.

But surely that proved that he was exactly who he thought he was. Just another Furlan. Full of himself and unworthy of anyone else's love and regard.

Fear and awe in the corporate world had sustained him this long. Surely he should need nothing more.

"You deserve far better than me," he managed to grit out.

"And you deserve to believe that you are capable of loving another person without destroying them," she said, her voice intense, her green eyes steady. "Because Ranieri. Listen to me. *You are.*"

He felt something move through him, like a deep shudder. As if he was breaking into pieces when he knew he wasn't. Because she was holding him—with that gaze, with her hands in his.

She was holding him, and because of that, he was whole.

Even when he didn't feel as if he ought to have been.

"You visited my father every single day you were in this city," Annika continued, her voice low and fierce. "He was in a coma. There was no possible advantage to be gained from visiting him. No corporate reason that would explain it. I suspect you loved him. Because you went and sat with him. Every day you could, Ranieri. For five years."

He had done that. And had explained it away a thousand different times. He'd spoken of respect. Of proper behavior.

He would never have called it love. He had no experience with love, in any case.

But now, looking back, he couldn't think what else it could have been.

Because now he knew what love was.

Annika had showed him.

"You could have laughed off those additions to my

father's will," she said. "So could I. Yes, I love Schuyler House, but there were other ways I could have gone about taking charge of it. But we jumped right into this marriage instead."

"Passion fades, Annika," he said, urgently now. "And then what are you left with?"

But she only shook her head at him. "Passion fades not because passion itself is temporary. But because it can't be the only thing that links two people together. If it is, then of course, in time, it will fade. But what if it's sustained by other things? Love? Respect? Genuine affection? Why would that fade?"

He moved without meaning to, freeing one hand so he could gently cup her face. "Because you're the expert on these things."

Her gaze lightened then, but she didn't smile. "I'm an expert on you, Ranieri. I've studied you for years. Falling in love with you was a slow process that took most of my life, and then a whirlwind these few months. But it was always inevitable."

"Annika. *Amore*," he managed to say. "I cannot bear the idea that one day, without even meaning to, you and I will become my parents."

"That will never happen," she assured him, with another flash of that ferocity he loved to see in her. "Because you are not a small man, forever looking to others to make you large. And I am not a dissatisfied woman, looking for others to blame." Her lips curved then. At last. "And I always know that if all else fails, I can always roll out the unicorn initiative and get you right where I want you."

Ranieri shocked himself by laughing. Because that was what she did to him.

And suddenly, he got it. In a way he never had before. This whole time, he'd reeled from one emotion to the next, convinced that being with her was fracturing. That she was breaking him down into all these pieces—and he could only assume that this was how it began. Losing his sense of who he was, and then, and inexorably, turning into all the things he liked least about his family.

But now he knew better.

The trouble with his family was that they felt nothing. They thought only of themselves. But with Annika, he felt everything.

Everything.

He had thought of little but her since the day of that will reading. If not long before, during his five years of acting as some kind of guardian to her.

And loving her, with everything he was, with all these different parts, was the only way he would ever be anything like whole.

"Annika," he managed to say, because he got it now, and he was filled and whole and new, "I love you."

Her smile then was so brilliant, so bright, it drowned out the city outside.

"I know," she whispered. "I know you do. I love you, too."

Ranieri only remembered at the last moment that he was in the conference room in the middle of the Schuyler Corporation offices. The walls were made almost entirely of glass and half the company was right on the other side, no doubt watching every moment of this.

It would be the very opposite of appropriate to handle this moment the way he wanted to, naked and horizontal.

So he did the next best thing.

Fully aware that he would likely see a video of what he was about to do on the nightly news, Ranieri Furlan swallowed back the damnable pride that had done nothing for him in all his life, and dropped down to his knees.

"You have already married me," he said, gazing up at her as her gaze widened. "But Annika, I want you to be my wife. In full. No restrictions, no rules. I want to build a life with you and I want it all. All those words we said in our vows, I want to make them real. Sickness. Health. Richer and poor. I want them all. And I want you by my side, always."

She looked down at him, her eyes sparkling, that fathomless green. "Where else would I be?"

"I want to love you as well out of bed as I do in it," he told her gruffly, not sure he could even put into words these things he felt. But he could try. "And I promise you, I will not let the Furlan pride tear us apart. I vow it with all that I am."

"Oh," she said, though she was smiling big and bright, "you don't have to worry about that."

He gripped her hands. "Since that day in the law firm, when I heard your father's wishes, I have worried about little else."

But she smiled down at him. His wife. His love. His future.

And her smile was beautiful, as it always was, but there was steel in her gaze.

"I have my own pride," she told him then, very matter-of-factly. "And I do not intend to let you go, or to suffer in silence in some cottage in the hills, no matter how beautiful it is. If we're going to do this, Ranieri, then we do it together. All the way. Or not at all."

"That sounds like an ultimatum."

But he was smiling up at her, and she could have given him a thousand ultimatums then, for all he cared. He would have met each one.

"It's only an ultimatum if you think it's a choice," she replied, grinning. "I'm speaking of facts. That's the way it's going to be with us. I'm going to make sure of it."

"And I am going to hold you to it, Annika. Every day. For the rest of our lives."

She leaned down to kiss him, sweet and hot, and when she pulled back, they were both grinning wide. Because this was how it was going to be.

This was the beginning of the beautiful life they would build—together, this time.

Ranieri knew it. He had already created fortunes out of thin air. He defied expectations as a matter of course. He had somehow won the love of this woman when he knew he could never deserve it, or her—though he intended to dedicate his life to the art of trying.

Forever would be a piece of cake in comparison.

He would make sure of it.

CHAPTER TWELVE

ON THE FIRST anniversary of their wedding, Ranieri presented his wife with a dahlia in a pot, this time a deep shade of purple.

She only smiled, then gave him his present.

A rainbow unicorn figurine, of course. This one the size of a football.

He placed it on his desk in his office and dared anyone who saw it to comment, but they never did. No one dared.

The Schuyler Corporation had come to the conclusion that his announcement that he was leaving was a bid for better compensation, and Ranieri had felt so guilty about that that he'd donated the difference to charity—and upped the rest of his charitable contributions by double-digit percentage points.

Because at this point, he couldn't lose his fortune if he tried. So he figured he might as well try harder.

He and Annika carried on together, exactly as planned. Only with more laughter than he could have imagined. More love, more light.

That was their life together. *More.*

And on their second wedding anniversary, she presented him with a daughter.

They moved out of his Tribeca loft with the daughter who had been lovingly created in the rooftop bathhouse, back into the Schuyler Apartments on Fifth Avenue.

Where they had three floors, after all.

It was no wonder they did their best to fill them.

Ten years later, Ranieri stood in the sitting room outside their bedroom in the house in the Italian hills, where it was their custom to spend the summer far away from the demands of his job, and hers. Far away from city life and the distractions of too much technology.

He heard Annika coming, calling out as she went, corralling the children and issuing her usual commands.

When she arrived in the sitting room, she looked flushed and disheveled and more beautiful today than she had been all those years ago. She smiled when she saw him, the way she always did, and handed him the baby she held on her hip.

Their final baby, they had decided. After three girls, all of them stunners like their mother. And three boys, all of them impossible, Annika liked to say, just like him. This last had been their tiebreaker.

Accordingly, he was the most mischievous of the lot.

Ranieri loved him, as he loved all of them, with a love so deep it bordered on grief—and he had learned how to live with that.

"Are you all right?" Annika asked him now.

He followed her into their bedroom, watching as she bustled around. He found he loved this season of their lives, where the passion he always felt for her only grew—but he was always having to wait. Until the children were in bed. Until they had a moment alone. Until she took that nap she would pretend she didn't need, but always made her feel refreshed.

But Ranieri had discovered something he never would have known without her. That delayed gratification only made it better.

"I am all right," he assured her. "In every possible way."

Annika threw him a look, but she didn't comment further. Then again, she didn't have to. The longer they stayed together, the more they simply knew each other. Better and better by the day.

He couldn't wait to see what that looked like twenty years from now. Thirty.

And perhaps later, when they were alone in their bed and the children were safely tucked away in theirs, he would tell her what it was like to see his parents again as they had today. To see them the way he did these days. To feel nothing but pity.

He had vowed to Annika in a conference room in New York that he would love her forever, and he would. He did.

But what he never could have guessed—what seeing his diminished parents only made clear—was that love, deep and sure and not afraid of what life might throw at them, with vulnerability in place of pride, was pure joy.

She came past him on one of her bustling loops, and he stopped her with his free arm, pulling her face to his to kiss her, deep and long, while their baby chortled with delight.

When he pulled away, her eyes were dreamy and still that glorious green. And her smile made him start imagining all the things he planned to do to her later. In detail.

"What was that for?" she asked softly.

"For you," he said. He kissed her again. And only pulled back when the baby started squawking. "Always for you, *mi amore*. Light of my life, I cannot thank you enough."

"You never need to thank me," she whispered. "You don't need to do anything but love me, Ranieri. Always."

"I will," he promised her, the way he did at least twice a day. "Forever."

And then, after they put all their babies to bed, he stretched out with her in that bed in the back of the house that they had made a home, not a hiding place, and he showed her.

Again and again, because forever took the best kind of work.

And he was just the man for the job.

****

COMING SOON!

We really hope you enjoyed reading this book.
If you're looking for more romance, be sure to
head to the shops when new books are
available on

Thursday 1ˢᵗ September

To see which titles are coming soon, please visit
millsandboon.co.uk/nextmonth

MILLS & BOON ®

Coming next month

THE KING'S CHRISTMAS HEIR
Lynne Graham

Her cheeks were pink, her striking eyes downcast as she disconcerted him by reaching for the pen and scrawling her signature on the document that Dario had given him.

"You shouldn't sign a legal document without your own lawyer at hand to represent your interests," Gaetano remarked tautly.

"That's your world, not mine," Lara parried in a tone of scorn. "I don't require a lawyer to tell me I want to be free of you. You have disappointed me in every conceivable way, Gaetano –"

"I regret that you feel that way," he breathed curtly.

"No, your only goal is that I sign this form so that you can shed any responsibility you might have for me as discreetly as possible. That doesn't surprise me but I'm angry on my son's behalf!" Lara countered, throwing her head back. "He is an innocent party here and you didn't even look at him at the park!"

"You're trying to say that your son is also… my son?" Gaetano framed in open disbelief.

"He's sixteen months old, Gaetano. Who else could be his father?"

Continue reading
THE KING'S CHRISTMAS HEIR
Lynne Graham

Available next month
www.millsandboon.co.uk

MILLS & BOON

THE HEART OF ROMANCE

A ROMANCE FOR EVERY READER

MODERN

Prepare to be swept off your feet by sophisticated, sexy and seductive heroes, in some of the world's most glamourous and romantic locations, where power and passion collide.

HISTORICAL

Escape with historical heroes from time gone by. Whether your passion is for wicked Regency Rakes, muscled Vikings or rugged Highlanders, awaken the romance of the past.

MEDICAL

Set your pulse racing with dedicated, delectable doctors in the high-pressure world of medicine, where emotions run high and passion, comfort and love are the best medicine.

True Love

Celebrate true love with tender stories of heartfelt romance, from the rush of falling in love to the joy a new baby can bring, and a focus on the emotional heart of a relationship.

Desire

Indulge in secrets and scandal, intense drama and plenty of sizzling hot action with powerful and passionate heroes who have it all: wealth, status, good looks…everything but the right woman.

HEROES

Experience all the excitement of a gripping thriller, with an intense romance at its heart. Resourceful, true-to-life women and strong, fearless men face danger and desire - a killer combination!

To see which titles are coming soon, please visit

millsandboon.co.uk/nextmonth

LET'S TALK

Romance

For exclusive extracts, competitions
and special offers, find us online:

 facebook.com/millsandboon

 @MillsandBoon

@MillsandBoonUK

Get in touch on 01413 063232

For all the latest titles coming soon, visit
millsandboon.co.uk/nextmonth